# THE
# CRIMINAL
# MIND

THOMAS BENIGNO

Contact email for press, licensing, book clubs, or speaking engagements: tombenigno@aol.com

Cover by Nathan Wampler
Back cover script by Diana Benigno
Book formatted by: ebookpbook.com

ALSO BY THOMAS BENIGNO

THE GOOD LAWYER
THE CRIMINAL LAWYER

To Giovanni Baptiste Benigno,
My Stepfather-My Real Father
1917-1976
&
To the Veterans and Heroes of the Vietnam War
With Gratitude, Admiration and Love.
—Draft Lottery #238—

*It is a man's own mind,*
*not his enemy or foe,*
*that lures him to evil ways.*
*Buddha*

# PART 1

# THE MISSING

December 2007.
Somewhere in Upstate New York.
*I hear the voices again—coming from outside the box.*
*Men's voices in the cabin above me—getting louder.*
*The floor is creaking everywhere.*
*The ceiling hatch opens.*
*Footsteps descend the stairs.*
*I can smell the cigars and the liquor.*
*I can hear men talking and laughing. They're getting closer.*
*I shut my eyes and see my friends in the playground.*
*They're on the swings. The moon is shining brightly above them.*
*A drawer is pulled open next to me.*
*There's a grab for the keys.*
*I'll think of something else. I'll think of Christmas. I'll be home for Christmas.*
*A key misses the lock that is inches from my ear—then clicks in.*
*There's another lock near my ankles.*
*I'm slipping away again.*
*More laughter. More drinking.*
*I can hear the sound of liquor spilling.*
*The second lock falls off.*
*The lid opens.*
*The light is blinding.*
*Large blurry hands reach for me.*
*I'm walking in the playground.*
*I'm inside the box crying and screaming.*
*I'm on a swing pumping myself higher.*
*I hear the cries and screams of other children.*
*Fear grows inside me like a monster about to tear me apart.*
*I'm safe again—in the playground under a full*
*moon and a thousand twinkling stars.*

# CHAPTER 1

December 2017.
Midtown Manhattan.

The seventy-two-year-old, legs amputated above the knee, tightened his grip on the wheelchair's push-ring. His daily battle: Not letting the New York City traffic finish what the Viet Cong tried to, but failed.

Competing with a cacophony of blaring horns, tires screeching and pedestrian chatter, he blurted obscenities as a plume of exhaust discharged indiscriminately from a passing city bus. But the instant he lifted a hand to swat the noxious cloud, the wheelchair sped toward the curb-cut only seconds away from being T-boned by all manner of vehicles that raced up Eighth Avenue.

"I got you," gasped the young female voice behind him as she grabbed the chair by its grips and yanked the old veteran back onto the sidewalk.

"Damn it," squealed a passing businessman as the wheelchair toe-crushed one of his Bruno Maglis. Carrying an attaché case and wearing a long buttoned-down coat over a suit and tie, his face took on a disgusted yet constrained look. The target of his ire: The teenage girl and the bearded old man in the chair gazing up at him.

As he calculated the wisdom of complaining further, his eyes settled on the veteran's worn camouflage jacket and oversized sweatshirt, which was emblazoned with the faded cartoon heads of Minnie blowing Mickey a kiss, crossed over with an 'X' in black magic marker. But it wasn't the sight of the old man, his trouser fatigues sewn shut above the knees, or the young girl gripping the chair that restrained him from leveling an expletive as the sting in his foot intensified. It was the message on the face of the wily veteran: *Just give me an excuse and I will be only too happy to vise grip your executive balls.*

Seeing no percentage in further discourse, the businessman hurried off while the teenager uttered nervously: "I'm really sorry. I thought I had a good grip."

As a scraggly mix of white-and-gray hair spilled out of a trucker's cap, the old man jostled in his wheelchair and cocked his head back. His stern gaze fixed on the petite girl behind him, intent on navigating them both across the busy avenue where an assorted mix of cars, taxis, buses and trucks were halted at the light.

Where normally he would have barked a gruff "fuck off" at the slightest encroachment to the sanctity of his world, when he arrived at the opposite corner, he merely adjusted his seating position and turned to size up his chair's uninvited caretaker.

With straight, shoulder length brown hair, large brown eyes, and a light olive complexion, she was straining with determination as she steered the chair through the crowded sidewalk until a spot alongside a storefront window came into view where it could be safely parked.

"Whew. I wasn't sure I would make it," she said, as she pressed the sole of her sneaker down on each of the chair's brakes while the old man reached for a bag of M&Ms he had stuffed into his jacket pocket. "Are you okay now?" she asked, while smiling down at him. "Do you want me to wheel you somewhere else?"

*She looks like a sweet little angel,* he thought to himself. In a pink ski jacket, designer jeans and clean white sneakers, she reminded him of his younger sister, who had been about the same size and age, and had smiled the same pretty smile the last time he saw her.

"Want an M&M?" he asked matter-of-factly.

"Yes, please," she answered.

He dropped several into her open hand.

It was early December and snow was in the forecast for the New York

Metropolitan Area. Add 20-odd degree winds, and that Eighth Avenue corner was beginning to feel closer to zero.

"Are you sure you don't need any more help?" she asked. "I can push you farther if you like."

"You can, can you?" The old man spoke with the haughty air of a cranky granddad.

"Sure," she said cutely.

"I'm good." His voice had a hoarse, raspy quality that would've seemed more than a bit disconcerting to most teenage girls. But not this one.

Charlie Malone was a grouchy, unkempt amputee in a wheelchair— one among many people considered different and unusual who traveled along a midtown Manhattan street, which had a much higher bar on the level of 'different and unusual' than just about anyplace else.

As a passerby casually knocked into the arm of the chair, causing Charlie to scowl at everyone and everything around him, the young girl looked down at him unfazed. "You get mad a lot, don't you?"

He spun his chair in her direction and studied her for a moment, uncertain of what to say and do next until he saw something in her eyes that hadn't been there before. Her face had become hardened and intro-spective. Her shoulders rose as if toughening up for a fight. Tilting her head to the side, the sweet teenage girl who had been standing before him suddenly took on the pugnacious demeanor of someone twice her age. But as quickly as this change came, it disappeared. Her shoulders dropped, and her facial expression softened as if nothing had happened in the interim.

The veteran looked warily at her. He had his suspicions about what he saw but decided to act none the wiser. "How old are you? Fourteen, fifteen?" he asked.

She didn't answer.

"And where did you come from anyway?"

She gulped like a reluctant child and pointed east. "I live a few blocks down."

"You mean like on Fifth, or maybe Park, or Lexington?"

"On Park." There was a hesitant tone in her voice.

"You live on Park Avenue and you're over here slumming on Eighth?" He threw his hands in the air. "Well then, I'm revising my age estimate.

You must be younger than fourteen, because only a foolish little girl would be hanging out on Eighth Avenue with me, while a Park Avenue apartment was waiting for her at home."

"What does where I live have to do with anything, not to mention my missing a 'thank you' for helping you across the street?"

"I thought I said, 'thank you,'" he said pensively.

"Well, you didn't."

"Oh…then…thank you." He spoke with uncharacteristic politeness, and instantly became both uncomfortable and embarrassed for doing so.

"You're welcome." She looked away.

"Okay, now tell me," he said. "What's your name and what are you doing up here?"

"My name is Mia Langley, and for your information, I'm actually doing homework. I'm supposed to meet someone new and different, and write about them."

"Oh, so you weren't just being a Good Samaritan?"

"Yes, I was, and it wasn't until you offered me the M&Ms that it occurred to me to write about you…maybe." Charlie's jaw dropped, a look of incredulity on his face. "But I want to write about someone good." She hesitated, not sure how he would react. "Different, kind of, but interesting and good."

He laughed, following up with a warm smile that made him seem less the curmudgeon, and said: "Regardless, you shouldn't be talking to strangers. And you shouldn't be out on the streets of Eighth Avenue alone, school or no school."

Mia was blank-faced, standing with her hands in her jacket pockets, one dug deeper than the other due to a torn inseam and a nervous habit of pushing her hands down as she walked. "I may not look it, but I just turned eighteen," she said, as she bobbed her head in confirmation.

"Still, your mother is okay with you roaming the streets all by yourself?"

"My birth mother died a long time ago. I'm adopted, and my adoptive mother trusts my judgment. She just doesn't want me out late."

Charlie smiled, extended his hand and introduced himself. "Since your trusting mother's okay with it, I'm Charlie Malone." At the risk of being the subject of her homework, he told Mia a sanitized version of his life story, including his time in Vietnam—how he lost both his legs, and now lived in a center for veterans with disabilities on Eighth Avenue and 54<sup>th</sup> Street, made possible by the generosity of a rich benefactor.

Mia stared down at him. "Did it hurt?' she asked, her thoughts drifting to another place and time.

"Did what hurt?"

"When you lost your legs, did it hurt?"

Normally, Charlie would have been outright annoyed at such a personal inquiry from a stranger, and would have reacted in kind, but the young girl's innocence and apparent empathy evoked an altogether different response. "Not really," he answered. "I was in what you would call 'shock' when it happened. Then everything went black. The hurt? That came later."

"The hurt came later?" Mia asked herself as she glanced up at the sky. "I know what that's like," she added, gazing indiscriminately at the street traffic as she leaned against the storefront window and popped another M&M in her mouth. She then said, matter-of-factly: "Before I was adopted—when I was little—I used to get hurt a lot." There was a peculiar sadness in her eyes.

The old veteran looked at her curiously, while another New York City bus roared by, exhaust billowing behind it, its tires inches from the curb.

Then as if a starter's pistol had just gone off, Mia stepped away and ran after it.

Careful to remain outside the line of traffic, she sprinted on-and-off the sidewalk, dodging street vendors, pedestrians, a crowd of Japanese tourists—and even a police officer on a horse.

Quite capable of moving quickly in his wheelchair when he had to, Charlie pumped the push ring as hard as he could and gave chase.

Struggling to catch his breath, he caught up to her at the next corner.

The bus had come to a stop at the curb, and she was pacing back and forth on the sidewalk beside it. She had an anxious look on her face, as if she was searching for someone.

"Why did you take off like that?" he asked. He was red-faced and breathing hard. "You scared the crap out of me. I thought something happened. I didn't know what to think."

Mia took one look at him, hurried into a nearby coffee shop and returned with cup of water. "Here, drink some of this."

Charlie took a few gulps, then crumpled the cup in his hand and tossed it away. "Now what's going on with you?"

"I thought I saw someone, that's all."

"What do you mean, 'saw someone'?"

"On the bus, in the window. This isn't the first time."

"What in God's name are you talking about?" Charlie's speech was labored as he huffed in exasperation.

"She tried to protect them," she said, in a tone a few octaves lower.

"She? Who is she?" Charlie was becoming increasingly agitated.

"Mia," she responded blankly.

If not for the longing in the young girl's eyes, he would have lost his patience entirely. "I thought you said *your* name was Mia."

"I never said that." She shook her head, then stepped behind him, and grabbed the chair's handgrips. She began talking to the back of his head as she turned him around and pushed him back in the direction they had come from. "One moment they're there, and the next they're gone."

"Who and what are you talking about?" Charlie was facing forward but talking to the young girl behind him.

"I can't say," she muttered.

"You said you tried to protect them. Who did you try to protect?"

"I said that?" She brought the chair to a stop and looked around. "Oh yeah. I guess I did. We'll talk more the next time I see you."

"Why next time? Tell me now. Who was it you were trying to protect?" Charlie shouted to be heard over the street traffic.

Mia ignored him and resumed pushing the chair until they returned to the corner beside the storefront window. "You okay to get back home?" she asked.

Charlie did his best to hide his concern. "Of course I'm okay. I got here by myself, didn't I?"

"Not exactly. I helped you cross the street, remember? So, maybe next time you could help me with…something." Mia smiled, and then with a half-moon wave of her hand, said "bye," and hurried off.

For reasons Charlie wasn't fully aware of, he was heartbroken to see her leave. He remained on that corner until sunset—when the city lights became unbearably bright, and the cold December night made sitting idle in a wheelchair on a midtown Manhattan street corner nearly intolerable.

But he couldn't stop thinking about Mia, her peculiar personality, her er-rant youth—and her brash innocence.

He grabbed both push-ring and slowly pumped himself back home.

As Charlie approached the entrance to the Veterans' Center, he tightened his grip and worked his way up the handicap incline. Hurrying past security and ignoring the nod of the receptionist at the front desk, he sped down the hall.

"Take it easy, Charlie!" she shouted.

Given how he made his way around the city on a daily basis, it was a wonder that Charlie had any strength left in his arms at all. His veins, like green tracer wire, lined his biceps and forearms in such a grotesque fash-ion they often looked as if they were going to pop.

At seventy-two years of age, the strength in Charlie's upper body was a reminder to him—and a signal to all—that he was still vital and a force to be reckoned with, whether it was in the jungles of East Asia or back home in the real world. Though his caseworker had time and again of-fered to requisition a motorized chair, Charlie refused to even consider it. 'Use it or lose it' would echo inside his head as he rebelled in words and actions against the muscular atrophy that accompanied his disability and advancing age.

Once inside his apartment, he easily picked himself off the chair and vaulted onto the bed with the mere use of his arms. Since he was almost always sweating—regardless of the temperature outside—he grabbed a bag of baby wipes from the night table, dropped flat on his back, and used one to cool his forehead while continuing to wonder about Mia. Was she running toward or away from something when she chased after that city bus? But more puzzling was her sudden transformation—referring to herself in the third person—her face and persona altering from one personality to another.

# CHAPTER 2

I am a lawyer, but I don't practice law anymore. The purpose of the profession I dreamed of as a little boy has long since eluded me. Having spent my career and most of my life as a criminal defense lawyer—four and a half years as a Legal Aid lawyer in the South Bronx and another twenty-five in private practice—successfully advocating for the guilty to go free while powerless at times to protect those who weren't—I realized I could do more good and save more innocent lives another way. No bitterness. No second-guessing. I left behind a career I had aspired to and loved, and one that has defined me more than anything else ever has, or ever will.

The veterans' facility that Charlie and ninety-nine other disabled veterans called home was the result of a plan I had launched years earlier with my wife, Eleanor. It began with the purchase of a building located on the west side of Eighth Avenue between 54th and 55th Streets that had previously housed over 300 City College students. Though acquiring the property at a reasonable price was no easy task—having to battle higher bids from Fortune 500 retailers, tech giants, real estate barons, and several worldwide hotel chains—our project was finally green-lighted when the New York Post published an article outlining our intentions: The creation of a home for impoverished and disabled American combat veterans.

Fortunately, no one ever questioned the source of our funds, especially where I was concerned. Eleanor was the product of old Southern money—the beneficiary of an estate that would make even the Wall Street turn-of-the-century robber barons froth at the mouth. As for me, my humble Brooklyn roots notwithstanding—an inheritance from my mobster uncle (my mother's younger brother) precipitated by decades of crime and violence, was much easier to part with, and so I did so at every chance I got—this son of a high school cafeteria lady who tossed a little extra into every student's dish. Abandoned by my biological father while I was still in diapers, Mom met my stepfather, John Mannino, one year later. A second-generation Sicilian, he was strict, but loving, generous, and the only father I ever knew. Consequently, upon turning 18, I made an application in Supreme Court, changed my last name to his, and have been known ever since as Nicholas Mannino.

Having invested my mobster uncle's inheritance wisely—resulting in a tenfold return since his death—a serendipitous consequence that provided the seed capital to build the Veterans' Center and bankroll numerous investigations into missing adults and children, I just never thought I would, on occasion, be risking my life in the process. But in the end, it was always worth it, and each time I parted with the product of decades of criminal activity and laundered money, it was like slowly ridding myself of sheaths of heavy armor that I had been sentenced to wear uncomfortably for the rest of my natural life.

As a teenager in the 1960s, the implacable Vietnam lotteries would be forever etched in my memory—the precarious bouncing of bingo-like balls inside two plexiglass barrels that on March 8, 1973, combined to give my birth date the random number 238. Numbers 1-95 were placed in "a readily inductible pool" to be drafted, or so we were told. It didn't matter if you were an only child. It didn't matter if you were in college. It was a matching of birth dates and numbers—a lottery of life and death, plain and simple. As a result, I had always been sympathetic to the plight of Vietnam veterans, especially those who were poor and disabled, which is why I insisted that the bylaws of the not-for-profit corporation that ran the Center make specific reference to the "forgotten heroes of the Vietnam War."

Though I never thought that any accomplishment in my life would have been greater than obtaining a law degree—with its 100 studio apartments, grand dining room, visitor's lounge, regulation basketball court, squash courts, and game room—the Veterans' Center was one shining success story. And it gave me the best opportunity to put the money I inherited from my mobster uncle—which I never expected, wanted, or needed—to the best possible use.

It was during the construction of the facility that Eleanor and I purchased an apartment in Manhattan. Since we wanted to oversee the development of the Veterans' Center, and both our adult children were now living in the city, this served a dual purpose. Then in 2016, after battling pneumonia and a failing heart that had been cruelly and unknowingly beating with oncoming finality for years, Eleanor was taken from me.

And when she left to meet the angels, all I wanted to do was go with her.

But the God of life and death had other plans for me.

It was after Eleanor's passing that I found myself visiting the Veterans' Center more often—on a daily basis whenever I was in New York. I enjoyed spending time with the veterans and ate lunch with them every chance I got. If not for my high lottery number and the de-escalation of the war in 1972, I might have been one of them. While it broke my heart to see these great men and women in walkers and wheelchairs, the more I got to know them, the more I came to appreciate their individual trauma, their struggle, as well as their courage and perseverance. And in no other veteran was this more evident than Charlie Malone.

An often cranky and outspoken man who never took off his marine fatigues (may I never again make the mistake of calling them army fatigues), Charlie was the genuine article. He was smart, tough as nails, and caring about the facility and everyone in it—almost to a fault. We quickly became friends. Our lunch meetings and the banter that ensued was a singular source of solace and comfort to me during the saddest and loneliest time of my life—and more than I cared to admit at the time.

I came to know Charlie quite well, and the story of how he came to join the Marines was as tragic and unforgettable as he was.

It was on a rainy afternoon in March when I decided to hang around long after the other veterans had left the cafeteria—some escorted by aids, most of them moving on their own in wheelchairs and on crutches—that

Charlie and I had a heart-to-heart. Maybe it was the loneliness we shared—although I quickly came to learn that Charlie's had no equal—but we sat and talked for hours. I fessed up about my Mafia uncle—something I had never done before with anyone except Eleanor. Charlie in turn bore his soul about the most painful time in his life—before he ever considered joining the Marines and serving in Vietnam.

"I grew up north of Syracuse, in the Village of Phoenix, New York, where the Oswego and the Seneca Rivers combine," he began. "My father's name was John, same as your stepdad's. He had a small landscaping business. My mother, Frances…she was a homemaker who made extra money babysitting children after school. A real beauty, inside and out, she had such a natural way with kids…so much so that many figured she should open up her own daycare center. But she wouldn't have it. Being a mother to her own two children 'to raise them proper,' she'd say, 'was a full-time job in itself.' But the real reason: No wife of John Malone was going to work. That was the man's job, and with his landscaping business running full-speed from the spring through the fall, and snow removal keeping him busy throughout the winter (and Lord knows there were plenty of snow days in and around Syracuse) we rode out the worst of times, year-after-year. There was even a little extra for a vacation drive to Niagara Falls, or Canada. We even went to Florida once. 'But every family has at least one cross to bear,' my mother would often say."

"I heard my own mom say that very same thing," I added, woefully.

Charlie nodded. "That cross was my younger sister, Peggy, though my mom would never admit it. You know, it wasn't easy for moms back then, and my dad…he was no prize package either. I tried not to be more of a burden to either of them. Peggy tried, too. I know she did. Three years younger than me, she was physically indistinguishable from other girls her age. Though only five foot two, she excelled at every sport she played… soccer, tennis, and especially track. There seemed to be no limit to her energy, and boy, was she determined! By her sophomore year in high school, she had made all the varsity teams."

"She sounds like a real star to me," I added. "So what was the problem? Did she have a learning disability?"

"Unfortunately, yes. Peggy barely passed her classes, and it wasn't for lack of trying. With each school year, the harder she worked, the harder it was for her to skirt a failing report card. She just couldn't seem to concentrate. And sitting with my mother for hours after school didn't help. As my father once crudely put it: 'We just have to face facts. Peggy isn't very smart.' And because my uncle on my mother's side had been diagnosed as mentally retarded, my father was quick to blame Mom's genetic line for all of Peggy's problems. Though 'learning disabled,' like you said, would have been a more accurate diagnosis, it was 1965, and the world then was not a kind place for those with special needs. As for Peggy, adding to the complexities of her life, was her not-so-little junior year secret. His name was Howard."

"That doesn't sound too bad," I said with a sigh of relief.

"You never met my father," Charlie continued. "Howard was a senior and captain of the high school football team. His dad owned the lumberyard in nearby Cartersville. Put simply, they were 'well-off,' to say the least. The problem was that Peggy had yet to turn 16, and because of her learning disability, my parents wouldn't let her date. Though my mom would appear to soften at times, as far as my father was concerned, she suffered from a mental illness, and a boyfriend-girlfriend relationship at her age, especially with an older football player, was out of the question. My dad was part of the first Marine division, who fought in the grueling Battle of the Chosin Reservoir during the Korean War, where the allied losses were so great, its survivors were known as 'the Chosin few.' Tough as nails, he felt it was his duty to protect his daughter, and no one was going to take advantage of her on his watch. Frustrated by this wall of objection, Peggy would sneak away after school to meet Howard while claiming that she was headed to her girlfriend's house to do homework. When a family friend spotted the couple on Howard's motorboat as it passed through one of the Oswego Canal Locks, Peggy was grounded for a month. Afterward, the two had to settle for necking by their lockers and in the school's stairwells."

"Like you said, your mother had her hands full."

"It gets better, or should I say, worse…much worse," Charlie said sadly. "The day after Peggy turned sixteen, Howard showed up at the door to ask my father for permission to take her to the senior prom. My mom let him in. Howard began by apologizing for seeing Peggy on the sneak and then swore that he would have her home by eleven. It was as if he was begging for his life. As for my father, cemetery headstones displayed more emotion as he sat stone-faced in his favorite chair while Howard, standing before him, pathetically pled his case. Whether it was the perverse image of my sister being deflowered on prom night floating around in my father's head or not, I couldn't tell, but the look of unflappable consternation never left him. Then, all of a sudden, my father got up, pointed to the front door and shouted: 'I've heard enough. You get the hell out of my house right now!' My mom, who was standing by the kitchen door, dropped her head to her chest. Peggy was devastated but undeterred. Come the night of the prom, she put on her favorite pink dress, called Howard, and lied. She told him that, thanks to my mom, my father had finally changed his mind. Howard said that he would pick her up in under an hour. Of course, Peggy told him not to…that one of my father's conditions was that my mother drop her off."

"I'm going to need more coffee," I interrupted. "Depending on where this is going, maybe a shot of rye. I'm not sure."

"Well, you'd better get it then, but all you'll find is coffee, and you'll have to go in the kitchen for it," he answered. "They cleaned up out here already."

Even though Charlie didn't ask for one, I left and returned with two cups. Mine was the light and sweet one. The black coffee was Charlie's. He thanked me and continued.

"Howard rushed to shave, shower and dress, and then waited, all the while imagining Peggy stepping out of my parents' car looking as radiant as an angel. After an hour passed, he called the house. I picked up the phone in the kitchen. Confused and concerned, I told him to hold on, and then without uttering a word to either of my parents, I ran up to Peggy's room. Her bedroom window was open, and she was gone. Now I knew that the relationship between Peggy and Howard was a hotbed of controversy, so I went to check on my father first and found him in his usual spot—sitting in his favorite chair, watching television. I then checked the rest of the house. My mother was nowhere to be found but before I could breathe a sigh of relief, I looked out my bedroom window and there she was—digging in the front garden with the family car parked in the driveway. Wearing an apron, patches of dirt on her face and hands, she hadn't gone anywhere. I rushed back to the phone. 'Peggy must be walking,' I said nervously.

'Maybe you should give her a little more time.' Howard immediately hung up the phone, got in his car and for over an hour drove up and down the roads between his house and ours, hoping to spot her. But he never did. No one ever did. Peggy was never seen nor heard from again."

"Dear God!" I moaned loudly, causing two members of the kitchen staff to peek into the room. "I am so sorry, Charlie. Your sister...your only sibling..."

"A woman in town, who had a small sewing shop, said that she saw a young girl who resembled Peggy chasing a crosstown bus later that same day. She didn't say whether the driver ever stopped to pick the girl up. But as time passed, and it became apparent to the authorities that this wasn't the case of a runaway teen, search parties were formed. As word spread about Peggy's disappearance, the newspapers picked up the story, and local television stations flashed bulletins on the 'Case of the Small-Town Missing Teenager.' My mom even pleaded on-air for Peggy's return, but to no avail. My parents became depressed, angry and frustrated, which over time turned into guilt and accusation. Six months later, a skull was found near an off-road construction site on the outskirts of town. Dental records identified it as Peggy's. The following day, my father went into our backyard, held the point of his favorite hunting knife against his chest, and fell on it. He wanted his death to be painful. Nine months later, my mom sold the house and moved to Florida. Since I refused to go, just before she boarded her plane, she kissed me on the cheek, handed me an envelope filled with two-hundred-dollars cash and made me promise to take care of myself. I was nineteen years old at the time."

As Charlie went on to tell it, it took him all of one hour to deposit the money in the bank and join the Marines. Ten months later, he was in the thick of the Vietnam War, crawling through the jungle in the rain, a rifle in his arms, all manner of dirt, mud and insect life making a home in his boots and trousers. But it wasn't until his fourth combat tour in January of 1968 (the record was five) that he lost his legs during the TET Offensive in a field outside Hanoi. All he remembered before his world went dark was seeing the ground explode around him amid a barrage of gunfire.

According to his VA file, he had been diagnosed with post-traumatic stress disorder.

It was also during one of our lunches at the Veterans' Center, sometime in early 2018, that Charlie first mentioned Mia to me. "Maybe it was her age, her size, and her big brown eyes that reminded me of Peggy," he said.

Or maybe it was the pain of losing his sister at such a delicate moment in their lives that always stayed with him. Or maybe he was just one old cranky bastard looking to revisit a time of wistful innocence before tragedy came that destroyed his family, and forever changed the world as he knew it. Now this old man, who earned medals for bravery and a Purple Heart, was at the tail end of his life and had nothing and no one, until a petite eighteen-year-old girl came along with a simple act of kindness that reminded him of the sister he lost but could never forget. Mia's innocence, her youthful energy and an apparent inner struggle seemed to crack open a door of purpose and meaning in Charlie's life.

I understood him more than I cared to admit.

What he remembered about his sister came from a time so long ago it must have seemed like a horrible dream that came and went like an inexorable reminder he could not vault away—no matter how hard he tried, no matter how overwhelming life became with its struggles and complexities, no matter how many bombs went off, no matter how muddy the ground beneath him, no matter how many legs he lost.

He still felt the pain of that nineteen-year-old boy whose life suddenly and without warning was blown to bits.

# CHAPTER 3

I suppose that when tragedy strikes, whether you've lost your legs, or your wife, we all have our coping mechanisms. Mine were frequent trips to the Veterans' Center. It was a delicate time for me—less than a year after Eleanor's death.

Early in our marriage, and after my very first confrontation with a serial killer as a young lawyer in 1982, I'd made a promise to Eleanor that I would leave all forays into the legal defense of the innocent and capture of the guilty behind me. But it wasn't long before I broke that promise and again selfishly immersed myself in my work in callous disregard of wife and family. Since I hadn't been a man of my word, she was a woman of hers, and—to my foolish surprise—she left me in the summer of 2005. After we reconciled five years later, determined to keep her by my side, I sold our Long Island home and moved us into the heart of the South—Franklin, Tennessee, to be exact—something I never thought this New York born-and raised-kid would ever do. But it was Eleanor's unspoken wish to return to her Southern roots, and I loved her that much.

For months after her passing, I wallowed in my own self-imposed exile of despair that was so debilitating, I do believe there were times I enjoyed the suffering. It was as if I deserved it: The cataclysmic loss, the ultimate emotional defeat—the absolute deepest and darkest depths of sadness.

*My mother was a survivor, and so am I,* I repeatedly told myself. So some-how, some way, I had to pull myself out of the dungeon of depression I was in.

Idyllic Franklin—its gray Civil War history and its classic Main Street—a cardboard cutout from a 1950s movie with its town theater, antique shops, restored Victorian buildings, and historic public square. Sometime after Eleanor's passing, I began taking early morning walks, at the end of which I'd stop at the local diner where a waitress named Maureen kept regular hours. She would often sit with me, if merely to chat about absolutely anything and nothing, and bring me a slice of fresh morning pie, whether I asked for it or not. Those pieces of pie back then were the only thin rays of light in my otherwise bleak and solitary existence. So out of sync with the world was I, that it took me weeks to realize that it wasn't the pie, but Maureen—with her bright blue eyes and charming smile—that provided the welcome trickle of joy in my morning. And I'll swear before a firing squad that I hadn't an impure thought about her—at first. But as winter turned to spring in Franklin, she continued to fill my thoughts at all hours, and for no apparent reason.

When I asked her more about her life, I discovered that those eyes and that smile were masking the pain of a messy divorce from a habitu-ally unfaithful husband who treated his wife like the sports car he loved: a trophy possession he refused to part with and was his alone to drive. Even more distressing was her teenage son's voluntary induction into the Army two years earlier to escape the daily barrage of marital acrimony.

In time though, during my daily breakfasts at the diner, I learned a few things more about Maureen and her situation. When she had gotten married twenty-five years earlier, she gave up a career as a teacher to be a stay-at-home housewife and eventually mother—wholly dependent on hubby for food, clothing, and shelter. It's what he insisted upon. (Eleanor would have *hated* this guy!) And Maureen trusted him to provide. In turn, he screwed every woman who would let him and eventually her, too. She walked away from the marriage with a mere nine-thousand-dollar settle-ment and a thousand per month in alimony. It was just enough to get her a three-room apartment above the hardware store in town. But what mat-tered most to her was that this was a life that was stress-free, aside from the daily worry that comes with a son who was serving overseas. She even waived all claims to her ex-husband's pension and any other assets of the marriage. She wanted out that badly.

A regular at church every Sunday, she prayed for her son on a daily basis and volunteered at the local children's hospital one afternoon a week. When I met her in 2017, she was 49 and I was 62. I should have been grateful she was even giving me the time of day.

We began with dinners, mostly—nothing fancy. We'd then take in a movie afterward. She loved going to the movies, and it was a welcome distraction for me as well. Eventually, I felt close enough to encourage her to get back to teaching, but she seemed to have lost her confidence. "It's elementary school—how hard could it be?" I asked, and she didn't get offended in the least. She just laughed and said: "If it was easy, everybody would be doing it."

Though she poured her heart out to me on many occasions, other than my wife's passing and living alone in Franklin while my son and daughter lived in New York, I told her very little about myself—at first. My past life as a lawyer, my funding of searches for missing adults and children, and those responsible, along with my net worth, were off the table.

And classy lady that she was, she never pried.

As more time passed and we grew closer, Maureen would occasionally sleep over at the house. That we were developing a strong romantic connection was undeniable. I just didn't feel comfortable building upon it just yet. When it was time for me to go to New York again, I bid Maureen goodbye to a genuine disappointment in her big blue eyes. And though it saddened me to leave her, I just wasn't ready to take her with me. I wasn't ready to have her to meet my children.

When that sadness kept recurring—and not from missing Eleanor, but from leaving Maureen—I felt as if I had somehow betrayed my one great love: When I was with Maureen, I found myself not thinking about Eleanor.

On the evening before I left for New York for the last time without her, we drove into Nashville and had dinner at The Palm Restaurant—fancy, and yes, expensive. We dined on filet mignon and flourless chocolate cake. We drank. We laughed. I had never seen Maureen happier. Since we each had at least three drinks, and it was a warm May night, we decided to walk it off on Nashville's Broadway lined with open bars and live entertainment, until we came to the Riverfront Railroad Station that ran along the Cumberland River. Arm in arm we stood there, taking in the night and looking out across the water at the colossal Nissan Stadium, home to the Tennessee Titans. Twenty minutes later, we returned to my car and headed back to Franklin.

When we got to the curbside door that led up to Maureen's apartment, I told her that I was sorry I had to go. Though she never asked why I was leaving, she knew both of my kids lived in New York and I guess that was enough for her. After giving me a goodnight kiss before she went upstairs, she did something she had never done before. Though she had every reason to believe that I was coming back, she made me promise to return anyway. "Don't you leave me here now," were her parting words, punctuated with a smile that was both sweet and sad at the same time.

When I boarded my flight at Nashville International Airport, headed for JFK, I thought about the evening we spent together and how much I would miss her company. I was grateful to have met her and wondered if in some far-off alternate universe, Eleanor was pulling the strings on my behalf, which wouldn't have surprised me in the least. But amid the feelings of gratitude, longing and loss, I recalled an uneasiness that had drifted through me as I walked to my car after Maureen and I said our goodbyes. Experiencing so many new and conflicting emotions that night, I shrugged it off as butterflies—the result of a post-Eleanor conundrum—but it had nothing to do with Eleanor.

I had a strong sense that someone was watching us and monitoring our every move from Franklin to Nashville, and back.

# CHAPTER 4

After I landed in New York, I went right to the Veterans' Center, wheeled my suitcase into the front office for safe keeping, and headed straight for the cafeteria. It was lunchtime. I was hungry. As I entered, I spotted Charlie and took a seat across from him.

Scores of disabled veterans, mostly men, filled the room. As always, Charlie was donning his scraggly beard, his wild hair combed back, and wearing his marine fatigues. He moved his wheelchair closer to the table. "Six times I ran into this teenage girl on the streets of Manhattan. What are the odds of that in a city of millions?" he asked. "I think she wants to be found."

Mia's story, as divulged to Charlie, came from Mia's own lips, but it wasn't only Mia who told it. According to Charlie, each time he met up with her after their first encounter on that Eighth Avenue corner, she looked the same—no makeup, straight, shoulder-length hair, wearing a pink ski jacket and jeans. They would engage in small talk, after which he was politely dismissed with a casual: "See ya."

But the fifth time was different. Bright pink lipstick covered her lips, rouge was on her cheeks, black liner was around her eyes, and her hair was tightly pulled back behind her head. Her jeans appeared to be brand new. Her jacket was Canada Goose, and she carried herself with a prominent air of youthful sophistication. Charlie had caught up with her as she was exiting a drugstore carrying a small plastic bag with the store's logo on it. When he called out her name, she did a double take then greeted him with an outstretched hand.

"Hello Charles," she said in a tone evoking a maturity that was well beyond her years.

"It's Charlie, but you know that already," he answered.

"I like Charles better." She looked him squarely in the eyes.

"You look different," he said.

"Different? How? This is how I always look. Is there something wrong with the way I look?" She spun around to showcase her clothes.

"I don't know," he hesitated. "I'm not sure. I had been wondering about you, that's all. I still ask myself why you chased after that bus the first time we met."

"You must be thinking of someone else," she said firmly.

Charlie huffed and leaned back in his chair. "No, it was you, and you said your name was Mia Langley, and that you were adopted." He nodded his head emphatically.

The teenager stepped closer and leaned against the drugstore window, her eyes wide with inscrutable innocence. A small plastic shopping bag was hanging from the crook of her finger. "Let me end the mystery for you," she responded. "Mia said and did those things, not me. My name is Melanie."

"What is she? Your twin sister or something?"

"Or something." She rolled her eyes and grinned.

"Okay, if you're Mia's sister, then tell her that I'm looking for her. Tell her I want to see her again."

"She probably knows that already, Charles. But I'll try to get her your message. We're not always in the playground at the same time, you know."

"Playground? What playground? What in God's name are you talking about? I don't think this is a nice game you're playing, and I wish you would stop it."

"This is not a game, Charles. A game is something you do for fun. What Mia, the others, and I have in common—has nothing to do with fun."

"The others?" Charlie's uneasiness had quickly turned to frustration and even anger as the volume of street noise around him seemed to intensify, and the sidewalk appeared to fill with pedestrians walking much faster than they actually were.

The teenager looked down at him, her faced filled with empathy—not for his physical condition, but for his lack of understanding. "Charles," she said politely. "There are now only five of us. There's Judy, Marion, and—well, the names don't matter right now. But there used to be more—a playground full of six or seven—struggling to keep Mia alive. If you want to know more about us, I suggest you speak to her psychiatrist, Dr. Sylvia Field." She closed the conversation with resolute finality and walked off.

Charlie rolled his eyes at me and shrugged as a gesture that he was done. The cafeteria had thinned out. Engrossed in his story, I had let the temperature of my coffee drop to lukewarm. I took a last worthwhile sip and sat back in my chair. "This is crazy stuff," I said.

"I know," he answered.

"So, wait," I added, determined to understand. "What you're saying is that Mia has either a lot of sisters, or some kind of…multiple personality?"

"That's right!" he said emphatically.

"You're kidding. Really? Charlie, this is hard stuff to swallow."

"As you may or may not know, "he added. "Multiple personality disorder is usually the product of a severe trauma that occurred in childhood. The different personalities are probably the only thing that prevented Mia—or whoever she is—from going completely insane, especially when you hear what happened to her."

I wasn't sure if I had instantly turned pale, but I certainly felt like I had. "Are you sure this young girl wasn't just pulling your leg? There are those who believe that 'split' or 'multiple personality disorder' is a hoax."

"Are you one of them?" he asked.

"Let's just say that I've read very little about it and haven't ever given it much thought."

"Well, I have. It should be of no surprise to you that I have a lot of time on my hands," he said firmly. "I also suppose you're not ready to hear what actually causes it. You should keep an open mind until you do. I ran into Melanie a second time—or should I say, she ran into me. There's much more to Mia's story, and it's not a pretty one. When this girl was just a child, she was driven Upstate to a cabin in the woods."

"A child? How old? Kids aren't the most reliable witnesses, you know."

24

"She was six or seven, old enough to remember. And I believe her, whether it's Melanie or Mia I'm hearing it from. The drive took hours, she said. Melanie remembers talk about a town called Cartersville. She was taken on these trips by a so-called uncle of Mia's, who wasn't really an uncle, but a boyfriend of her mother's. When they got to this cabin in the woods somewhere, Mia was put in a locked wooden box. Melanie says she is not sure for how long. There were many instances of this. I'll spare you the gritty details right now of what happened to her, but I know the area she is talking about. Cartersville, in Upstate New York, was practically my hometown growing up."

"How do you know that Mia or Melanie, or whoever, isn't just making up stories? How do we know that this isn't just a convincing fantasy of one of her alleged personalities?"

"Like I said, I believe her." Charlie was adamant. "The part about the cabin and the box came from Mia herself, not an alternate personality. You are just going to have to trust me on this."

I was sufficiently scolded, and instantly reminded that I wasn't as tough in mind as I once was. Or maybe I just wasn't ready to delve back into a life consumed by horrible crimes again. Maybe I had spent too much time in Franklin, Tennessee, living the idyllic small-town life. Maybe those years without rancor and stress had softened me. Maybe I didn't want this any-more—another dark adventure to get personally involved in. Either way, I had heard enough, and got up to leave when Charlie grabbed my hand and squeezed it hard.

"I want to help this girl," he pleaded. "I believe I keep running into her because she wants me to."

"She's under a doctor's care, isn't she?" I answered, as he released his grip. "We can't change what happened to her, Charlie."

As I walked away, I noticed a tear form in the corner of Charlie's eye that I was convinced had less to do with Mia, and more to do with who she reminded him of—his late sister, Peggy.

I left the Center and enjoyed the long walk back to my apartment. It was a warm spring day, and I always loved how the buildings in Manhattan glistened in the midday sun only to cast broken shadows across the avenue. It was a day better suited for a long walk or window-shopping, or an afternoon in the park—not one for hearing about horrible atrocities against a young girl. Not that there ever is one.

I thought about my son, John, the idealistic young lawyer (I was one of those once), and my daughter, Charlotte, the hedge-fund manager as beautiful on the inside as in every other way. I thought about how much I missed them, and how I always wanted them to be proud of me. I thought about how adamant they were that I leave all forays into crime-solving in the past—close the vault—contain the ghosts that might spur me down another dark and dangerous path once again.

# CHAPTER 5

It was 8:00 a.m. and the ground was still wet from the rain. The tractor's shovel bore deeper than the driver intended, and when it rose into the air, the rectangular box of gray-aged wood was lifted but otherwise undisturbed. It was a clean scoop, and when the excess dirt and rocks were shaken loose, the box remained largely unscathed. If not for a break in the clouds and the early morning sun, it might have gone unnoticed, routinely dumped in a waiting truck to be hauled away and dropped into an even larger pile of dirt, sand, and unearthed gravel.

Diego was a Mexican American and a citizen of the United States for over fifteen years. The home he shared with his wife and five kids was in a suburb just outside Ithaca, New York. Every morning he woke up at 4:00 a.m. to start his shift at 7:00 a.m., seventy miles away outside the small town of Cartersville. This day, his foreman put him on the tractor. The last thing Diego wanted was to find a box in the dirt that resembled the coffin of a small child. Two years earlier, he had buried his son in one the same size. The boy had died of brain cancer and was three years old.

At first, Diego thought he had found a hidden crate of rifles. He was tempted to put it back, bury it deeper, and not get involved as a witness against 'the wrong people.' Then he thought again. Perhaps these were the remains of someone whose family could not afford a proper burial.

He leveled the shovel to just a few feet off the ground. Arms wide, he stepped off the tractor, gritted his teeth and gripped the sides of the box. It was lighter than he expected. He gently placed it on the ground. After hesitating for a moment, he tried to lift the cover off. But it was nailed shut. He thought about calling his foreman, who cared only about time and money and keeping on schedule, and then thought again. Although Diego feared the ramifications of what he might find, he was a religious man and would not be able to live with himself if he dumped the box without knowing.

He climbed back on to the tractor, grabbed a large screwdriver from his tool bag, stepped off and pried open the box only to have his worst fear realized.

Inside he found the skeleton of a young child, and alongside it a tarnished copy of the children's book, *Christmas Moon*.

# CHAPTER 6

When I entered the cafeteria the following day, Charlie raced toward me. After bumping past a few other veterans in wheelchairs, he screeched to a stop at what had become our usual table. "I wanted to call you," he said frantically. "The supervisor here wouldn't give me your number."

"I'll give you my number if you want it, but what is it? What's going on?"

His voice was grating and raspier than usual. "They found a box of bones in a construction site in Cartersville. It was the skeleton of a small child, five or six years old."

"When was this?"

"Yesterday, and get this. Less than a hundred feet away, *another* box was dug up with more bones in it."

"Another child?"

"The authorities aren't saying. Once the second box was found, the police shut the press out and refused to release any other information. They have the area barricaded. No one can get within a quarter mile of the site. Very strange if you ask me. I have a sneaking suspicion they found more bodies and are keeping it under wraps."

"What kind of boxes are they anyway?"

"Wood crates, like you would ship produce in."

"Listen, if you run into that teenage girl, I wouldn't tell her anything about this. It's too upsetting."

"Fuckin' A, Captain. Don't you worry." Charlie was about to say something else, but caught himself.

"Okay, Charlie. What is it?"

"There's just one problem. She was the one who told *me*. And now she wants to meet you."

"But how does she know about me?" I asked, raising my voice.

"Let's just say, she knows," he answered sheepishly.

Seconds later, Charlie called Mia from his cellphone and in less than half-an-hour she was standing right in front of us exactly as I pictured her—a lovely, petite, teenage girl. After approaching and firmly shaking my hand, her face draped with empathy as she looked around the cafeteria filled with veterans, mostly men, eating their lunches in wheelchairs or with crutches by their sides. "Nice to meet you, Mr. Mannino," she said as she sat down. "I'm Mia Langley."

"Nice to meet you, too. And how are you doing today?"

"I'm fine, thank you, and how are you doing?"

"I'm good," I answered. "Charlie tells me that you wanted to meet me."

"I read in the paper about that boy found in the box. Charlie said that you might be able to find out what happened to him."

"He did, did he?" I looked over at Charlie, who instantly raised his eyebrows in an expression of fake apology.

"And he said that if I wanted to, I could speak to you directly."

"I see," I answered, none too happy about the direction the conversation was taking. "I'm sorry you had to read about that, Mia." I thought again. "By the way, how do you know that it was a boy found in that box? From what I understand, there were only bones inside."

"I just know it, Mr. Mannino. And that box—it's the same type of box that I was put in as a child. The very same."

Mia then went on to tell us a bit more than we ever expected or wanted to hear.

# CHAPTER 7

Disturbed by Mia's story, once I got back to my apartment, I immediately called Paul Tarantino.

A Secret Service agent in the President's detail from George Bush Sr. until Junior's first term, Paul was one of the very best private investigators money could buy. More like a high-priced fixer, in 2010, he proved invaluable in the hunt and capture of the Jones Beach serial killer. With his contacts in government and law enforcement—along with the assistance of Jasmine, his crack computer hacker—he was able to accomplish what the police and the FBI failed to. In the end, we both risked our lives and brought to a violent conclusion the serial killings of young women on Long Island—all prostitutes plying their trade in and around New York City and God knows where else.

Though Paul was a stranger to me when we met, I paid him handsomely and added a huge bonus if he was successful in finding the killer—an offer he ultimately refused. Paul didn't need any additional incentive, and with his expertise in criminal investigations, no one is more adept at finding a missing person than he is.

Six times since 2010 I hired Paul to find missing children, and six times he succeeded. Success, however, doesn't always guarantee that the child will be found alive and well, as I sadly discovered. I left him a voicemail stating that I would be in need of his services and added that this investigation might be the most disturbing he'd ever conduct.

He called me back in less than two minutes. "Going soft, Nick?"

"Maybe I'm just getting old," I answered.

"You're not that old. Stop hiding behind your sixty-plus years and that dye job of yours."

"My brown hair is a genetic aberration. Put up serious money and I'll prove it to you."

"I prefer you use your money for more worthwhile ventures. Now, why'd you call me? What's so disturbing?"

"I heard the most horrible story. At first, I couldn't listen. Funny thing, even with our history, I wasn't ready."

"The last time we worked together, we were in a basement torture chamber." He was referring to the Jones Beach killer's underground bunker. "Maybe you are going soft."

"No. It's probably because I've been languishing in the real world for a change and the nightmares are finally behind me. And I'd like to keep it that way."

"Nick, there's nothing you're going to tell me that I haven't already heard or seen."

"I don't know about that. Apparently, this young girl, now 18, was repeatedly kept in a locked wooden box when she was little."

"Repeatedly? Was she someone's prisoner? Was she kidnapped for a long period of time?"

"Actually, no. It's complicated."

"It always is, but that doesn't answer the question of how someone did this to her and got away with it many times over."

"It may be more than just one person who's responsible. For that reason and others, I'm afraid this particular investigation is going to be exceedingly difficult."

"They're all difficult."

"Not like this. I have a sinking feeling that we're not just dealing with a sick criminal or two, but an entire enterprise."

"And when exactly did all this supposedly happen?"

"It happened when she was six or seven years old. She lived in Manhattan at the time, and still does. As far as being kept in a box and the abuse she suffered, that happened somewhere in Upstate New York, in or near a town called Cartersville."

"And how do you know all this?

"First, from one of the veterans at the center who knows her. His name is Charlie Malone. Then, from the young girl herself…and her witnesses, you might say."

"Witnesses?"

"Yeah, alters."

"Alters? You mean like other personalities? Nick, what the hell are you involved in now? Are you telling me that we've got witnesses who aren't really witnesses?"

"Maybe. And Paul…with this one, I have a suspicion that the small-town police force up there isn't going to be of much help, if they're not already part of the problem."

# CHAPTER 8

I just had to see my son and daughter while in New York. Both had late night meetings, however, so I didn't press them right away for a get together.

John had to prepare for oral argument in the United States Court of Appeals, while Charlotte and key members of her staff were wining and dining a super-rich investment type in the hope of gaining his business. I suppose everyone has his or her own journey. I don't doubt that my Charlotte will retire young and filthy rich (even richer than she is now), while John will keep working until his head hits the desk for the last time. My predictions—as far as my children are concerned—have been wrong before, and I suspect will be wrong again.

While in Manhattan, I stayed, as I always did, at my apartment on 51st Street and Second Avenue, a two-bedroom penthouse with spectacular views of the city.

Though I had planned on going right to bed, after my phone call with Paul, I just couldn't get Mia out of my mind. The next morning, I rented a car and drove out to Long Island to see him. His offices were still in the same village where Eleanor and I once had a home and raised our kids.

I hadn't been back to Garden City since recuperating from my serial killer injuries, and then selling the house on Hillcrest Place. When I entered Paul's suite of offices, they were exactly as I remembered—file boxes in the corners of every room. Jasmine, the computer genius, was at her desk in her own neatly kept private office.

In her mid-30s and as fit as Broadway dancer, with skin a glowing shade of terracotta, Jasmine was a woman of very few words. But when she did speak, it was to parse out pearls of invaluable information no one else could find.

A strapping figure in his custom fitted suit, at six-feet-two, Paul greeted me with a firm handshake as I walked past the reception area. "You look good," he said loudly, and then gave me a warm hug. "A hell of a lot better than the last time I saw you."

"Serial killers have that effect on people. And hospital beds aren't meant to be flattering."

"How's the leg?" he asked, as we walked toward his corner office.

"I can't seem to completely shake the limp that everyone else seems oblivious to but me."

"What limp?"

"Thanks, but it comes and goes. And I know you're full of shit, anyway."

"I don't see a limp. You want me to lie?" Paul was a good liar.

"Let's talk about Mia, the young girl I called you about." I entered his office and sat down. Paul leaned against the wall. "We're going to have to be very careful with this one." My tone was ominous.

"You make me laugh," he said, as he walked around his desk. "We almost got killed last time, and now we have to be careful?"

"Laugh all you want, but this is no laughing matter."

"Nick, this is very sketchy stuff...alternate personalities? C'mon, and this whole thing about the box—"

"Now listen. There's more. They found a kid's bones in a wooden crate just outside Cartersville—the same town Mia said she was taken to. She also said she was put in a box exactly like the one they found the bones in. As far as I'm concerned, this changes everything. We've got to get up there and see what we can find out. This poor girl still has the scars on her arms from the lit cigarettes."

Paul just stared at me blankly.

"Listen, I know we have a whole lot here to substantiate," I added. "But this teenager, Mia...she may be unusual, but she's very bright. And she believes the abductions are still taking place. And you know what? I think she may be right."

# CHAPTER 9

I was pleased when Paul immediately brought Jasmine up to speed on the purpose of my visit. Paul's confidence in her was not lost on me. She knew how to hack and tap technological sources in ways that were impenetrable to almost anyone else. Without Jasmine's help, Long Island's Jones Beach killer would still be murdering young prostitutes.

After I left Paul's office, I couldn't resist. I drove up to Hillcrest Place and passed by the home that Eleanor and I raised our children in—our house on the hill that abutted the Garden City Country Club and golf course. I had purchased it in 1985 as a show-off gesture to my in-laws, even though I used a portion of my Uncle Rocco's inheritance to do it.

And it hadn't changed a lick since I sold it back in 2010.

I pulled over and parked. Memories of my life with Eleanor came flooding back, putting me in a melancholy trance, while the reel of a blurry home movie I directed and wished I could do over, ran in my head. Consumed by my work, I ignored my wife on bad days, and on good ones took her for granted, giving back little to nothing in return. In a futile attempt to console her, I once overheard my daughter, Charlotte, say to her mother: "Dad loves you in his own way." The truth is, I loved Eleanor in every way. I just had a hard time showing it.

After a few minutes that seemed like hours, my trip down the crooked path of memory lane took a turn when my cellphone jolted me back to reality, and another old friend was returning my call.

Back in 2010, when the bones of four prostitutes were found stuffed inside burlap bags and left to rot along the South Shore Beaches of Long Island, Lauren Callucci's sense of hearth and home had been irreversibly altered. Her sister was one of the dead.

With the help of a seasoned yet semi-retired criminal defense attorney (yours truly), and a former White House Secret Service agent turned private investigator (Paul Tarantino), the truth behind her sister's disappearance was unearthed, and eventually, so was the identity of the killer.

In the end, Lauren lost a lot more than just the sister she loved. Though both were victims of child abuse, one had turned to drugs and a life of prostitution, while the other became a reporter for Long Island's largest newspaper and then a CNN foreign correspondent. But even after the Jones Beach killer was eventually brought to justice, Lauren's psychological and emotional damage remained. The truth (cloaked in the identity of the killer) was one grim reaper, and the connection Lauren and I had made was regrettably destroyed by it.

The same age as my daughter, Charlotte, when Lauren left New York in 2010 to take the job overseas, it saddened me to see her leave. I wanted to help her—mentor her back to psychological health—whatever the cost. But when she escaped to the Middle East and a land of sand, bombs, and artillery fire, all I could do was hope that in the pursuit of a greater purpose, she would find some inner peace—some resolution.

When in the spring of 2018, I heard she was back in New York, I reached out to her. Only this time, unlike 2010, it was I who was seeking her help.

# CHAPTER 10

Framed caricatures of actors, agents, producers, directors—all part of the Broadway community—filled every square inch of available wall space throughout Sardi's Midtown Manhattan restaurant. Central to the Theater District, it is one of the most famous dining establishments in the world. Eleanor and I had eaten there often, and I was pleased to find that the well-groomed maître d' remembered me as soon as I walked in. When he asked if Eleanor would be joining me, I told him no, and why. Genuinely saddened, he grabbed my hand and arm in a sympathetic embrace. "I'm so sorry," he said. "She was a lovely woman. I will pray for her." Consequently, that hollow empty feeling that I thought I had successfully kept under quarantine returned. I should have known better. Returning to New York had its own memories. As the maître d' escorted me to a table in the corner (a favorite of mine), I tried in vain to shake off images in my head of Eleanor walking in beside me, sitting down, looking at the menu, and ordering the apple pie with vanilla ice cream for dessert.

"I'm here on business," I told him. "I also see that the person I'm meeting has just walked in." I waved to get Lauren's attention.

When I last saw her, she was twenty-eight years old and carrying more emotional baggage than anyone should ever have to. Eight years later, she looked even younger. Gone were the faded jeans, the T-shirt and the dowdy, pugnacious look. Well-dressed in a blouse and skirt, she was also wearing makeup—the first time I had ever seen her do so.

She greeted me with a big smile and a warm hug. Standing before me was a Lauren I had never seen before.

"So glad you could come. It's great to see you," I said. "When I heard you were overseas and in Aleppo, I was worried about you."

"I was worried about me too," she said as we both sat down.

"Is it as bad as I've seen on the news?" I asked.

"Worse."

"So why did you stay so long?"

Lauren looked away. Then she looked back at me. "After my sister's murder, there was nothing left for me here in New York. I had to get away to a place where my reporting could make a difference—do a hell of a lot more good than it was doing here—and in the process maybe find some meaning to this life."

"There will always be meaning to your life. That's because of the extraordinary woman you are. Don't ever forget that."

"Thank you, but some us have to search and find it on our own terms. In Kabul, and then in Syria, I understood what it was like to live in a country at war—to be entirely at its mercy, to have no control over your life—and how insignificant that can make you feel. You think you matter, and then you don't. I also understand now why soldiers get drawn to the field of battle, even seduced by it. Life is so much simpler when bullets are flying past your ears and bombs are dropping from the sky, and your only goal is to stay alive. It's an odd confluence of feelings."

I patted her hand. "The important thing is that you're back home and in one piece."

"Never thought I would appreciate New York so much," she said. "So many bad memories, you would think I would never want to come back."

"Time to make some new ones. What are you, thirty-four?"

"Thirty-six this year."

"The greater part of your life is still ahead of you. And from what I read on CNN's website, you're back in investigative journalism—your first love. Am I right?"

"Why do I sense you're going somewhere with this?"

"I'm just so very happy for you."

"Thank you," she said with amusing hesitancy in her voice.

"You heard about Eleanor?"

"While overseas, I read *The New York Times* every day. I was so hungry for stateside news. I even read the obituaries. I'm sorry, Nick…truly sorry about Eleanor."

"Thank you. I'm just beginning to learn how to live past the sadness. I was depressed…I don't know…for many months after she passed. That was the hardest—that hollow feeling of hopelessness."

I then remembered that Lauren became uncomfortable when the conversation got too personal, so it came as no surprise to me when she changed the subject. "And your son and daughter?"

"They're good, very good. Thanks for asking. I'm having dinner with them tomorrow."

"Glad to hear it," she said with a broad smile. "Now tell me…what else is on your mind?"

I told her about Mia.

"In Manhattan, young women go missing on a regular basis in numbers that would be considered shocking—mostly prostitutes and runaways," she said. "Many of them are eventually accounted for, but yes, cases of missing children north of New York City and Westchester County are always coming across the *Associated Press* wire."

"I've also got Paul Tarantino on it," I said.

She didn't seem surprised. She remembered him from 2010. Not that Paul was hard to forget.

Since I didn't want Lauren to think that Mia was the only reason I had asked her to dinner, I changed the subject, and before I knew it, we got so caught up in conversation that the restaurant nearly emptied out, and only a handful of non-theatergoers remained.

As Lauren went on to tell it, her time in Aleppo, Syria, was especially disturbing. While leaving the country, she even tried to sneak a little girl out in the hope of saving her and someday reuniting her with her mother—but the Syrian government's armed forces were unyielding and yanked the child from her arms at the airport in Damascus.

I squeezed her hand. "Despite all our good intentions, and no matter how hard we work at it, we can't save the world. It's something we have to live with, but it doesn't mean we have to stop trying." Lauren patted her eyes with a napkin. "But you're right," I added. "As much as I wanted to see you again, there's more to this dinner invitation that just catching up. If you must know, I could use your help."

"You said that you read about my new job, but I don't think you know the half of it," she answered. "I met with the head of the news division yesterday. They want me to produce a show similar to *Dateline* and *48 Hours*, and they want me to do it for CNN."

"That's great. So, you'll also be in front of the camera?"

"Probably. If they deem me camera-ready, so to speak." Lauren made quote signs with her fingers.

"Trust me. You're camera-ready, and I mean that like a proud uncle. You either don't know how beautiful you are, or you don't care. Either way, that's one of the traits that makes you so special."

"Okay now, that's enough, Uncle Nick. I only told you by way of explaining why I may not be in a position to help you right now."

"I understand," I said, while not the least bit convinced. I handed Lauren notes I had on all I had come to learn thus far about Mia and the recently discovered bodies. "I have a sneaking suspicion that the more you dig—and the more you find out about what happened to this young girl and others—as a true investigative journalist, you won't be able to stay away."

# CHAPTER 11

As I entered my apartment after the dinner with Lauren, I reflexively glanced over at the couch where Eleanor would sip a glass of red wine before turning in. The two-bedroom penthouse high above the city had always provided the quiet seclusion we both loved; and she never looked more comfortable and at peace with herself than sitting there and drinking that glass of Merlot. Sometimes she would catch me staring at her and make a face as if to say: "What, you never saw me drink wine before?" And the answer I always thought to say but never did was: *You look so content and happy. At least now, I haven't failed you.* As I stood in the entryway and sadly reminisced, that sinking feeling that came with the realization of irreversible loss returned. Then I heard my *Moon River* ringtone and pulled my cellphone out of my pocket. According to the area code, the call was coming from Franklin, Tennessee.

A nurse was on the phone.

Maureen had been physically assaulted in her apartment. She was in Rolling Hills Hospital, and in stable condition. That's all the nurse could tell me. She had no idea what happened, nor could she comment on how badly Maureen was hurt. I asked her to pass along the message that I would be boarding the next flight to Nashville. Unfortunately, that next flight was not until 6:00 a.m.

After I hung up, I immediately called Maureen's cell, but got no answer. I kept trying until the calls went from busy, right to voicemail. When I called the hospital back, I was told that Maureen had not opened an account for a bedside phone.

The next morning, I was in Tennessee and walking into Maureen's hospital room just as breakfast was being served. I breathed a sigh of relief. She was awake in her bed and didn't have any bruises or injuries that I could see.

"I thought you were in New York." She seemed surprised and happy to see me. She even lifted her head up.

"I volunteer here and didn't want to miss my shift."

She smiled weakly. "You're funny…and I would laugh, except I was hit in the head, and I'm afraid it might hurt if I do." She reached for my hand. "So…you're back?"

"Just to see how you're doing. Then, I'm sorry, but I have to return to New York."

"It was so sweet of you to come. My God, that last-minute flight must have been expensive. You didn't have to. I'm fine, really."

"What the hell happened?"

"I have a concussion. It's not serious. They ran tests. No internal swelling. Just a bump."

"Otherwise though, you're okay?" I leaned over and kissed her gently on the lips.

"Oh, yes. I don't even think anything was taken. I guess I scared him away."

"Did you get a good look at him?"

"I got no look at him—assuming it was a him. I heard movement and then got hit from behind."

"You look fine though. Really."

"Thank you, but Nick, can you do me a favor? The police were nice enough to bring me my purse. Can you take my keys and get me some clothes? I asked a girlfriend to do it, but she was too afraid to go in the apartment. I'm told the police dusted for fingerprints, but they're done; so I figure it's okay to go in now. They're letting me go home soon and I'd love to have something fresh to wear."

"Of course. I came back to help in any way I can."

"And I'm so happy you did." Maureen squeezed my hand.

"And when you get released, you're coming back home with me."

Maureen sighed with relief. "Thanks. I would like that."

I called a taxi from the hospital lobby to take me home. When I arrived, I didn't even bother going into the house. I got in my car and drove to Maureen's apartment on Main Street.

Upon arriving at her building, I first checked the outside door and then her apartment door on the second floor to see if either the lock or the doorframe showed any sign of a forced entry. They didn't. Once inside, I looked around—and not only was there no sign of a break-in, there was no indication that the police had been there.

After I went into the kitchen and grabbed a garbage bag, I went about packing a few things on a list she had given me. As I continued to move about the apartment that consisted of merely a bedroom, living room and kitchen, the absence of any indication that the place had been burglarized began to concern me even more. Before I left, I made a point of checking the windows. They were all locked.

When I returned to the hospital, I handed Maureen some fresh clothes to wear. While she was in the bathroom changing, a short, stocky, clean-shaven man in his 50s with gray crew-cut hair came into the room. He introduced himself as Detective McCormick. I introduced myself as "Maureen's ride home."

When she exited the bathroom, she smiled at the detective and shook his hand. She seemed to be walking well and appeared to have her energy back.

"I just wanted to fill in you and the Mrs.," he said.

"I'm not a Mrs.," Maureen countered. "I'm divorced." She then gestured in my direction. "This is my good friend, Nick."

"We've met," I added.

McCormick spoke plainly. "I'm glad to see that other than a nasty bump on your head, you seem to be doing fine."

"Let's hope she stays that way," I said. "With a concussion, it's hard to tell."

"True. Very true," he answered. "It is hard to tell." I wasn't sure if the detective was being sarcastic, insensitive, or just blunt. He then turned to

Maureen. "There was no damage to your doors or windows. Did anyone else have a key to your apartment?" The detective looked at me. "Your ex-husband? Any of your children?"

"My son is in the military and overseas," she answered. "No one has a key to my apartment but me."

"We'll have the fingerprint results in a week or two, but I have a feeling we're not going to find anything there either," he said. "Do you have any medical history that might have caused you to just pass out, fall and hit your head?" He seemed to be expressing sympathy while asking what could have been interpreted as an obnoxious question.

"No," Maureen responded. "And that's not what happened. I felt a blow to my head caused by something hitting it, like a hard object. I passed out right after."

"Did you hear anything unusual before you passed out?"

"Uhm, no."

"Your neighbor, the widow on the top floor, found you because your door was left open."

"There you have it. I never leave my door open," Maureen said. "And I clearly remember being home for about a minute or two before I was struck. And I also remember locking the door behind me after I came in, like I always do."

"Well then," he added, while shrugging his shoulders. "Please let me know if there's anything else you recall, whether you think it's important or not. Can I reach you at your apartment, if I need to?" He handed Maureen his card.

"I'm not going right home," she said. "I'm staying with a friend tonight." Maureen glanced at me.

McCormick took notice. "Do you want to give me the address of where you're staying, in case I have to get in touch with you?" he asked.

"You can call her on her cell," I interrupted. This detective was fishing, as if trying to piece together a love triangle that had gone bad. Either way, in the age of cellphones, his request for her address seemed a bit peculiar.

Maureen glanced over at me. "Yes, just call and we can talk then," she said. "No one wants to know who broke into my apartment and knocked me unconscious more than I do."

I eyeballed McCormick and smiled. "I'd also like to know."

46

After Detective McCormick left, the head nurse came in and Maureen signed her release papers. She took home instructions for post-hospital care and received an appointment for a follow-up visit with the attending physician. As we were about to leave, she looked around the room. "My cellphone…I thought I left it on the table by the bed."

"You think someone took it?" I asked.

"Everyone was so nice," she said. "I certainly hope not."

"Are you sure you had it with you when you were taken to the hospital? I tried calling you a few times yesterday, but there was no answer."

"Positive."

"Since I've been here, I haven't seen it. I'm sorry, Maureen, but are you sure you had it with you? You suffered a concussion, after all."

"I know, but I'm sure I had it."

"Then someone must have taken it…but why?"

# CHAPTER 12

I f it were nighttime, outdoor lights would have illuminated the entire perimeter of the stately colonial that Eleanor and I had called home for over six years.

A stickler for security, I installed an alarm system immediately after we closed on the house, along with cameras around the periphery, which meant that every exterior movement would be recorded and saved on a DVR for at least 30 days. Installing a house alarm in Franklin, though not unheard of, was rare. But cameras? Aside from famous country western singers, many of whom made their homes in and around Nashville, Eleanor and I were the only people we knew of who had them. After all, this was not New York. Franklin, Tennessee was considered one of the safest communities in the country.

Jump to 2018, and I'm coasting up the long driveway to my home atop two acres—not with Eleanor, but with Maureen—and with her assault less than 24 hours old, all I could think about was keeping her safe.

I didn't have to ask myself why I cared for Maureen, although her similarities to Eleanor were few, and her differences many. Maureen was no heiress. She lived paycheck-to-paycheck. My mom and stepdad lived that way their entire lives. As for Maureen's ethnicity, I never asked. I would have guessed Irish or Scottish, although her eyes had an oval shape that seemed more Eastern European than Celtic. But what did it matter? I cared about her, and I was determined to protect her as long as she would let me.

"As usual, your house looks beautiful," she said as she gazed up at it through the windshield.

"With the perimeter lights, cameras, and alarm, you'll be safe here," I said.

"I sometimes wonder if you're expecting a Russian attack," she said, jokingly. "I know you didn't do all this for me."

I chuckled. The Russians were about the only people I wasn't afraid of. "Being a retired criminal defense attorney from New York might explain it, I suppose."

"I do recall you saying something about that, though you're not big on detail," she said cutely.

"I suppose you can always Google whatever else you want to know about me." I was feeling awkward and showing it. I should have expected this to happen as I developed stronger feelings for her—recent events notwithstanding.

She took my hand. "Nick, I'm not going to Google you," she said with gentle seriousness. "Did you Google me?"

"Of course not." I sounded defensive, probably because I regretted bringing the subject up in the first place.

"Whatever you want me to know about you, you'll tell me," she said. "Whatever you don't want me to know, I'm sure I'll eventually find out anyway." She laughed and kissed me twice on the cheek.

If it were ever possible for me to forget about Eleanor, those two kisses and that laugh would have done it for me.

# CHAPTER 13

After spending the afternoon nestled together in the den, Maureen and I ordered dinner from a local pizzeria. I insisted on cleaning up. I wanted Maureen to rest. At 9:00 p.m., she thanked me profusely "for everything," gave me quite the passionate kiss, and then went to bed in the guest bedroom we often shared when she slept over. The master bedroom was never an option. I couldn't even bring myself to show it to her and was grateful that she never asked me to. She even claimed that she had never slept better than in the guest bedroom's four-post canopy bed that faced east and the early morning sun.

Since I wasn't nearly as tired, I went back into the den to sort through the mail that had accumulated over the last couple of days in my absence. Searching for the letter opener, I heard my *Moon River* ring tone again. It was my son, John, and he wasn't happy.

"You've got to be kidding me, Dad."

"You got my voicemail."

"I got it, alright. You come to New York then leave without seeing Charlotte and me, not to mention Sofia, who's always asking about you."

"That was not by choice. I planned to see all of you, but a friend of mine down here had some trouble and I had to take the next plane out."

"Well, is he okay?"

"It's Maureen, and she was struck on the head by a burglar, but she seems to be doing fine."

"Holy crap. Where are you now?"

"I'm in the den. Maureen is sleeping in a guestroom upstairs. I couldn't let her go back home just yet."

"I can understand that." John was sounding more agreeable by the second.

"Looks like she's going to be okay though. It doesn't seem to be a bad concussion, or the hospital wouldn't have released her."

"Let me know if I can help."

"That's very nice of you, but we're good for now. I'll be back in New York very soon. I have some business there."

"What do you mean by very soon?"

"A day or two. I just have to figure out what to do with Maureen. I don't want her going back to her apartment. If she's up to it, I may take her with me."

"Really? And how well do you even know this woman?"

"Well, we've been seeing each other for a few months now. So, I know her fairly well, I suppose."

"What's a few?"

"Six."

"Six isn't a few, Dad. Listen, just call me when you get back to New York, and if you bring Maureen, I want to meet her. I'm sure Charlotte does too—and I don't have to tell you how pissed *she* is."

"Both of you should know better. I would never leave without seeing you if I didn't have to. I miss you guys, and you know how fond I am of Sofia. Apologize for me."

"We miss you too, and maybe, just maybe, your son and daughter will get to meet this mystery woman."

Though I had a greater and more significant mystery weighing on me—like that of buried children in Upstate New York—I answered cheerfully. "Sooner than you think. I promise. And give my best to Sofia."

After having fallen asleep in the den while watching *The Godfather* for the umpteenth time, I woke up the following morning at 8:00 a.m.—thoughts swirling around in my head about misbegotten men and unfulfilled dreams.

I must have grabbed the blanket I kept on the arm of the sofa and covered myself, because I awoke hot and uncomfortable. After a quick shower, I brewed coffee in the Cuisinart and waited until about 11:00 a.m. before I went to check on Maureen. I knocked on her door and asked if she would like some eggs for breakfast. She sounded groggy and unsure of how to answer. "Oh, that would be great. Yes. My God, I can't believe I slept this late."

"Rest is good for you. Come down when you're ready and I'll start breakfast."

"That's wonderful. And you're wonderful!" Maureen shouted back.

I knew I had to get right back to New York, and waited for Maureen to finish her breakfast before I broached the subject with her. When I did, I saw instant disappointment on her face, and even worse—fear.

"You don't have to go back to your apartment," I added. "I didn't mean to suggest that. You can stay here...as long as you like. You can look after things for me."

"You mean I'll be alone in this big house." She looked around and shrugged her shoulders, then thought again. "I'm sorry. I'll be fine." She stared down at her empty plate, avoiding eye contact. And the longer she did, the worse I felt.

I got up from the table. "The hell with staying here. Come with me."

She looked up, but her sad expression remained. "I can't, Nick. And wouldn't the plane fare be expensive on such short notice?"

"Don't worry about that. I've got points. It won't cost me anything." I was lying and hoping to avoid further talk about the fare.

"I don't believe you and I can't let you do that. I can't go. I just can't. I have my job here."

"Under the circumstances, I'm sure your boss will understand."

"I already made plans to stay with a girlfriend."

"I see, so you don't want to go back to your apartment."

"And the expense. I'll never be able to pay you back."

"My dead uncle won't mind. It's all inheritance anyway." I wasn't nearly about to tell Maureen the whole truth and hoped a light explanation would end the discussion.

"I don't know. I just don't know." She was looking down again.

I put my hand under her chin and gently guided her head up to face me. I looked her in the eyes. "It will be great for you to get away, especially now."

"I'm also supposed to make an appointment with the doctor the hospital gave me."

"We have doctors in New York, and I hear they're pretty good."

She chuckled. "You are persistent." She dropped her head, but her eyes stayed fixed on me. "I'm sure it would be nice to go with you." Then, with a deep conciliatory breath, she added: "But I'll still owe you, okay?" She had a determined look on her face that I found endearing.

"Absolutely," I answered. "I'll send you my marker." I then walked over to the built-in desk beside the kitchen counter. Eleanor's laptop was still sitting there. I flipped it open and booked two seats on the 3:00 p.m. flight out of Nashville.

"Do you have a lot of business in New York?" she asked.

"Now and then." As to the reason for my trip, she wasn't even close to getting the truth out of me. Eventually, I figured I would fess up. For the moment though, she seemed pleased to be going, and I didn't want to spoil the mood with unpleasant talk about missing children.

Maureen tapped me on the shoulder just before I closed the laptop. "Nick, how long will we be away? I'll need more clothes for the trip."

"Just bring enough for a few weeks."

"A few weeks?" She thought again. "And where will we be staying?"

"I have an apartment in the city."

Maureen eyes widened. "Oh..."

Other than a stale smell, everything seemed the same in Maureen's apartment as the day before. Since she seemed hesitant to enter, I went in first and wondered if she would ever be able to sleep alone there again. She quickly packed a suitcase while I waited in the small living room that merely consisted of a coffee table, couch and a wing chair.

Though I found it hard to believe that her ex-husband and father of their only son would strike Maureen over the head hard enough to render her unconscious, he was still at the top of my suspect list.

She told me that his name was Larry Brooks, and despite the recent trauma Maureen had suffered, she was still able to recall the last four digits of his social security number. She also said there was a time when she could easily recite his checking account number too, since she was the one who made the deposits, signed his name, and paid all the bills. "But make no mistake about it," she said. "His name alone was on the accounts." At one time, she even knew his American Express number, including the four-digit security code, but when she started questioning some of the charges—which she suspected were from his many dalliances—the card disappeared. When the new one came, it was in the name of his business—an account, he said, she didn't "need to concern herself with."

Despite Maureen's firm belief that her ex had nothing to do with the assault, when I got back to New York, I would pass this information along to Paul.

# CHAPTER 14

T he moment the plane's tires hit the runway, a call came in on my cellphone. I had purposely kept it off 'airplane mode' just in case. The flight attendants were still strapped in their seats, or a gentle scolding would have been in the offing—gentle, because we were flying business class.

Maureen had been sleeping, and my *Moon River* ring tone wasn't exactly startling. She didn't so much as flutter an eyelash when the sound of Mancini's symphonic strings rose from my pocket. I suppose I should have been more worried every time she did go to sleep, considering the concussion she suffered only three days earlier. She had good color though, and I was keeping a close eye on her—checking her breathing—while admiring how pretty she looked as she slept. Since it warmed me all over when she opened her eyes, I let the phone play a few bars more before I answered the call.

It was Charlie, and, as usual, he sounded anxious and cranky and (again) began talking without even a perfunctory hello—another Charlie idiosyncrasy. "Hey Captain, we've got to get up to Cartersville. No telling how many more kids are buried up there."

"Am I hearing 'we'? C'mon Charlie. You can't be serious? And there's no need to call me Captain."

"You're *my* captain now, and I'm dead serious. No one knows the area better than I do. Like I told you, I grew up there, and I can take you to all the places you need to go, including the construction site where the bodies were found." I could hear the anxiety in his voice heighten. "I bet it hasn't changed a lick in the last fifty years."

"I don't know, Charlie. Are you okay to travel?"

"What do you mean, am I okay to travel? I made it back from Vietnam, didn't I? Syracuse is a 45-minute plane ride. Besides, I'm in a wheelchair. I'll go to the head of the line and with an airport escort to boot."

Maureen was still a bit bleary-eyed in the cab ride to the 51st Street apartment. As soon as we pulled up to the building, the doorman ran out to get her bags. As she stepped on to the sidewalk, she looked up at the building's 59 stories. The doorman—whose name was also Nick, and who was also Italian American—left Maureen's bags by the elevator. That was as far as he went; no way would he leave his post by the door. I gave him a twenty.

Since I had left my suitcase in the apartment when I rushed back to Franklin, I helped Maureen with hers—one large and one small—then hit the button for the 59th floor.

It was a warm night in early May, and once we settled in, I went out onto the balcony overlooking 50th Street and the southern views of a colorful and brightly-lit New York City that weren't blocked or overshadowed by taller buildings. Like lawyers, New York City sometimes gets a bad rap, which in the 1970s and 1980s—when it was on the verge of financial collapse and crime was at an all-time high—was somewhat deserved. But those were the 'bad old days.' The New York City of 2018 was a thriving assortment of neighborhoods—all on a developmental upturn. Broadway box office receipts were breaking records, tourism was at an all-time high, and loads of foreign money was flooding in. It was no surprise that the greatest city in the world still had its ups and downs, but whether I was seeing it from the sky or the water or the vantage point of a tall building's highest floor, New York had always been one beautiful shining metropolis to me, and I never had to ask myself why. It was, and always will be, a place of infinite possibility and boundless hope, no matter who you are or where you're from. And as I stood on that balcony and

56

pondered the reasons why I loved New York, an intractable sadness began to swell inside me.

It was in May of 1979 at a dance at Cardozo Law School in Downtown Manhattan when I first met Eleanor. She was in her third year at NYU Law at the time—and engaged to be married. Nothing ever came easy to me, and I don't expect anything that truly matters in this life ever will. We danced, talked, and ended the night with a kiss. Though we spoke on the phone almost every day thereafter (long distance between Long Island and her home in Atlanta), it wasn't until she broke off her engagement later that summer that we began dating.

Looking out over the city, I could still see her at the edge of that dance floor as clearly as if she was standing right in front of me. And as I drifted off into a state of melancholy, a squall of discontent washing over me, I could swear I felt her arms around me as I had so many times before on that very balcony. But they weren't Eleanor's imaginary arms I was feeling. They were Maureen's real ones.

"It's wonderful here. I can't thank you enough," she said. "You're like my knight in shining armor." She then rested her head on my back and began to cry.

As I turned to put my arms around her, the hollow lump of sadness that had begun to swell inside me seemed to dissolve away.

"Why are you crying?" I asked.

"Because my life is a mess, and I don't know what I would have done if I hadn't met you...if I hadn't gotten to know you over pie and coffee. And that scares me more than I care to admit."

"You mean you weren't just trying to fatten me up?"

She briefly laughed, then cried some more. I took her by the hand into the living room and we stood in front of the picture window facing the north side of Manhattan.

"Can you believe this city has a 20-acre park in it?" I said lightheartedly, trying to cheer her up. "We can visit it tomorrow if you like, and then have lunch at Tavern on the Green."

She turned to me and gave me the longest kiss I'd had in almost two years. And I didn't want it to end. She pulled back first, but not before giving me a shorter one on the cheek.

With my hands on her back, I continued clutching her close. The window beside us was open slightly and I felt a cool breeze across my face and neck that probably began somewhere along the East River. Though it only slightly rustled Maureen's hair, it was enough to ground me back to reality. I moved my hands slowly down to her waist, which only served to enhance my burgeoning arousal. We caressed each other and my head began to fog. But before I could move in for another kiss, the instrumental version of *Moon River,* normally meant to enhance any and all amorous moments, only served to interrupt one.

"How romantic," Maureen whispered.

"If you call bad timing romantic."

I pulled out my phone. The screen read: *Paul Tarantino.* Maureen gave me another kiss before I gently stepped away and put the phone to my ear.

"Did I catch you at a bad time?" Paul asked.

"Since when do you care how you catch me?"

"I don't, but I could swear I heard someone else breathing."

"It's just me. When you get old, you breathe this way." I turned to Maureen, excused myself, and went back into the bedroom. "So, what's up?" I asked.

"We confirmed that two crates of bones were found at the construction site, and according to the medical examiner's reports, they were the bones of little boys. Jasmine also picked up some encrypted email chatter off a police server indicating there may be more."

"So, when do you want to leave?"

"If you're serious about this investigation, first flight out tomorrow."

"I've got to see my kids. If I can have dinner with them tonight, I'll catch up with you later in the day."

"Fine."

"And I'll probably be coming with Charlie."

"The disabled vet? You've got to be kidding."

"He's the guy who turned me on to this investigation in the first place."

"That doesn't mean you have to bring him."

"He grew up in and around Cartersville. He could be an asset to us, and besides, he wants to come."

"It's your dime, Nick. I only hope he doesn't get in the way."

"From what I understand, he's very independent. He's also pretty rough around the edges, but who isn't these days?"

58

"All the more reason I should get a head start."

"Charlie also says he can show us around."

"Nick, the last thing I need is an escort, but if you insist on bringing him, bring him."

"I'll be wiring you the usual retainer. Look out for it."

"I'm not looking out for anything. If I can't trust you by now..."

I then whispered to him the info on Maureen's ex and ended the call. When I returned to the living room, she was still standing beside the picture window. "Who are you anyway, Nick Mannino? I couldn't help but hear some of that."

"Sorry, I tried to talk quietly." I squared up next to her. "Forget the call. What do you say we go out to dinner with my son and daughter and you'll find out all you'll ever want to know about me?"

"I say yes." Another kiss came—only this time we didn't stop there.

# CHAPTER 15

J asmine was what one might call a 'quiet genius.' She had been working
for Paul since he left the Secret Service during George Bush Jr.'s first
term. Her resume stated that she was an early Facebook recruit, and
at a time when how well you can hack at Harvard was a prerequisite to
employment, she was one of their best. In 2005, when Paul's sister, Julie,
was found wrapped in trash bags on the side of a dirt road in Central
Pennsylvania with her skull caved in, he called Jasmine.

But she was already on it.

Jasmine was Julie's roommate at Harvard. She never liked Julie's husband, Chris, and believed the rumors that he had date raped a University
of Massachusetts coed before he met Julie. The instant Jasmine discovered
that Julie was missing, she hacked into Chris's computer. On it she found
a history of online chats he had with women on websites dedicated to
sadomasochists. She also saw that he had downloaded TOR, the entry
browser to the dark web. Paul asked her to keep at it to see what else
she could find.

And she found out plenty.

Despite being in serious financial trouble, Julie's husband, Chris, also
loved the '1-900' telephone lines. When the lights in their house were
turned off, Julie discovered that the not-so-successful DDS had not only

let their personal bills go unpaid, he had also wiped out their savings. All that was left of value were their joint life insurance policies. When Julie's body was found, the information Jasmine uncovered was enough to make Chris suspect number one as far as Paul was concerned. With help from the FBI, Paul arranged to have a forensics team sweep the house. With the use of luminal spray and an ambient light, images of blood puddles and splatter that had been thoroughly washed away appeared, which provided conclusive evidence that Julie was murdered inside the house. Once confronted with the luminal proof, Chris confessed to the murder.

While Maureen and I were headed out to have dinner with my kids, and Paul was booking his morning flight to Syracuse, Jasmine had already begun hacking the servers of police departments, news organizations, and a variety of intelligence-gathering governmental agencies. Her goal: to gather whatever information she could find on missing children in Upstate New York, outside Syracuse, and in and around Cartersville.

Our investigation had officially begun.

# CHAPTER 16

Maureen and I dined with my children at Café Luxembourg on 70th Street and Amsterdam Avenue, where the food was delicious (and also expensive). It was Charlotte's choice. The last time I dined there was with Eleanor, and the actor, Liam Neeson was sitting at a table across from us with his sons. His wife, Natasha Richardson, had just died in a skiing accident and his boys were no more than ten or twelve years old. The site of the three of them eating alone was both lovely and sad. Thoughts of Charlie and Mia must have been weighing on me, because my mind then drifted from the Neesons to Upstate New York and the many buried crates that inexplicably contained the bones of little boys.

I was pleased when my son grabbed my attention and began chatting about a case he was handling. As I proudly listened, I kept glancing at Charlotte and Maureen, who were pleasantly talking away the evening. Apparently, Maureen was telling an abbreviated version of her life story—mostly the second half—and I was pleased to see that Charlotte appeared genuinely interested (whether she was or not). I was hoping John would break away and join in. My fondness for Maureen was apparent. Charlotte, the tougher of the two to please, appeared to be warming up to her quite nicely. I also noticed John looking over and taking in some of the conversation (or so it seemed). He then turned to me and asked: "So why are you really in New York, Dad? And don't tell me it's just to visit the Veterans' Center and your friend, Charlie."

I thought about dodging the question, but what was the point? My son was a grown man, and like the best of friends, our loyalty to each other was without bounds. I fessed up about Mia, her alters, and the discovery of the wooden boxes.

He thought for a moment. "You said this teenager, Mia, had turned eighteen this year," he said, placing emphasis on her age. "No doubt she's been seeing a psychiatrist with her multiple personality disorder and all that she's been through. Am I right?"

"No doubt," I confirmed.

"Dad?" John said my name as if to ask a question, but it was more of an indication of what he was thinking.

We stared at each other for a few seconds until it dawned on me. "That's brilliant!"

"It's not brilliant, Dad. I'm just thinking like a lawyer—and apparently so are you."

"Still, this should have occurred to me already. Now that Mia has turned eighteen, if she waives doctor-patient privilege, we can find out all that her alters told her psychiatrist—not to mention the doctor's notes and records. It could be a treasure trove."

"Psychotherapy notes will be harder to get," John added. "The patient does not have an absolute right to them. What you *can* get is what Mia would have said about crimes committed against her and others— what she said to the doctor when one of her alters was talking. Don't even bother asking for the doctor's written observations and conclusions. Without a continuing case of patient child abuse, you won't get them."

"Got it." I answered.

"But will Mia waive the privilege?" John asked.

"She is as anxious as anyone to find out what happened to those little boys, and should the doctor refuse to cooperate in spite of the waiver, we'll get the FBI to issue a subpoena. Paul Tarantino's got the hooks."

"Any resistance from the doctor—and I would also get Mia a lawyer. I'd have her bring an action as well. She's the patient, after all, and no one is more entitled to the doctor's notes and records than she is."

Busting with pride at my son's reflexive command of the issues, I sat back and wondered to what extent I would get the doctor's cooperation, with or without a court order.

As John and I clicked our glasses in acknowledgement of our legal brainstorming, Maureen excused herself to go to the ladies' room. Feeling hopeful and emboldened, I popped an entirely unrelated, yet significant question to my beloved children.

"So, what do you think of Maureen?"

In unison and to my utter astonishment, they replied: "She seems nice, Dad, but you do know she looks just like Mom, don't you?"

# CHAPTER 17

After we returned to the 51$^{st}$ Street apartment, I broke the news to Maureen that I had to leave the city on business. Though she seemed both surprised and disappointed, she pulled me close and gave me another slow, soft kiss that seemed to stay on my lips long after it was over. Though another round of lovemaking seemed to be in the offing, I felt thrown off balance by my kids pointing out her likeness to Eleanor. Maureen seemed tired anyway, so I told her that I had to make some calls and that she should not wait for me to turn in—even though the only one I intended to make was to Charlotte. But before my fingers touched the phone, a call came in from Lauren.

"No way you read my notes on Mia and Upstate New York and are bailing on me this quick," I began.

"Oh ye of little faith. I did some digging, got the dope on Mia, and you wouldn't believe who her adoptive mother is." Lauren sounded confident and self-assured, as always.

"Hillary Clinton?"

"Close, but wrong party. It's Beatrice Langley, Reginald Langley's widow."

"The former Secretary of—"

"The Treasury, yes."

"How the hell did that happen?"

"Meet me at the Skylight Diner on 34th Street tomorrow morning at ten, and you'll find out."

After I hung up with Lauren, I couldn't help but think to myself...*What in the world am I getting myself into?* I made a couple of quick calls, and then in an effort to clear my head, I went into the living room and turned on the TV. After flipping through the cable channels, I found that *The Godfather* was on again, and I picked up almost where I left off back in Franklin. But once again, age got the better of me and I dozed off. When I awoke, I checked on Maureen. She was in bed and in a deep sleep. I checked the time. It was only 10:45 p.m. Since I knew Charlotte would still be up, I called her and asked her to look in on Maureen "while I was away on business for a few days."

Charlotte answered as I expected she would. "You bring your girl-friend to New York City and then you leave her here? So, what is it? Are you serious about her or not?"

"Now you're embarrassing me."

"Well, she's goo-goo eyed for you, Dad."

"I can't believe you're grilling me like this—like I used to grill you."

"Believe it. It's happening."

"Alright...yes, I care about her very much. Now can you just check in on her while I'm gone, please? Have her over...take her out once or twice...and ask John to join in, too?"

"You're going to have to ask John yourself. He's not exactly onboard with the Maureen thing just yet—especially with the resemblance."

"Charlotte, I don't want her wandering around the city alone, so please—"

"I'll look after her, but it will have to be after work."

"Of course, after work."

"I'll do my best, Dad. Now have a safe trip."

The next morning, Maureen and I went out for breakfast. When we returned, I gave her two thousand in cash and told her it was for food and fun while I was gone.

"Nick, there is no reason why I would need this much money," she said. "I'll use some of it to stock the refrigerator, but that's it. When you come back, I'll be as plump as a pumpkin."

"Don't be silly. The Broadway shows are amazing, and my daughter, Charlotte, is going to give you a call also. She wants to take you out and show you the big city."

"That's sweet of her. I'd love that."

"As for the money? I'm really just a poor boy from Brooklyn who got an inheritance I can't spend in a dozen lifetimes. So, enjoy it while I'm gone. When I get back, we'll enjoy it together."

I was then the recipient of another of those long kisses that made me forget that a limo would be arriving soon with a crusty veteran inside. After Lauren had called the night before, I moved the flight to Syracuse from 11:00 a.m. to 5:30 p.m. There was just one problem: I'd forgotten to tell Charlie and the limo driver.

As expected, Charlie griped about being picked up so early, and then griped some more when I told him we had a few stops to make before we headed to the airport—first to see Lauren and then to pay a visit to the offices of one Dr. Sylvia Field, psychiatrist. I'd called ahead to make an emergency appointment. Didn't matter. She was booked. Then I dropped the name of Beatrice Langley, and like the parting of the Red Sea, at 2:00 p.m., a slot opened up.

After I told Charlie what I had planned, he could barely contain his excitement. Being part of the investigation seemed to breathe new life into him. Once we arrived at our initial destination, I watched as he moved easily onto his wheelchair from inside the limo. All I had to do was open the rear passenger door, move the chair close, and he did the rest. He also insisted on wheeling himself. He told me that this was something I had "better get used to."

The chrome storefront of the Skylight Diner was a throwback to the trailer car diners of the 1950s and 1960s. After we passed under a long blue awning, we went inside and joined Lauren at a corner booth. She hid her surprise at seeing Charlie, introduced herself, and shook his hand. His marine fatigues, scraggly beard and rough manner didn't faze her in the least. After all, she had just returned from war-torn Aleppo.

When the waitress arrived, Lauren and I merely asked for coffee, while Charlie ordered a pancake breakfast.

"Didn't you eat at the center?" I asked.

"So what?" he replied. "You never heard of anyone having two breakfasts? Besides, while the two of you are talking, I'll at least have something to do."

"What do you mean?" Lauren asked. "You're a part of this too, Charlie." Lauren then sent a smile in his direction, which caused him to blush.

"She's not flirting with you," I said blithely to Charlie.

"I can dream, can't I?" he answered, while shoving a fork full of pancake soaked in maple syrup into his mouth.

Lauren went on to explain that there was little that she couldn't find out while working at the center of one of the world's largest news organizations. The resources were endless, and there seemed to be no bottom to the well of information at her disposal—whether archived on computer servers, or collected from books and records dating back to the invention of the printing press.

She then spoke while referring to prepared notes that she later gave me.

"Now a widow going on nine years, Beatrice Langley came from what was dubbed in her social circle as 'good stock.' Regrettably, this term was not at all applicable to her husband, Reginald Langley, known to his friends as Reggie, whom she first met at a polo match in the Hamptons. Beatrice was quite the young beauty in those days. Standing next to Reggie, a handsome and fit polo player, the two looked like paper cutouts from a high society magazine—but for Reggie's background. Reggie was a professional gambler, and though quite the athlete (having played Triple-A ball for the Baltimore Orioles), he had barely enough money to keep up appearances. On the other hand, Beatrice's family had been in banking since the early 1900s and was downright filthy rich. Regardless of their differences, Reggie's ship was about to come in, and Beatrice's family was helping steer it to port.

"Prior to meeting Reggie, and to the dismay of her family, Beatrice had just concluded a scandalous affair with a Dominican chef who worked at one of the country clubs her father belonged to. The affair came to an abrupt end when her father called in a few favors, got the chef fired and ultimately deported. When rosy-cheeked Reggie came along with his athletic build, good looks and pearly white smile, it was all Beatrice's family could do to keep the two together. Once Reggie caught wind of the catbird seat he was in, he proceeded to shake down her father for a half-million-dollar dowry, and married Beatrice. Shortly thereafter, Reggie began the career in finance he was dreaming of, starting as an assistant vice president in one of his father-in-law's banks. Bright, charming and even hardworking, he quickly rose up the ranks, impressing both Beatrice's father and the local political machine. This explains why, five years into the marriage, he ran for Congress and lost, and then two years later ran for the U.S. Senate and lost—all the while climbing New England's political ladder in lockstep with his rise in the banking industry.

"Then the marriage lottery paid off—and paid off big—when one fine day a certain U.S. president (who was returning a favor), nominated him for a cabinet position. Fortunately for Reggie, that president's political party was in control of Congress and his appointment was easily confirmed. Reginald Langley, gambler and gold digger, had become the Secretary of the Treasury of the United States of America.

"As for Mia, Beatrice had been dead set on adopting the moment she discovered that she couldn't have any children. Reggie, the bastion of encouragement, had serious doubts as to whether she would be able to assume the grand responsibilities of motherhood over the long term, which is why he suggested she begin by giving foster parenting a try.

"With the help of a friend in local government, Beatrice was able to view a series of bios and photos handpicked from the files of New York City's Bureau of Child Welfare. Though Mia's backstory was troubling, Beatrice softened immediately after seeing a photo of the child's young, sweet face. Then they met, and Mia's emotional and psychological difficulties no longer mattered. As for Reggie, he never did meet Mia. At the same time that Beatrice was finalizing the paperwork to become a foster mom, Reggie's car was veering off a highway somewhere south of Albany on his way back from a hunting trip. Having crashed down into a culvert, he suffered severe head trauma and died a week later. Though Beatrice barely shed a tear, she footed the bill for the elaborate funeral befitting a member of the president's cabinet, and accepted all condolences graciously. Afterward, she was only too happy to be raising Mia alone."

"Damn," I said. "I can't believe how much information you found, and how fast you found it."

"It was easier than you think. Beatrice isn't the only one with contacts in Social Services."

"Ya gotta have friends," Charlie uttered, as he slurped down the remains of his coffee, and then cradled the cup in his hands. "You can always get a good cup of coffee here," he exclaimed.

"You've been here before?" I asked.

"Why should that surprise you?" he answered matter-of-factly.

Lauren had to get back to work, but before she left, I had one more assignment for her. "What you need to know, and what I failed to tell you until now, is that Mia suffers from multiple personality disorder."

"You're not serious." Lauren appeared surprised, but not deterred.

"I suppose when you get put in a box, and tortured and abused as a child," I answered, "you either go completely mad, or some force inside you comes to your aid—like white blood cells fighting off an infection."

"Oh my God," Lauren blurted. "This poor kid."

"And you wouldn't know it to meet her. She's lovely really. Of course, as Charlie can attest, sometimes you're meeting someone else."

"I can attest," Charlie interrupted, while widening his eyes in exaggerated fashion.

"This is the most fascinating, and at the same time, the saddest thing I have ever heard." Lauren looked down, thought for a moment, and then perked up and gave me her full attention. "Nick, I want in on this case, and I'm not talking about a news story. I want to help this girl."

"And we've also got to find out about those buried kids," Charlie added.

"I'm glad you feel this way," I said to Lauren. "Which is why I need you to do something for me. I need you to get Mia to sign a waiver of doctor-patient privilege, so we can find out what Mia's alters said to her psychiatrist about the crimes they witnessed, as well as who was responsible. Mia, of course, will tell us everything that *she* knows. The problem is that it was her alters who saw and heard the worst of it. If we can get the psychiatrist's session notes and maybe even compel the doctor to talk, we might just find out what actually happened to Mia, and many other children as well. Right now, all we've got is a little girl's limited recollection."

"I'm sure our lawyers at the network will have the waiver," she said. "I'll take care of it. Just tell Mia to expect to hear from me."

"We will," Charlie joined in. "Here's her info." Charlie pulled a pen out of his pocket, wrote Mia's telephone number on a napkin, and then handed it to Lauren.

"Thank you, but I have it," Lauren said. She then slipped me a piece of paper with Mia's address on it. "Take this too, should you need it," she said.

# CHAPTER 18

Charlie got back into the limo as easily as he got out of it by locking the chair's wheels, climbing on to the open doorframe, turning, and dropping himself on to the rear seat. And he didn't so much as break a sweat in the process. Even the driver marveled at his strength and dexterity.

Once the chair was placed in the trunk and we were all seated inside, I announced to the driver that our next stop would be Park Avenue and 60th Street.

"Why the hell are we going there?" Charlie asked, as he wiggled to get more comfortable.

"Lauren gave me Mia's address. Since our flight won't leave for a few hours, let's take a look. I have a feeling you might like her digs…at least what we can see from the outside."

"Fine with me." Charlie chuckled as he spoke. "And I must say, I like that Lauren."

"Either way, don't get too excited about the upscale visit," I said. "We've got time to kill before our next appointment, so we're just doing a drive-by. I doubt we're getting out of the car."

"A drive-by, huh. Should I be packing heat?" Charlie asked, as the driver, a man in his seventies, eyeballed us via his rearview mirror as he turned off 35th and on to Park.

"Funny, but not funny," I said.

Charlie looked out the side window on to Park Avenue. "Do you know why there are these big planters with flowers in them running up and down the center of the avenue?"

"No, I don't, Charlie. Maybe because it adds a park-like atmosphere to the two-way street called Park Avenue?"

"That's one reason, but not the main reason," Charlie said proudly. "In the mid-1800s, there was a railroad that ran up the middle of what was then called Fourth Avenue. In 1875, the train stopped running and the tracks were sunk into a trench and covered with dirt. Later, grass and benches were added to cover the trench—thus, the park-like atmosphere you speak of. Later on, when the high society-types moved in, the name of the street was changed to Park Avenue."

"Very impressive," I responded. "I didn't know you were such an urban history buff."

"I'm also impressed," the driver added cheerfully. "And may I add, sir, a 'thank you' for your service."

Charlie ignored the driver's 'thank you' and turned to me. "There's a lot you don't know about me, Captain, and there's a lot I know about Upstate New York that you'll find damn helpful once we get there—if we ever get there. Did I catch that we have another stop after this?"

"Patience, Charlie. We're killing three birds with one stone before we leave.

We'll be back in your hometown for dinner. You'll see."

Charlie continued to look out the window. "I've been up in this area many times, you know. I also know Mia's address. She told it to me once."

"You came all the way up here in your chair?"

"If you can walk it, I can ride it."

"Whatever you say." I looked down at the address, then up at the numbers on the buildings. I asked the driver to slow down. "Here it is, 510 Park Ave." The driver stopped beside an awning braced onto brass poles that extended from the curb to the building, where gold-trimmed front doors under an elegant, stained-glass Tiffany light welcomed all inhabitants and invited guests—of whom we were neither.

"There are marble floors, walls and ceilings inside," Charlie exclaimed with surprising familiarity. "There's even a spiral staircase leading up to the second floor. Of course, to go any higher, you have to use the bank of elevators. The rich don't like to be kept waiting."

"How on God's green earth do you know all this?" I asked.

"I followed Mia home once, waited, and then went inside. There are two doormen on at all times. One, who was working at the time, was also a veteran—Iraq and Afghanistan. He let me hang out and look around for a few minutes."

I shook my head in disbelief.

"Hey, I lost my legs. I didn't lose my arms, and I certainly didn't lose my mind."

"I suppose not, Charlie."

"No supposing about it. Where to now, Captain?"

I looked up at the building through the limo's skylight. It was about fifty stories high. "I'll bet my uncle's inheritance that Beatrice Langley's apartment is somewhere in the stratosphere up there." I then looked down at my notes and nodded to the driver. "Please take us to 81 Greenwich Street. I believe it's in the Village."

"It's in the Financial District," Charlie said.

"That's right, sir," the driver responded.

"Where are we going now?" Charlie asked.

"We're going to see a psychiatrist," I answered. "We have an appointment."

"This should be fun," Charlie said sarcastically.

"Let's see what she is willing to tell us—without a waiver," I said.

"I wouldn't hold my breath," Charlie answered.

# CHAPTER 19

Dr. Field's office was located in a four-story mixed-use building that housed a restaurant on the ground floor. After we entered the lobby through a separate doorway, a man sitting behind a counter in a security uniform took my name and directed us to the elevator. We took it to the third floor, where it opened into a waiting room that looked like it hadn't been updated since Ronald Reagan was president. Even the magazines were several years old, and the dust on the bookcases behind an empty reception desk was visible from across the room. But no sooner did I sit down and Charlie wheel up next to me, than a door opened up inside the wall of books and Dr. Field entered. She was in her mid-fifties, wearing a pantsuit and a loose-fitting vest that she habitually tugged on in an apparent attempt to hide her obesity. Her manner was less than welcoming. "Who are you two gentlemen, anyway?" she asked, and then paused for a moment to take in the sight of Charlie in his wheelchair. I do believe she tempered her remarks thereafter as a result.

I stood and extended my hand. "My name is Nick Mannino, and this is Mr. Charlie Malone."

"I don't shake hands," she said abruptly. "And Mr. Mannino—are you here for a session or not? Because I checked with Beatrice, and she hasn't the foggiest idea of who you are."

"I'm sorry for any misunderstanding, but we do need to speak to you—provided of course, your answers do not compromise the delicate doctor-patient privilege." I had no idea why I was speaking sarcastically. I either didn't like the doctor's manner, or for some reason I just didn't like her. Either way, this was not an appropriate way for a PI to begin asking questions, especially of someone who could rightfully hide behind the cloak of legal confidentiality. But I wasn't a PI. I was a retired lawyer flying by the seat of my pants as a private investigator, just as I did the last time I teamed up with Paul. Evidently, in my six-year layover, I had grown quite rusty at the task. Even Charlie's expression conveyed his disappointment in me.

As for Dr. Field, she wasn't letting up. "So, what you're saying is that you dropped Beatrice's name just to get me to clear this hour for you."

"Yes, and no. Actually, this is about Beatrice. Her adopted daughter, Mia, is your patient. I assume that Beatrice is not."

"Beatrice is my friend." Dr. Field's emphasis on the word 'friend' was a sign that we shouldn't expect her to be breaching any unwritten oaths of personal loyalty. I also didn't expect professionalism to rule the day either. While Charlie was as cool as a cucumber, I was using every ounce of self-control I could to contain my resentment of a doctor who probably listened for years to atrocities against children, all the while indifferent to whether it was continuing or not.

"I'm not asking you to talk about anything that would make you feel uncomfortable, and nothing that Beatrice wouldn't have to answer to if she were subpoenaed herself."

The doctor's eyes widened, as did Charlie's. I questioned the wisdom of raising the specter of a subpoena at this early stage. It was a gamble, and one that I hoped would result in getting Dr. Field to talk, though there was a good chance it would backfire, and I'd immediately be shown the door. But since honoring subpoenas, or bringing motions to quash them, have a way of producing large legal bills (not to mention the lost billable hours when doctors are called away to testify), Dr. Field relented and asked us to step into her private office.

Once inside, the décor changed to 'contemporary minimalist,' and was a bit too sterile for my taste. I like wood, and since there was very little of it, I sat on her circa 1980s couch instead of one of her thinly designed Art Deco guest chairs.

Charlie, to his credit, let me do the talking, but no sooner did we settle in than Dr. Field tried to turn the tables on us. "I knew your name sounded familiar," she said, as she walked behind her desk and plopped down in a plump leather chair. "You're the guy who caught the Jones Beach killer." She pointed at me with her upturned hand.

"A lot of people are responsible for catching the Jones Beach killer," I said, trying to hide my discomfort. "I was just someone dumb enough to confront him who wound up getting a couple of knife wounds to show for it."

"That's a lot of bull," Charlie interrupted. "He went in to save his friend."

I waved Charlie off. "Regardless, we're here because we're investigating cases of missing children in Upstate New York."

Dr. Field's demeanor softened. "Fine. If I can help you regarding missing children, I will. Of course, I will, but I want you to know I'm not crazy about subpoenas. My ex-husband was a lawyer, and I don't need or want to contribute any more to that ugly profession than I have to. So, ask me what you will. I'm just not sure how much I can help you. My sessions with Mia are, of course, confidential."

"I understand and respect that," I said. "So, let me ask you this: Can you tell us how Mia came to be adopted by Beatrice Langley?"

Lauren had given us plenty of information on it, but I was certain that Dr. Field had a more complete version to tell. Besides, this seemed like a safe question to start with, since it gave Dr. Field an opportunity to put Beatrice in a positive light.

"See…this I can answer, and it's also a matter of record, though those records, too, are confidential." As Dr. Field spoke, with head back, elbow on the arm of her chair and pen dangling in her hand, I suspected that Charlie and I were about to get a whitewashed version of the adoption backstory. But that was fine with me. At least we got her talking. We could then take our openings as we found them. And as she continued, eyes rolled back and looking in all directions but ours, you would think she was theorizing on a landmark event in history to a class of college seniors. "I can help you with this because I know Beatrice wouldn't mind, and neither would Mia. You see, Beatrice started out as Mia's foster mom," she said definitively. "It was a supervisor-friend of hers at Social Services who started the adoption ball rolling after Mia's mother passed away. Mia's birth name was Mia Archer. She was named after her mother, who was an actress—and who also had a terrible drug problem, courtesy of her drug dealer boyfriend. His name was Greg, and all I can safely tell you about him was that Mia called him 'Uncle Greg.' He would often conduct his drug business out of their crappy apartment off 10th Avenue. When a neighbor reported both him and Mia's mother to the Bureau of Child Welfare, Mia was removed from the home."

"Did this 'Uncle Greg' hurt Mia in any way?" I asked.

"I can't speak to whether he did or not without Mia's permission."

"Then what you're saying is that he did hurt her," Charlie said curtly.

"I already answered that question the only way I can," Dr. Field responded.

"Please tell us whatever else you can, Dr. Field." I was hoping politeness would work better than sarcasm and anger.

"Regretfully, shortly after the adoption was finalized, Mia's mother overdosed. The police showed up to question old 'Uncle Greg,' but he was nowhere to be found."

"Did Beatrice have any second thoughts about adopting the daughter of a drug addict, considering her husband's high-level position in government?"

Dr. Field adjusted her sitting position. She seemed to be suddenly uncomfortable in her chair. This was a question she was not expecting and as soon as I asked it, I was sorry I did. It was just too in-your-face. "It's common knowledge that Beatrice and Reginald didn't get along during their marriage. You could ask anyone that knew them. It's no secret. Besides, he died before Mia came into the picture. He never even met her. He was driving back from a deer hunting trip—at least that's where he told Beatrice he was going—when his car careened off the road. He passed away in the hospital shortly thereafter. Funny thing, though he didn't own any rifles, deer hunting was something he did year-round. Peculiar if you ask me. Then again, so was he. He had told Beatrice that he used a friend's rifles once he got there. He said he preferred it that way because he didn't like traveling with weapons. He also told Beatrice that the site of the hunting ground was somewhere just south of Albany. When she asked him why he insisted on driving instead of flying up, he brushed her off with different excuses—like the drive wasn't that long…he enjoyed the scenery…and the fares were too pricey on such short notice."

"Are you sure he was going deer hunting?" Charlie asked. "Better yet, was Beatrice sure he was going deer hunting?"

"Yes. I even heard him say so myself when I was visiting once. It was during the month of May if I recall correctly. I was looking out the front window on to Park Avenue and admiring the flowers on the medium. Come to think of it, I also remember hearing Reginald say that he was a terrible shot."

"And you specifically remember him saying he was going deer hunting in the month of May?" Charlie asked.

"Yes. It was May, definitely."

Charlie wasn't done. "Dr. Field, are you aware that the New York State Department of Environmental Conservation only allows deer hunting in this state from late September to late January?" Charlie apparently knew a lot more about New York State's environmental conservation laws than I did, which wasn't saying much. I had never hunted in my life, though I did recall a cousin of mine from Staten Island once remark that the price of a good deer kill was freezing his nuts off in the process.

"No," she answered. "But that might explain things."

"How so?" Charlie asked.

"Considering that the location of Reginald's fatal car crash was just ten miles south of Cortland, on Route 81—though he wasn't lying about going Upstate—he seemed to be about his exact destination."

"If he were coming from a hunting ground near Albany, he would have been on Route 87, not 81, which leads down from Cartersville and Syracuse," Charlie added.

Without being asked, Dr. Field also stated that she and Beatrice Langley had been friends since their teenage years, when they attended the same private high school for girls in Connecticut. As a result, Beatrice would always confide in her, she said, like "close friends do."

"So, what's the explanation for Reginald being on 81 then?" Charlie had his suspicions, but nevertheless pressed Dr. Field for an answer.

And Charlie got one, but not the one he expected.

"Reginald was having an affair, plain and simple. At least that's what Beatrice thought. The so-called 'deer hunter' was cheating on her with another woman. Beatrice was convinced of this and refused to accept any other explanation. As far as she was concerned, the marriage had become one of mere political convenience."

"I don't buy it," Charlie said under his breath.

"That must've been hard on her," I spoke up, hoping my expression of sympathy would override Charlie's cynicism, while keeping Dr. Field chatty and engaged. There was no doubt that Dr. Field knew much more than she let on, and it wasn't merely the issuance of a subpoena that she feared. It was the truth. Fortunately, she wasn't finished with passing along what she believed we would assume was harmless information about an affair. But as she continued to talk—not as up to date on the news coming out of Cartersville as we were—she couldn't have been more wrong. "Beatrice's suspicions about an affair escalated one morning when she went to the dry cleaner and picked up one of Reginald's dinner jackets that he had worn on his last so-called 'hunting trip.' Seems the presser had removed a receipt from one of the pockets and stapled it to the plastic wrap. It was a receipt from Toys 'R' Us for the purchase of several children's books. Once Beatrice found it, not only did she suspect that her husband was having an affair, but that he had a second family as well."

"What were the names of the books?" Charlie asked.

I looked at him as if to say: *Why would that possibly matter?* And Charlie continued to prove himself smarter than I gave him credit for.

"Let me look," Dr. Field answered matter-of-factly. "I still have the receipt. Beatrice gave it to me to hold eons ago, should she one day get up enough nerve to file for divorce." Dr. Field pulled a cash register tape that was about eight inches long out of the recesses of her bottom desk drawer and read it out loud. "Oh look…there's a couple of my daughter's old favorites here." She read off the titles light heartedly. *"Freddy Spaghetti, Love You Forever, Dumbo,* and lastly…*Christmas Moon."*

# CHAPTER 20

C hristmas Moon was, in fact, a popular children's book that had been published in 2005. Was it a coincidence that Reginald Langley, who was lying about his Upstate hunting trips, also purchased a copy of the same children's book that was found buried along with the bones of a little boy? Was it also a coincidence that Mia, who was also placed in a box of the same type, happened to be adopted by his widow?

Paul was right. We needed to get up to Cartersville—and fast.

Near the conclusion of our meeting with Dr. Field, Charlie took a bold step. "And what about Mia and Upstate New York?" he asked.

Dr. Field was adamant. "That's confidential, and I do not have Mia's consent to discuss that with you."

"And if you did?" Charlie asked.

"That would be different," she said. "But Mia can't give that consent while she is still a minor. You will need Beatrice's permission."

"Mia turned eighteen in December," I said, careful not to sound adversarial.

"Then if she is of sound mind, and she puts her consent in writing, perhaps that would change things." Dr. Field rose from her chair. "Now one of you please write me a check for my time, as I have other appointments to attend to."

"And how much is that, Doctor?" I asked.

"Seven-hundred-and-fifty dollars," she answered.

"That's pretty steep. Isn't the going-rate much less?"

"That's Mia's rate, and since you used Beatrice Langley's name to get this urgent appointment, that's my rate to you."

I wrote a check to cash and handed it to her. "I suppose I should be grateful that my ailments are only physical," I said wryly. "What is your usual rate, anyway?"

"Three-hundred-and-seventy-five an hour."

"So, Mia pays double?" Charlie asked.

"Her mother does and that's because Mia is a special case."

"I'll bet," Charlie uttered under his breath.

"And you've been having sessions with her since she was what, seven?" I was guessing wrong on purpose. "Isn't that when she was adopted?"

"Try age ten. And we had two—sometimes three—sessions per week," she answered stoically.

Charlie could contain himself no longer. "That's eight years, which means we're talking between five-hundred-thousand and a million in fees. Yeah, I would say she was special, all right."

The doctor's response was deadpan. "Goodbye, gentlemen."

# PART 2

# THE TOWN

*This place is so different from the city.*
*Less people.*
*Lots of trees.*
*No traffic.*
*Mia wishes her mom were here. I can feel it.*
*Uncle Greg is driving, though he's nobody's uncle.*
*I don't know why we've come here.*
*Such a long trip.*
*The height of the mountains passing by us scares me.*
*I heard Uncle Greg say something about cash and lots of it.*
*Maybe that's what these packages are for.*
                                        *Melanie*

# CHAPTER 21

The flight time was less than forty minutes. Since I wanted Charlie to be comfortable, and there was no first class, the only upgrade was a seat with extra legroom—not exactly one Charlie would appreciate. When we boarded the plane and the attendant saw him in his wheelchair and wearing Marine fatigues, however, she placed us both in the first row after moving two paid passengers, whether they liked it or not. I only wished Charlie would have said "thank you," so that I wouldn't have had to say it twice. I was also grateful for the short flight because Charlie didn't stop talking the entire time we were in the air.

Paul had already booked us into the Red Mill Inn when we arrived. Though located in Cartersville, it was not my first choice. I was hoping to keep the purpose of our visit secret for as long as possible and would have preferred a major hotel where we would have been taken for just a couple of businessmen—no questions asked. When I confronted Paul about it in the hotel lobby, he posed a question that had its own answer: "What major hotel?" There was none.

From the outside, The Red Mill Inn looked more like a big barn than a mill (not that I had seen many mills in my life). The rooms were large, clean, and had a fresh look and feel to them, as if recently renovated. The staff was exceedingly nice, but they wore their curiosity like a signpost.

And who could blame them? Two casually dressed men and a disabled Vietnam veteran in a wheelchair were not exactly everyday visitors.

With a population of less than eight thousand that encompassed a mere 3.2 miles, Cartersville is a town within the county of Onondaga, New York, and is also considered part of the Syracuse metropolitan area a mere eighteen miles away. These stats were delivered by Paul minutes after Charlie and I arrived. "It's located right on the Seneca River," he added. "It runs right through it and is a tributary of the Oswego River." When I asked him why I needed to know all this, he simply answered: "When you come to a place for an investigation, it's important to know its geography."

I noticed Charlie's duffel bag hanging off the back of his chair and asked him if he was going to be okay. He absolutely refused to have a bellman help him with it. "Why wouldn't I be okay?" he asked indignantly.

Paul then gave us his first directive: "Meet me back in the lobby in an hour. I made an appointment to speak to the sheriff."

"About what?" I asked.

"About the Memorial Day Rotary Festival. Did you see the poster?"

"So now you're a comedian," I countered.

"No, but I figured I'd break the ice with talk about the festival, then move on to the topic of dead children."

It hit me hard in the gut to hear him talk so callously, but I just figured he had his own way of coping and keeping a level, dispassionate mindset amid the most dreadful facts and circumstances.

I had yet to develop such a mechanism.

# CHAPTER 22

The Sheriff's Department of Cartersville, New York consisted of a one-story tan brick building located on the main drag, Carter Road. Of course, 'main drag' for Cartersville meant that it got about the same traffic as any side street on Long Island. It was no secret that Dr. Horace Carter was big in these parts since both the police station, the road it was on, and the town, were named after him. His claim to fame—building a dam across the Seneca River in the mid-1800s that provided a central energy source for the entire area.

Whether any of that energy had made its way into the sheriff's station had yet to be determined. About forty years old and looking more the brawny fireman type than the pot-bellied elder I expected, George Rifts was quick to clarify that he was the 'interim sheriff.' The actual sheriff had passed away a month earlier from sepsis. Paul introduced himself while flashing his private investigator ID and former Secret Service credentials. I questioned the wisdom of displaying the latter until I came to realize the means by which we obtained this meeting (i.e., a secret call from a contact of Paul's at the FBI—the reason Paul insisted that Charlie remain at hotel).

There is what may be called an 'investigative underworld,' the importance of which cannot be discounted as a means to an end. It is a channel of communication among governmental and quasi-governmental agencies that is laced with relationships founded on decades of trust, joint benefi-cial interests—and even monetary gratuity, when and if necessary. There is also an underworld of untouchables, dangerous by virtue of their ability to get away with murder when cloaked in high-level grants of documented and undocumented immunity.

Paul had worked with the FBI before. On many occasions, his personal connections had proved invaluable to the Bureau. Because of his prior Secret Service clearance, he was a trusted source who provided leads and information on all levels of society—especially the rich corporate elite. As long as he wasn't betraying his own client's trust, Paul worked hand in hand with the Bureau, while having no problem backing off when his con-science told him to. In turn, the FBI would help Paul by providing access to law enforcement agencies at every level, even in small-town Cartersville, where Interim Sheriff Rifts seemed more than accommodating.

"We appreciate your assistance, Sheriff." Paul was polite and direct.

"I'm only the sheriff until the special election in September. Then someone else is taking over. But as long as I'm here, you'll have the full cooperation of the department." Sheriff Rifts was refreshingly sincere, and I found it curious that the powers-that-be weren't running him for the full-time position. On the wall outside Rifts' office was a photo of the for-mer sheriff. With his button-popping beige shirt and white mustache, he looked more like a turncoat lawman in a backwoods revenge flick than the keeper of the peace. Rifts caught me staring at the gone-but-not-forgotten Sheriff Hall.

"I just hung that photo," Rifts said, as he stared up at it with a quirky sense of pride. He then turned to Paul. "Funny thing the way he died, though. Went out to dinner, got a stomach attack, and two weeks later he was gone. Other than getting the blues sometimes, he always seemed fine. But he was seventy-five years old, you know. And when your time is up, your time is up, I suppose."

"Had he confided in you about any of the cases he was handling?" Paul asked.

"He confided in me about a lot of the cases he was handling. I was his highest-ranking deputy."

"Any case that may have been a particular source of stress for him? That could be why he had the stomach attack."

"You heard about those boxes of bones found by the construction worker?"

"I think I may have read something about it." Paul was playing dumb. "Did you say boxes?"

"Yes, there were two boxes. The first box was dug up intact. The second was broken in two by the tractor shovel. We figure that they were buried there quite some time ago by a family who couldn't afford the proper services."

"But they were just discovered. Am I right?" Paul asked.

"Yes, just last week. This is the kind of matter that would have gotten the sheriff's goat but good, I can tell you that."

"Is forensics examining the bones?" Paul was careful not to push too hard and alert Rifts to our real reason for being in Cartersville.

"I heard something about the county marshall possibly stepping in, since the boxes were found within a mile of our jurisdictional line, so I'm leaving that to him. That's our policy here. But there's also no reason to believe a crime was committed. All that the medical examiner was able to tell was that they were the bones of little boys."

"I'm only asking because we're looking for a missing boy ourselves." Paul was making this up and I thought it clever of him to do so. While keeping our true purpose under wraps, it gave us a plausible reason for being in Cartersville and asking questions.

"You're looking for a missing boy, you say?" Rifts responded pensively. "Well, talking about Sheriff Hall getting upset…about two months ago, we found the body of a boy who was about five or six years old in another wooden box by the banks of the Seneca River. We suspected it was also a poor family burial. The boy was found fully clothed, but for some reason the sheriff asked for an autopsy and toxicology tests on the remains. We don't usually do that unless we suspect a crime was committed, and even then, it depends."

"You mean you don't do autopsies on a regular basis when a child is found dead?" Paul modified his tone to hide his shock and surprise.

"Not always. People are more religious up here than in the city. If we can ID the body, we try to honor the family's wishes and not have the remains sawed or cut into if they express their disapproval. I figured, because there was no ID on that boy found by the river, that Sheriff Hall ordered the autopsy. But it was only when the autopsy results came back that he then decided to order the toxicology."

"Why is that?"

"The autopsy didn't show anything. No sign of any sickness or disease or evidence of any crime…just some indication of malnourishment. I only know what the Sheriff told me, but it was when he got that report that he called forensics."

"Can I read the report?" Paul asked. "Just to see if this is our missing boy. His parents are torn up not knowing what happened to him. They live in Syracuse."

"Certainly," Rifts answered. "It got filed away after the sheriff passed. I haven't read it myself but let me get it for you."

Rifts went down the hall and into another room. After I heard the distant sound of a filing cabinet drawer opening and then closing, he returned with the report and handed it to Paul.

"Can I take it with me?" Paul asked.

"I suppose I can trust a member of the FBI with it, so why not?"

Paul just said, "thank you." No need to correct the interim sheriff.

While I drove Paul's rented SUV back to The Red Mill Inn, he read the report and jotted notes down on a yellow pad. When we got back to the hotel, we found Charlie in the lobby, sitting in his wheelchair. He was drinking steaming hot coffee out of a mug and appeared anxious to see us. Paul took one look at him and asked to speak to me alone.

"I didn't fly up here for the small-town atmosphere," Charlie squawked. "I got enough of that growing up. If you've got information, I want to hear it, too. Do I have to remind you guys that you're up here because of me?"

"This is pretty rough stuff," Paul said to Charlie. "You sure you want to hear it?"

"Rougher than losing your legs in fucking Vietnam?" Charlie gulped down the coffee and then slammed his mug on the arm of his chair.

"Charlie's right, Paul," I said. "We are here because of him and Mia, and I know he can be trusted."

With that, Charlie's expression went from angry to cautiously respectful. It was the kind of look I'd seen in the movies when a soldier, without saying a word, expresses his undying loyalty to his commander. No brave general, I welcomed it nonetheless.

"Okay, if you say so," Paul said. "Here goes." I braced myself for the worst. And that's exactly what I got. "The last child, the one the sheriff spoke of—found about a month ago in a wooden box by the river." Paul swallowed. "The autopsy report states that urine deposits were found in the box."

"Well, that's not so unusual, is it?" I asked. "When the body decomposes it releases fluids."

"True," Paul answered. "Your muscles relax. Your brain isn't controlling anything anymore, and the dead body usually pees and craps itself."

"So, what's your point?" I asked.

"The traces of urine were not only found on the bottom of the box, but also on the top of it."

"How could that be?" I asked.

"Whoever buried him, buried him fully clothed, whereas the other two bodies found at the construction site—or should I say bones from what once were bodies—had no discernible clothing on them. But what is especially unique and disturbing, is that not only was the body found by the river positively identified as a boy, but when his clothes were examined, the fly to his pants was found wide open."

"Are you saying—?"

"He's saying," Charlie interrupted. "That while the kid was in the box and on his back, he pulled out his pecker and took a straight-up piss."

"You mean…" I uttered incredulously.

"Yes," Paul said firmly. "It appears the boy was buried alive."

# CHAPTER 23

I've got to get out of this business, I thought to myself, as I looked over at Paul, who appeared stoic, but was nevertheless shaken by the report.

I needed no education on how dangerous this world can be for the weak and the innocent, but this was all too much evil to swallow, even for Paul. Charlie held up better than both of us. I suppose that's what a tour in jungle warfare gets you.

"There's one small consolation—or comfort, you might say—in all of this," Paul said.

"You can't be serious," I countered.

"But I am," Paul said. "The medical examiner found traces of Rohypnol."

"What the hell is Rohypnol?" I asked.

"Somebody gave the kid a roofie," Charlie answered.

"That's right," Paul said. "The kid was out of it before he died."

"And there also goes the 'poor boy burial' explanation," Charlie said disdainfully.

"Seriously," I bellowed. "Can this get much worse?"

"Looks like were going into a black fucking hole if you ask me," Charlie added.

Paul's cellphone rang. It was Rifts.

When Paul had explained the medical examiner's report to us, I had never seen his face go so white. But there was a deeper pale yet to show itself. "Thank you, Sheriff," Paul said. "I'd like to head right over there, if you don't mind."

Paul thanked the sheriff again, ended the call, then turned to Charlie and me. "Another kid has gone missing. He's a ten-year-old—a neighborhood kid on his way home from a friend's house after school. His bicycle was found on the side of the road."

"You see?!" Charlie shouted. "You see what we've got here?!"

"We don't know if this latest missing kid has been kidnapped," Paul said.

"Come on, really?" Charlie insisted. "What's with all these dead kids anyway, and who knows if this one's even still alive." As cold as it was to say, it was even harder to hear, not that Charlie's presumption wasn't well-founded.

Paul turned to me. "I say we get over to the crime scene and see what we can find out. And we do it now." He pointed at Charlie, who appreciated being considered. "Next time, my friend. We'll be back before you know it."

# CHAPTER 24

Paul stopped his SUV about fifty feet from a string of yellow crime scene tape and an unmanned sheriff's patrol car parked alongside it.

One look at the bicycle lying on the shoulder of the road told the story.

It was a two-wheeler with shiny red metal fenders that didn't have a scratch on them. There was a red reflector on the back seat and another on the steering column under the handlebars, where multicolored streamers hung from the grips. The bike was on its side with the front tire turned under it. There's no way a young boy with pride in his ride would leave it this way. It would have been set down gently, wheels straight and aligned with the road. The boy who claimed this two-wheeler as his own was either pulled from it or knocked off it.

It was just after 7:00 p.m., and the boy had been reported missing only an hour earlier. His name was Billy. When he didn't arrive home for dinner at five, his stepfather went out looking for him. Billy had been at his friend's house, and there was only one way home. As his stepfather told it, when he found the downed bicycle, he panicked and ran full speed into the woods alongside the road screaming the boy's name. A few minutes later, he called the sheriff's station.

We arrived just before the local detectives, which amounted to two deputies on temporary assignment. Rifts had told them to expect us. Both were in their mid-to-late forties with stocky builds. The one who greeted us had short brown hair and an ID badge that read: TAYLOR. The other seemed a bit perturbed by our presence. He wore a badge that read: CARTER.

"Just don't disturb the crime scene," Carter stated curtly.

Paul looked at me as if to say: *Disturb what? They haven't done shit so far.* Paul's answer though was far more polite. "Of course, we'll be careful, but if you don't mind, I'd like to take some photos with my cellphone."

"Knock yourself out," Carter said.

Paul turned to the friendlier officer, Deputy Taylor, and asked: "Do you have a spot?"

"A spot?" he asked back.

"A spotlight, or a strong flashlight. It's beginning to get dark," Paul answered.

"Of course," Taylor said. He went to his patrol car and returned with a large wide lens flashlight.

Paul took it and began to walk casually along the edge of the asphalt roadway with seemingly no clear intention in mind. But I knew different. As he shined the light at the downward slope of the grass shoulder, I'm sure he was thinking the same thing I was: No way was this boy riding on this unleveled grass when the roadway above it was flat and smooth.

Paul used his cellphone to click off over a dozen photos as he back-tracked and circled the area surrounding the bicycle. He then proceeded to walk further down the roadway, flashlight on and cellphone in hand. He stopped at a distance about thirty feet away. Since I had remained standing outside his rented SUV, he turned and waved me over.

"Come, walk with me," he said quietly. I followed alongside him until he stopped and asked me to hold the light. "I'm going to take some random photos while you shine the flashlight down along the shoulder, but when I tell you to stop, just light up the ground right in front of me. Okay?"

"Sure," I answered. Evidently something had sparked his interest that he did not want the deputies to catch wind of.

"Taylor seems okay, but I'm not sure what's going on with Carter," he whispered. "Is he simply a dick or is there a reason he doesn't want us here? Either way, I'm not taking any chances."

"What's sparking your interest?" I whispered back.

"I'll show you back at the hotel," he said.

I continued to walk beside Paul, and when he told me to stop, I pointed the light down in front of him as he asked. He then clicked off several photos. Afterward, we turned and walked back while I kept pointing the light and he kept snapping photos with his phone.

"Mind if we take some close-ups of the bike?" Paul asked Deputy Carter.

"Like I said, knock yourself out." Carter responded.

Paul took the flashlight from my hand and asked me to wait by the roadway while he walked to the edge of the wooded area and then around the bicycle, taking pictures with his phone.

"Any witnesses? Any cars or trucks pass that may have seen something?" Paul directed his questions to Deputy Taylor.

Carter answered for him. "Thus far, no."

"We'll ask around though," Taylor offered. "Maybe put out a bulletin."

"Sounds good," Paul said.

"We know what to do," Carter added abruptly.

Unfazed, Paul shut the flashlight and handed it back to Taylor. "Good night, Gentlemen. Thanks for letting us look around."

"No problem," Taylor answered.

As we walked back to the car, Carter grumbled something under his breath that I couldn't understand.

During the drive back, I could tell that Paul was mulling over whatever it was he had seen. What I didn't know was that he was also thinking about what he had heard as well.

# CHAPTER 25

Charlie waited for us in the lobby again. This time he was keeping company with an open bag of pretzels. It was 8:15 p.m., and he didn't waste a second. "So, what did you find?" he asked anxiously.

"I'll be more than happy to fill you both in, but let's order a pizza first," Paul replied. "I'm starving."

It had suddenly occurred to me that neither of us had remembered to eat dinner.

"I'm fine," said Charlie. "I had a calzone delivered, and even better, when the delivery man saw me, he wouldn't take my money." Charlie reached into his pocket and handed Paul a torn piece of paper. "Here's the number. And tip him good because I sure as hell didn't."

Paul called in the order, and we moved to a conference room behind the lobby's huge centrally located fireplace. Before I sat down, I checked my phone. Though there was no ring tone, I could see that a call was coming in. It was Charlotte's number, but it was Maureen calling. I stepped away to answer it.

"How are you feeling? Is Charlotte showing you around?" I asked.

Despite my upbeat tone, hers wasn't. "I'm just fine, and Charlotte is great. She took me out to dinner and tomorrow we're going to a Broadway show. But Nick..."

"You sound worried. What is it?"

"I called the hospital to see if anyone found my phone, but it seems to have disappeared."

"Is that what's bothering you? Just get another one. Use the cash I gave you."

"No, it's not that."

"What is it, then?"

"I miss you. That's all."

"I miss you, too. And I wish I could tell you how long I'll be up here, but I can't."

"And that Detective McCormick...I called him too. I just don't think he's doing all he can to find out who broke into my apartment. I'm not sure I trust him."

"That's probably just his way. Besides, what does it matter? You're in New York and safe. And I'm sure your phone will turn up. Meanwhile, call your carrier and report it lost."

"Okay."

"So, let's talk tomorrow. Our pizza should be arriving soon, and I haven't eaten all day. Now get a good night's sleep. You'll feel better."

"I will." She sounded disappointed that our call was coming to an end, which broke my heart a little. After a few seconds of silence, she uttered: "Talk tomorrow. Love you."

Then, as if I had said it a thousand times before, I whispered back: "Love you, too."

# CHAPTER 26

Since I was closest to the lobby door, I accepted the pizza delivery, walked back into the conference room, and laid the pie on a large mahogany table.

"You're blushing," Charlie said.

"Must be the phone call with his girlfriend." Paul said.

"You can both go to hell," I barked back. "Now tell us what you found, Paul, while I still have my appetite."

"First, let me find the photos," he said, taking out his phone and waving us closer. "Here it is." He widened the image on the screen with his fingers. "See that tire track?" He looked at me, then at Charlie. "See the indentation in the shoulder where it meets the grass? It's from the tire spinning out slightly. In other words—the driver left in a hurry. But now: Let's look at the markings where the vehicle first came to a stop. You can see the tire more clearly. It's a common tread, probably from an SUV. Now let's look at another photo of the same tire after it moved forward a bit." Paul swiped his cellphone's screen a few times.

I looked closely at the image he stopped at. "Why are there only partial tread marks?" I asked.

"Because there may be something caked onto the tire," Paul responded.

"You mean like mud—hardened mud?"

"Either that, or the tire has a bubble." Paul said.

"But how do we even know that the vehicle we're talking about has anything to do with the missing boy?" Charlie asked. "Someone could have just taken off after they pulled over to piss."

"I can't be positive, but these look like fresh tracks," Paul said. "When no one was looking, I knelt down to get a closer look and felt the ground to be sure."

"Then wash your hands before you touch our pizza," Charlie barked.

Paul continued. "And don't you think it was a little unusual that big mouth Deputy Carter let me get so close to the bicycle—especially after he warned me not to disturb the crime scene? I actually walked right up to it and he couldn't give a damn. Who lets a private investigator do that?"

"So, what are you saying?" Charlie asked.

"That the investigation into this missing boy is all that we saw and heard, which amounts to next to nothing," Paul said firmly.

"You mean they're just going through the motions?" I asked.

"I'd put money on it," Paul said. "Oh, I'm sure there'll be reports filed that document how they canvassed the town, questioned a dozen or so people et cetera, et cetera. They'll file a bunch of photos of the scene, of course. Then…case closed. Another kid bites the dust."

"What about the public?" I asked. "Doesn't anyone care?"

"There's a local paper—*The Cartersville Courier*," Paul answered. "It hasn't publicized a serious crime committed up here in decades. It could pass for a travel brochure for all anyone knows."

"That makes no sense," Charlie said angrily.

"I thought the folks in Upstate New York were supposed to be honest God-fearing people," I said.

"I guess not *everywhere* in Upstate New York," Paul responded with a sly smile.

# CHAPTER 27

I was dozing off to sleep when at 1:00 a.m. my cellphone rang. It was Lauren calling. "Sorry…I know it's late, but I've got more on that Upstate matter we've been talking about." She was all business and sounding more like the Lauren I remembered.

"Don't be sorry." I widened my eyes and shook off the cobwebs. "I'm here in Cartersville and I want to hear everything you've got."

"What do you mean you're in Cartersville? Why didn't you tell me you were going? I could have gotten a camera crew and joined you."

"Thanks for the offer, but that's the last thing we need up here in Small Town, USA. It's going to be hard enough to get people to talk to begin with."

"Forget the cameras," she said. "You could have introduced me as another investigator on your team. Just leave out the reporter part."

"You *are* on my team, whether you like it or not. I wouldn't be lying."

"I'm going to tell my program manager that I'm going on assignment. I want to come up there."

"Come then. You *should* be here. There's no one I trust more, and—like I once said—we're the same, you and I."

"Oh God, early morning sappy. I can tell you just woke up."

I was twice Lauren's age, yet I was convinced that I understood her better than she understood herself. Broken home. Abandoned by her biological father. Molested by her stepfather. Though I had suffered through an ass-kicking or two by my own stepfather, it was the knowledge of my mother's protracted childhood abuse by her oldest brother that affected me deeply and made me feel connected to Lauren in more ways than one.

Never one to mince words, Lauren quickly got to the purpose of her call. "According to my research—and I pulled every newspaper article, census, and death record I could find—young boys have been going missing in and around Cartersville since the mid-1950s, and almost all of them had resided in orphanages and foster homes, with no records of who their parents were."

"What about the kid whose bicycle was found by the roadway?" I asked.

"I just read about that. He's an anomaly—living at home with a natural mother and stepfather. You know, it could be that he is not a victim of the same serial kidnappers."

"Serial kidnappers? You really think there's more than one?"

"Neither of us need a lesson on good and evil," Lauren said morosely. "Over fifty years, there has to be—and this is based on records I actually found—some that even predate the Kennedy assassination. There's no telling how many young boys went missing who there are no record of. Let's face it: One horrible human being cannot be responsible for all these missing boys." Lauren sounded much too certain for my comfort level. "But we need more," she continued. "More proof—and not just from legitimate sources. If at all possible, we need to hack the cyber underground. Have you heard of the dark web?" I instantly thought of Jasmine, Paul's computer hacker genius.

I told Lauren that I had indeed heard of the dark web, and when I asked her to fully explain its implications to me, she did so in a rather colorful but precise narrative. "The dark web is both cunning and diabolical. Astonishingly, thousands of hackers engage in keeping a segment of web traffic totally confidential. They volunteer their time to provide hidden cross chains and complex avenues of web travel so that tracing the identity of users is virtually impossible—and I mean that literally. This is done largely over a network called TOR, which is an acronym for "the onion router"—a program developed by the U.S. Navy for government use in the 1990s. In 2004, it was open sourced. Put simply, it went pub-lic. Normally, when you connect to the internet, your IP address is your source identity—but when you're on the dark web, the browser takes a few circuitous routes with at least three random detours that causes your web search to bounce around the world like a pinball knocking in and out of random networks. As a result, this makes your site request work, but your source address virtually untraceable. In short: The dark web is a per-fect vehicle for criminals to traffic in, especially if their crimes are against children."

# CHAPTER 28

S ince there was no keeping Lauren away, she flew in the following morning and joined us at The Red Mill Inn. We were sitting in the corner of the lobby when she arrived and immediately handed me an envelope. In it were notarized doctor/patient privilege waivers signed by 'Mia Langley, formally known as Mia Archer.'

"How did you get this done so fast?" I asked.

"Network news lawyers don't sleep. The minute they sent these to me, I called Mia. She had already heard from Charlie and couldn't have been more cooperative. She met me at CNN headquarters, so I made her day by giving her a tour of the studio. Some of my co-workers even thought she was my little sister. We went out to dinner afterwards. She's a sweetheart, and smart as all hell. We really took to each other."

"Wow, that's great to hear," I said. "Charlie here is also quite taken with her. I met her just once, but I could tell she was special."

"She's just great," Charlie added. "Been to war and back like me, poor kid, and hasn't lost any of her wholesome innocence."

"Also like you, right Charlie?" I chuckled.

"Oh, yeah. Wholesome and innocent...that's me." Charlie smiled back and sarcastically nodded in assent.

"Just one thing," Lauren said. "Mia told me not to expect any cooperation from her adoptive mom, Beatrice Langley."

"No surprise there," I said.

"Tough shit on her," Charlie said.

"Yeah, but I have a feeling she's a force to be reckoned with," Lauren said.

"Well, so are we," Charlie exclaimed. "So are we."

Paul then suggested that our next step should be to canvas the town, speak to the residents, and see what we could find out. We discussed this door-to-door strategy for almost an hour. Convinced that the police would be of no help and that there was one deputy who could not be trusted, we decided to take it to the streets on our own. In doing so, we knew word would quickly get out about our investigation. Consequently, this was a dangerous move—dangerous for all of us. What we were counting on was that someone with a conscience would speak his or her mind, one-on-one and in confidence—whether it was to a journalist, a private investigator, a disabled marine veteran, or even a retired lawyer—and maybe, just maybe, a cage would be rattled, and we would get a peek under the cloak of evil behind what appeared on its face to be decades of kidnapping and murder.

We agreed to spread out in different directions, which wasn't hard to do in a small town like Cartersville. I took the north side, Paul the south, Lauren the east and Charlie the west. In his Marine fatigues and wheelchair, Charlie was determined to go toe-to-toe with all of us in questioning as many inhabitants as he came across. Even though we were already on the west side, I feared that him going out on his own, pumping his wheels from house-to-house, and in some instances up and down driveways, would be too much for the seventy-two-year-old. When Paul suggested that Charlie team up with one of us, however, we all bore witness to one angry vet tirade. Having calmed down a full half-hour later, Charlie compromised and let Paul drive him to a highly concentrated area where he would have less wheeling around to do. Paul also gave him a stack of PI business cards and told him to introduce himself as an employee of Franklin Investigations, which was Paul's PI firm located on Franklin Avenue in Garden City, Long Island.

Charlie seemed pleased to be part of the team, and I couldn't help but respect his independence and strong will. I only hoped (and prayed) that he would come back in one piece. That he tended to be cantankerous and feisty is an understatement, and I was not looking forward to possibly dealing with one of his post-traumatic episodes. We would all soon realize, however, that despite all our well-placed concerns, we underestimated both Charlie and Cartersville—the latter of which wasn't necessarily a positive.

Since we were all carrying our cellphones, we each agreed to call if any of us were even remotely in any kind of trouble. Where Lauren and Charlie were concerned, Paul and I made them promise that if they felt the least bit uncomfortable, they were to reach out immediately. Though I believed Lauren would, I wasn't so sure about Charlie. He actually scoffed at the notion.

This broad canvas approach to investigating was not something I was entirely comfortable with. Paul disagreed and said so. "We're focusing our attention on this town and its people. There is no doubt that there are those who know something but are either too afraid or simply don't care enough to speak out. You don't have this number of kids go missing and its citizens not know something is awry. So, we're going to shake this town's goddamn tree, and see what falls out. And believe me, something will. Hopefully, it's something we can use."

The instant I was out of Charlie's line of sight, I took Paul aside. "We're letting a Vietnam veteran with PTSD out alone on these streets to inquire about kidnapping and maybe murder?"

"First of all, he's only asking questions, and these streets cannot be more dangerous than the streets of New York City. Let's not forget that Charlie's been on his own for his entire adult life. He may be a little rough around the edges—"

"A *little* rough around the edges?"

"He'll be fine. Besides, you're the one who brought him. *You* tell him he needs a babysitter. I tried that and look where it got me. By the way, have you seen his arms? I bet he can press two-hundred-plus from that chair. Now let's not worry about Charlie and see what we can shake out of this one-horse town."

Since Lauren had her own rental car, before she headed east, she dropped me on the north side in an area comprised mostly of residential homes on plots of land that ranged from as small as a quarter-acre to as large as five acres, some of which abutted the Seneca River.

The balance of the morning passed slowly, but by noon Paul had already stopped at over three dozen homes where, for the most part, people were polite—yet cautious. When I checked in with Lauren, she informed me that her efforts thus far had been for naught. As for me, after several hours of ringing doorbells to no avail, I was becoming increasingly frustrated. Consequently, my patience was running thin.

I continued to question this tactic of Paul's and I called him to tell him so. "Foolhardy and somewhat reckless" was how I referred to this method of scattergun investigating.

He took no offense. "Standard police work up here, however incomplete or incompetent it may have been, has thus far turned up nothing," he said. "We need to go a bit rogue and see what happens."

I had no doubt that Paul had done his homework and knew Cartersville better than any of us, including Charlie, who hadn't been back in over fifty years. But his approach to investigating what appeared to be the most chronic and prevalent case of missing children in the country—and maybe the world—was unconventional and even odd, to say the least. Every case is different and has its difficulties, and based on Paul's track record, I should have had more faith in his judgment and choices. But my head was spinning that morning. My thoughts drifted from crates of bones to the dark web to Billy's downed bicycle. This bucolic small town with the river running through it, its acres of green grass, its quiet homes set back hundreds of feet from the road was beginning to seem like a bleak and disturbing place that I was wandering aimlessly and dangerously through.

So, no matter what Paul said, I was becoming increasingly convinced that canvassing this small town in Upstate New York was one useless venture.

But I would soon come to realize that I was wrong.

# CHAPTER 29

Paul drove his own rental car to the south side of town—the low-income area of Cartersville—where, during his random door-to-door investigation, he inadvertently ran into the charming ex-wife of the arrogant and obnoxious Deputy Carter.

When she pushed the screen door open, Paul knew he would be getting an earful, but about what, he had no clue. Standing before him in her bare feet and smiling, was a petite blond who wore a white nighty that barely reached halfway down her thighs.

"What can I do for you?" she asked in a sexy tone that was clearly an invitation to more than just casual conversation.

After identifying himself as a private investigator, Paul announced to the merry divorcee that he was canvassing the town for any information that might lead to the finding of a missing boy.

When she asked Paul to step inside, he slipped off his wedding ring and dropped it into his pants pocket. If she thought he was single, maybe she would fess up more.

The house was a prefab, which meant it was built somewhere else, and then delivered and dropped onto a concrete slab foundation. As Paul entered what looked more like a railroad car than an actual home, the fetching lady of the house invited him to sit down in a tiny living room that consisted of a small sofa and a coffee table.

"It's nice to meet you, Paul. My name is Betsy, Betsy Carter. By the way, my ex is the deputy sheriff here in town, but don't let that scare you off." She giggled, sat down next to him, crossed her legs, and let her nightie creep up her thigh accordingly. Paul looked because he knew it's what she wanted him to do. He had to be careful, though. She might no longer be Deputy Carter's wife, but Deputy Carter was still an asshole.

When necessary, Paul could be quite charming, but in the confined recesses of his psyche, behind his handsome features, athletic build and six-foot-two frame, he was all business. Betsy wasn't the first flirty blonde to cross his path, and she most certainly wouldn't be the last.

Paul leaned forward and smiled. "Maybe you can help me with something, Betsy."

"Oh sure," she said softly.

"I'm a private investigator trying to find a little boy who went missing two days ago. Any information you might have about anyone or anything that could help—however insignificant you may think it is—would be very much appreciated." Paul closed with a smile.

"I heard about that," she said. "That boy's parents are teachers, aren't they?"

"That's right."

"So, you work for them?"

Paul didn't answer, which lead her to believe that he did. "I'm here for the boy, to help find him," he said solemnly.

"The parents must be out of their minds with worry."

"Do you know them?"

"The mom teaches at my son's school. He's in fourth grade. She teaches first. I think the missing boy may be her only child."

"Actually, there's also an older sister. She's a teenager. The dad is their stepdad."

"Thank God there's another child in the home."

"What do you mean?"

She looked away, got up, walked toward the kitchen, then spun around.

"Can I get you something? I have some bourbon if you like. Oh, but you're working." She looked away and giggled again. "I'll add ice."

"No, thank you, but what did you mean by: 'Thank God there's another child in the home?'"

Betsy adjusted her nightie by pinching the shoulder straps. "Just...you know...good thing they have another child to comfort them."

"At a time like this, a teenage girl may not be much of a comfort. I'm sure she misses her brother, too."

"Yeah, you're right, I suppose. What do I know?" She threw her hands in the air and the nightie rose in unison.

"Besides," Paul added. "We're going to find him."

"Find who? The kidnappers?" She dropped her arms.

Paul looked at her inquisitively. "We're not sure he was kidnapped. He could have just run off."

"Of course. True, maybe he just ran away. That's possible."

Paul made a mental note that Betsy said *kidnappers*—not kidnapper. He looked around and then focused on the clock on the wall. It was 3:30 p.m. "I guess your son will be coming home from school soon."

Betsy glanced at the same clock and said: "He probably stopped at the park with his friends. We still have some time to talk—if you like." She smiled and leaned back against the kitchen counter that abutted the living room and everything else in this tiny house. Paul smiled back, while wondering why she wasn't the least bit concerned about her own son walking home from school alone, when a boy his age had gone missing less than forty-eight hours ago.

# CHAPTER 30

Disheartened by the early path of the investigation (the evidence gathered thus far consisting of a bulging tire tread), I could barely put one foot in front of the other as I went door-to-door on the north side of Cartersville—until I came across the Johnsons—a family of devout Baptists who gave me a welcome that was so warm and inviting, I wanted to forget why I was there.

At first, I was skeptical. Were they setting me up for a fat contribution for the upcoming church fair? For the most part the folks in Franklin, Tennessee, were a lot friendlier than my neighbors on Long Island, but inside the Johnson house, friendly was taken to a whole new level.

After inviting me to sit on a couch that had more pillows than seating space, Mrs. Johnson joined me in a nearby wing chair, while over a dozen other Johnsons—from grade school age to a grinning great-grandma—looked on.

Mrs. Johnson, a seventy-plus-year-old black woman, and matriarch of the family, began with a simple question: "Are you Baptist?"

"No Ma'am," I answered. "I'm Catholic."

"Well then," she said, smiling from ear to ear. "We both believe in Jesus and that's good enough for me." The rest of the family grinned and nodded in unison.

"Thank you, but I should tell you why I'm here."

"You're here," Mrs. Johnson said, "because God put you here." At this point, the front screen door opened and a seventeen-year-old the size of an NFL middle linebacker walked in with two school-age children, seven and eight years old.

Mrs. Johnson turned to the teenager then to me. "Marlon, this is... what is your name exactly?"

"Nick Mannino, Mrs. Johnson."

Marlon walked over and shook my hand. At five-foot-nine, I measured Marlon to be about six-foot-four. The two little boys with him said "hi," and then ran, bags in hand, to the rear of the house, where I figured a television inside a den was their intended target.

"Homework first, then TV!" Mrs. Johnson shouted.

"That's right," yelled another woman who was half Mrs. Johnson's age who followed the boys out.

"Nice of Marlon to pick up his younger brothers from school," I said.

"They're his cousins." Mrs. Johnson was quick to correct me. "And I just want my grandkids home safe is all."

"But isn't Cartersville pretty much a safe community?" I asked tentatively.

She took a breath and smiled weakly. The great grandma had stopped smiling entirely.

Mrs. Johnson looked at me with somber eyes. "You're here to ask me about that missing boy, aren't you?"

"Yes, I am, Mrs. Johnson."

"I figured as much. You don't exactly look like the welcome wagon." I smiled weakly back at her. "Little boys have gone missing around here before. But then a little white boy from a decent middle-class family disappears and someone like you shows up at the door. No offense to you, Mr. Mannino."

"Actually, that's not the only reason I'm here."

"Really?" There was cutting cynicism in her voice.

"Can I trust you with something, Mrs. Johnson?"

She gave me a look filled with both charm and indignation. "What do you think?"

"I think I can, but can we talk in private?"

She got up and escorted me through the kitchen, past the den where her grandkids were doing their homework, and into a large backyard with a small vegetable garden and a plush green lawn that abutted a deeply wooded area. We stopped midway into the yard.

"This is as private as it's going to get, Mr. Mannino. I don't like keeping things from my family. So, what is it that I can do for you?"

"I'm here because of those missing boys you spoke of. One is too many—but up here in this small community, it appears to be much more than that."

Mrs. Johnson took my hand into hers and looked me dead in the eyes. "And you don't know the half of it. You want answers, Mr. Mannino? Go to that home for boys along the river on the north side of town. It used to be an orphanage and has been run since by one crooked priest after another. No telling what happens there. Check their records—*if* you can get your hands on them."

# CHAPTER 31

After the cryptic counsel of Mrs. Johnson, I was done for the day and anxious to get back to the hotel. I was looking forward to meeting up with Paul, Lauren, and Charlie, hearing their stories, and finding out more about that home for boys by the Seneca River that Mrs. Johnson spoke of.

Upon returning to The Red Mill Inn, I couldn't help but notice the weak smile on the old man working at the front desk—an expression of mandatory politeness—unforced, habitual, but no less disingenuous. It wasn't the natural 'small-town smile' I was expecting. Maybe I was just getting a little paranoid. That can happen on investigations as you inch closer to the truth.

As I walked into the lobby, I saw Charlie sitting in his chair next to Lauren. I knew they weren't talking about their day when utterances that included "artillery fire" and "Syrian attacks" wafted into the air. As I went to sit down on a couch across from them, Paul hurried in from the parking lot, the keys to his rented SUV still in his hand. "There is definitely something going on up here that no one is eager to talk about. Considering how dangerous it may be, hopefully we can find someone stupid enough to tell us something."

"Maybe we're not looking for stupid," I said, as thoughts of Mrs.

Johnson came to mind. "Maybe we just need to find somebody with the goodness and courage to speak up."

"Courage and goodness?" Paul spoke much too loud for my comfort level, although his sarcasm was not lost on me. "We're talking about decades of heinous criminal activity that has gone virtually uninvestigated in a community of roughly three thousand people. Courage and goodness have been woefully missing in and around Cartersville, so I doubt it will suddenly emerge like some sunken shipwreck."

Paul then filled us in on his meeting with the deputy's ex. I followed by briefing everyone on my visit with the Johnson family—how their children needed to be picked up after school, while the deputy's son could wander home on his own—and just two days after a local boy went missing. Was Mrs. Johnson just being overprotective? Was the deputy's ex-wife simply an irresponsible mother? Not one of us believed either proposition—only that it seemed that some children were safe, while others weren't. "But why?" I asked.

"Because some kids are in the target group, while others aren't," Lauren said.

"And people go about their daily lives and just don't care how dangerous it is here for certain children?" I asked.

"You mean you're just beginning to figure out that most people aren't worth a damn, and the weak and the innocent are always screwed in this world?" Charlie's cynicism was not lost on me.

"I wouldn't be here if I thought that, Charlie, and neither would you," I replied. "All four of us have had to cope with close personal disappointment and tragedy in our lives, but we're still here, trying to put a halt to the cruelty and the madness."

I realized Charlie knew little of our pasts: Paul and Lauren's murdered sisters—one lost to a maniac husband and the other to a serial killer—while I still bore the emotional scars of my mother's childhood abuse. But truth be told, if you live long enough and manage to escape the curse of tragedy in its infinite forms, you are in the minority—at least as far as I can tell.

"What are we—philosophers?" Paul said jokingly.

Lauren laughed, and since I rarely saw her laugh, it was a welcome distraction that made us all take a breath.

As it turned out, Lauren and Charlie's day was no less eventful. Lauren met a man who had a special needs daughter, low on the autism spectrum, her communication skills limited to grunts and a few words. She was overweight and short for her age of sixteen. When Lauren asked the father about missing children, he evaded the question and asked her if she thought he would be able to place his daughter in a nursing home when she turned eighteen. He worked long hours installing underground hydraulic pumps and claimed he was unable to care for her properly.

Lauren responded with: "She seems to be doing okay the way things are."

He didn't like her answer and shouted back: "But I'm not!"

Startled by his outburst, Lauren quickly excused herself, but not before the father said: "Too bad there isn't a home for special needs kids, like the one they got upriver for them boys."

Then it was Charlie's turn. Seems his wheelchair didn't stop a white supremacist, who thought he had a sympathetic ear in one disabled Vietnam veteran, from almost having a go at him. The man was wearing what was known in my Brooklyn days as a 'wife-beater' T-shirt that barely covered a variety of tattoos up and down his arms, as well as a Nazi swastika down each side of his neck.

In excess of six feet, fat, bald, with a face marked by acne scars and patchy stubble, when he started trashing "the Jews and the spics," Charlie put his hand up. "You dumb fuck!" he shouted. "You forget who we fought in World War II. If the Nazis had their way, we'd be slaves to the Third Reich today."

"Only the niggers, spics and Jews—not us decent, pure-white Americans," the man answered, with an arrogance which only served to incense Charlie more.

They were talking through a screen door, and when the exchange got heated, the man pushed it open, only to have Charlie slam it shut with his wheelchair.

"Damn it to hell!" Charlie shouted. "You are one colossal dumbass!"

The man tried to push the door open again. In turn, Charlie smacked it closed again.

"Listen, shit for brains." Charlie wasn't done. "Why not try reading a fucking history book before you open your big, fat mouth?"

After Charlie wheeled himself away from the front door, the man freely kicked it open. "Lucky you're in that chair, you crazy fucker."

"Yeah, lucky me," Charlie answered. "Lucky me."

# CHAPTER 32

While we four were traipsing through Cartersville, two other investigations were in progress at Paul's behest—one in Franklin, and the other in cyberspace.

Paul had dispatched an investigator with instructions to get to Tennessee and find out what he could about the assault on Maureen. A retired FBI man, Donald Riggins was a spry seventy-five-year-old with a large stocky frame and a full mane of wavy gray hair. He was smart, patient, and best of all, unassuming. Unnoticeable and forgettable, he was in appearance and demeanor an every-man, but when it came to the delicate and difficult task of investigating, he was anything but. His success rate at solving crimes, finding missing persons—and identifying those responsible—was off the charts when compared to any other FBI agent. As a result, Paul had every confidence that Riggins would report back with valuable information.

While Riggins may have been our trusted man on the street, Jasmine was our cyberspace warrior—and she did not disappoint when it came to getting the lowdown on the home for boys by the river.

Her report back contained the following:

The Mount Seneca Seminary was built in the 1930s as a school for young men of faith studying for the priesthood. With a combined high school and college curriculum, the courses were almost entirely comprised of theological studies in one form or another. The lofty ideals of its founders, however, were not nearly enough to rescue the seminary from the scandal that occurred in 1953, when one of its priest-professors was caught bedding down with a sophomore. The seminary administration, along with the bishop, tried its best to sweep the incident under the sacristy rug, but were, for the most part, unsuccessful. The reason? The father of the young sophomore was none other than the editor-in-chief of the *Cartersville Gazette,* who refused to believe that his only son was a willing participant. In turn, he accused the priest-professor of rape—a bold and shocking allegation; especially in the early 1950s, and especially in a small town like Cartersville.

As word of the incident spread, and attendance at the seminary dropped to an unsustainable level, the monsignor decided the only way to survive financially was to turn the school into a state-funded orphanage for boys. Beginning in the late 1950s and early 1960s, however, orphanages were increasingly phased out and replaced by state-funded foster care systems. Therefore, what began as an orphanage in purpose, soon became a group home for boys. In consideration of the move, the state allowed the administration to keep its nontaxable religious status, which also made it eligible for large government state and federal subsidies. As an added bonus, those in administration were also allowed to take salaries commensurate with the number of young boys under their care. Since priests, unlike nuns, do not take a vow of poverty, as attendance at Mount Seneca rose to full capacity (over one hundred and fifty), so did the pay and net worth of the priests who ran the place.

Jasmine, however, found it hard to believe that in the 1950s—or at any time thereafter—there were that many homeless young boys in and around Cartersville and Upstate New York. Were they brought there from all over the country? Were any of the children ever eventually adopted? Records that dated back that far were either nonexistent, or in the case of adoptions—confidential. In her search for answers, Jasmine went a step further, and backchecked the staff records at Mount Seneca, and lo and behold, found someone on their books in 1953 who was still alive and still working. Her name was Fran Manz, and she was currently employed by USAdoptions.com.

Jasmine immediately called the company.

After a brief hold, a member of the executive board got on the line. Jasmine introduced herself as a PI investigating missing children in Cartersville, New York. After which, there was dead silence. Jasmine thought she lost the connection and repeated "hello" several times until the deep and succinct voice of an elderly woman cut in.

"I'm Fran Manz, and we need to talk. In person."

# CHAPTER 33

As Mia sat in the window seat of her adoptive mother's tenth-floor apartment, gazing down on Park Avenue, she thought to herself: *Could the flowerbeds separating the lanes of traffic be more beautiful?* Madeline, one of her alters, loved flowers, but hated heights, while Marion, another alter, couldn't care less about flowers, but loved money and wearing expensive clothes.

Mia chose to think of her alters as friends and wondered if they thought of her in the same way. What was in it for them anyway—a temporary life they had little control of? One moment they're here, and then in another, they're gone. Mia knew that she owed them a debt she had no possible way of repaying. She asked Dr. Field to tell her alters how grateful she was for their sacrifices—for the suffering they endured so that she could live on without going completely mad. But according to the doctor, each time an alter did surface, they ignored all questions and talked incessantly until they virtually disappeared.

All things considered, Mia never understood why Melanie—an alter who became hysterical at the slightest provocation—existed at all. Somewhat claustrophobic, she hated going outside for fear something would fall from the sky and strike her dead. As a result, she disliked all birds.

Lisa was Mia's favorite alter—kind, confident, and brave. Lisa handled herself with grace, poise, and intellectual bravado. If Mia could have melted away and morphed forever into Lisa's consciousness, she gladly would have.

Then there was the alter whose name Mia could never remember—the alter who got her into the most trouble in the secure and safe world she found herself living in after...

Perhaps it was the byproduct of a slow healing process, but as Mia got older, she gradually began to remember more. Images, like a short reel of movie clips, would surface in the darkness behind her closed eyes. They would come in small doses, like underdeveloped photos—each recollection ending with a box cover slamming shut with Mia trapped inside. It was as if her subconscious was helping her slowly build an emotional resistance to the horror she had suffered—like a spiral staircase she had to climb to rid herself of the emotional baggage the cruelty of her captors saddled her with. Maybe it was the beginning of the end for her alters—their cue that it was time to reconcile, time to begin the difficult task of shedding her paralyzing fears and surviving alone without her protectors. Maybe this was their way of slowly saying goodbye with each painful remembrance.

But could there be closure and permanent healing without Mia and the world knowing the truth about what happened to her, and why she survived when so many little boys vanished without a trace?

# CHAPTER 34

I missed Maureen and wanted her with me, but the more the investigation moved along—and the more I came to know—the less I wanted her anywhere near Cartersville.

Just before I went to bed that night, I answered a call from an unknown number. It was Maureen.

"I see you bought a new phone, but didn't keep your number," I said.

"I need a fresh start, so why not?"

Despite the assault and the loss of her cellphone, Maureen was still upbeat. It was one of her qualities that I admired the most. Optimism didn't exactly run in my family, nor did I pass it down. I thought of Maureen's son overseas and wondered how much he was like her. I then reminded her to send him her new contact information. She responded that she already did.

Since I wanted to see her, even if it was a virtual visit, I called her back on FaceTime. Once she popped onto the screen, I noticed that she was lying under satin sheets with her head on a fluffy pillow.

"I'm glad to see you're still at Charlotte's," I said.

"She's a dreamboat, Nick. She even bought me a present—a blouse. It feels expensive."

"My daughter is rich, Maureen. Her salary, plus bonuses at the hedge fund she manages, would make your head spin. Regardless, if Charlotte bought you something, it means she likes you, and nothing could make me happier."

"She told me that since her boyfriend is out of town, she enjoys the company."

"That's not it at all. I know my daughter. She is fiercely independent. She invited you over because she wants to get to know you."

"Are you sure it's not just because she felt sorry for me—being alone in New York and all?"

"I am sorry about that. Really, I am. And how are you feeling?"

"Oh, just fine. My headaches are almost all gone. Pretty soon it will be like it never happened. When I think about it though, I do get afraid. So, despite how nice your penthouse is, I'm glad I'm here with Charlotte."

"Good then. About the headaches…Charlotte can get you to a doctor."

"No. Not necessary. I'm fine. Forget I said anything."

"Okay, but just let her know if they continue."

"That's sweet of you, and with Charlotte, I couldn't ask for a better caretaker. There's a strong resemblance between you two, you know."

"Now I know you're going to need to see a doctor. Charlotte is all her mother, inside and out."

"Oh, I don't know about that." Maureen took a breath, and I sensed the conversation was about to veer a bit. "Nick…I…I hope I'm not talking out of turn, but I think Charlotte really misses her."

A lump formed in my throat. *I miss you, too, El.* "Then I'm sure you're a real comfort to her by being there," I answered.

It was sweet of Maureen to bring up Eleanor and to be concerned about Charlotte. Maybe it was the mother in her, or maybe she just wanted to get me talking more about my past. Or maybe she just wanted to keep me talking, period. "I know so little about you," she added. "You don't talk or act like I would expect a rich man would. And how you care about me brings me to tears."

"Of course, I care about you." I thought again. If I needed to worry about her in bucolic Franklin, Tennessee, maybe I should be just as worried about her in New York City. "You shouldn't be alone in my apartment, either. Why not just stay with Charlotte? I'm sure she'd love to have you until I get back. And when you go out, be careful. Don't go out alone if you don't have to."

"I love you for worrying, but you're worrying too much. Besides, Charlotte has to go to work. She has a very demanding position. And Nick, I also don't want to stay cooped up until she comes home either."

"I'm sorry. I know it seems like I'm being overprotective, but you can't blame me considering."

"You're the sweetest, but I have an idea that may make you feel better, and me as well. Since we both have iPhones, we can share our locations. This way you'll know where I am at all times."

"Really? Well, I like that, and yes, it would make me feel better." As Maureen proceeded to walk me through the app, a map popped up on my phone with her location on it—Charlotte's address. "I like this," I said. "And you know what? I feel closer to you already."

"Great, now you can stop worrying about me."

"I'm worried about you because I care about you. And by the way, I don't act like a rich man because I don't feel like one, and never will." Despite our many months together, I had ducked almost all discussions about my past. Since Maureen didn't like to talk about hers either, we kept it to a minimum. But it seemed like the right time to open up more, especially while apart. And so, I did—sordid history and all. Holding the screen image of her pretty face in my hand and watching her reaction while I gave the Cliff Notes version of my life was the best I could do at the moment.

In response, she appeared unfazed, told me she missed me, and asked if I knew when I would be returning.

"Not yet. I hope soon, but I can't say for sure," I answered. "Meanwhile, stay in New York, at least until we can figure out what went on in Franklin. And Maureen…"

"Yes."

"I miss you, too."

# CHAPTER 35

"Someone wants you back in Tennessee really bad, and enough to knock your girlfriend on the head to get you there," Paul opined, while the four of us were having breakfast at a local coffee shop. Having known and worked with Paul for almost eight years, I was no longer shocked or amazed at how glib he could be about otherwise delicate topics.

"What in the world are you talking about?" I asked.

"Someone knew you were seeing her, which means you were followed, and I bet on more than one occasion," Paul said.

"You're speculating," I answered.

"It was obvious you cared enough about this waitress to fly back to Tennessee the moment you heard she was hurt," Paul added.

"I don't like the sound of this," Charlie interrupted. "If what Paul says is true, someone down South knew that for this woman, you would drop everything in New York and hurry back."

"You're both reaching. Besides, she wasn't hurt that bad," I answered.

"That may be where they slipped up," Paul said. "She wasn't hurt badly enough to keep you both there."

Charlie was hanging on every word, and though Lauren couldn't help but listen, her eyes were glued to her cellphone. "Hey guys, sorry to interrupt," she said. "I just got an email from the process server I hired to serve Dr. Field with Mia's doctor/patient waiver."

"This should be interesting," Charlie said dubiously.

"Oh yeah," Lauren responded. "The doctor took one look at the papers and started screaming like a crazy woman, crumpled them up, and shoved the process server out the door."

"I have a feeling it's not the service of the waiver that upset her the most," I said. "It's the prospect of revealing information about Mia that her friend, Beatrice Langley, doesn't want her to." I turned to Paul. "With all these missing kids…any chance we could get the FBI involved?"

"I'll ask Riggins," he said. "But what we really need is proof we can count on that actual crimes were committed up here, and a whole lot more than a children's book that may or may not connect Reginald Langley to a buried little boy. By the way, Nick, speaking of Riggins, he's got more information for you on your girlfriend's assault."

"Why does it bother me when you call Maureen 'my girlfriend'?" I sounded obnoxious and didn't care.

"Probably because we're old friends, and I knew Eleanor," Paul said plainly. "I also know more than anyone how much you loved her."

"You can be a glib son of a bitch sometimes, you know that."

"You're only realizing that now?"

I took a breath and sighed. "So, now be glib when I want you to. What is it that Riggins wants to tell me, which I'm sure he told to you already?"

"While in Franklin, he paid a visit to Maureen's landlord. Retired or not, he flashed his FBI ID, then asked the landlord to accompany him to Maureen's apartment."

"You mean the landlord had a key?" I asked.

"This is Tennessee, not New York," Paul responded. "In Tennessee, you don't worry about your landlord stealing your stuff or walking in at odd hours."

"I don't give my key to nobody," Charlie said.

I let Charlie think what he would. At the Veterans' Center, the front office had keys to all the apartments.

"So, did the landlord let Riggins in? I asked Paul.

"Not really. When they got to Maureen's apartment door, the landlord pulled out his key ring, and what do you know? Maureen's was missing."

# CHAPTER 36

As a senior board member of USadoptions.com, Fran Manz worked mostly from her home in Garden City South, Long Island, which is why she suggested that Jasmine meet her at a small Italian eatery called Caffe Barocco only a few blocks away.

It was a small restaurant with a short wraparound bar, specialty wines, and a separate intimate dining room with a closed door for privacy. When Jasmine arrived, it was inside that room where she found Fran seated and waiting. Five-foot-eight, and with a girth as wide as a middle linebacker, at eighty-three-years old, Fran was quite the imposing figure.

"You are one very pretty young woman," Fran announced, as Jasmine sat down across from her.

"Thank you," Jasmine answered. She had been told this before.

Since the door to the private dining room was still open, a waiter popped in and asked for their drink order.

"They have the best salads," Fran said.

"I might have some pasta...maybe some lasagna," Jasmine responded.

"Yeah, right." Fran chuckled, turning to the waiter. "Bring us two glasses of red wine and two of my favorite salads." She turned to Jasmine. "Unless you want white?"

"No, red is fine." Food and wine were not what Jasmine came for anyway.

The waiter nodded, returned quickly with the two glasses of red, and then hurried off.

"I checked you out," Fran said, as she got up from the table and closed the door.

"What do you mean?" Jasmine asked coolly.

"According to my caller ID, you called me the other day from Garden City, so I figured this place would work for you."

"It's...fine," Jasmine said curiously.

"I didn't want to be seen coming or going from your office, just in case it's being watched."

"I doubt that, but this place is just fine. Not a problem."

Fran sat down and held a sly smile for a moment. "Not a problem, you say," Fran uttered. "When I was your age, we would just say 'okay,' or 'that's fine,' but today, 'not a problem' is the adage. Thank God, it's not a problem—one less thing to worry about." Fran was mimicking someone much younger. "But I guess in your line of work, all you deal with is problems—huge and ugly ones."

"Were you a Philosophy major in college?" Jasmine asked drolly.

"No, I was an English major, but I might as well have been a Philosophy major with all the existential nonsense we had to read."

"I was actually kidding, Fran. I would have figured you for a math or science nerd. Something about you—your carefulness, the uncompromising sense I get about you." Jasmine was serious, but at the same time she was trying to charm as well as disarm her lunch companion, whom she was beginning to feel a bit uncertain about.

Fran saw right through it and shook her off. "Like I said—you'll like the salads here."

Jasmine half smiled, and then got down to business. "Okay, you got me here in this private dining room with the door closed, while you know my office is investigating missing children in Cartersville, New York. So, tell me, Fran...There's a group home for boys there, but no records I can find on any boys being adopted. Is there something you know that could help us?"

"I know plenty," Fran said in a deadpan manner. "I was there during the scandal that nearly shut the place down for good. I even helped with the cover-up."

# CHAPTER 37

Jasmine had an incomprehensible poker face. Whether she was at her computer, either hacking into state secrets or culling from the laptop of a child molester who's been uploading images that would make a grown man shudder, her expression never wavered.

I have tried many times to crack her silent and serious shell, but to no avail. Considering how often I had financed her agency's investigations—and consequently paid her salary with bonuses—you'd think she would at least pretend to be friendly. Not a chance. Thus, it was in character that the sum total of Jasmine's reaction to Fran's revelation was merely to take another sip of red wine.

"It was a school when I worked there," Fran began. Keenly aware of the history of the orphanage/group home and its predecessor, the Mount Seneca Seminary, even Jasmine was surprised by Fran's next remark. "I was a nun then, you know."

In keeping with Jasmine's cool demeanor, she responded: "Now a nun…I would not have taken you for."

"Yeah, I know. I feel nothing like one today…and haven't for a long time," Fran said with a cynical air. "And I suppose I didn't feel much like one back then either, especially toward the end. 'Impure thoughts,' you might say. Who could blame me? I was young—all these college boys at the seminary. Some were damn good-looking, too. Go figure. Celibacy? What a crock! And as for that scandal that eventually brought the whole place to its knees—it was a small wonder no one got arrested."

"It was the 1950s. Priests don't even get arrested today. They sure as hell didn't get arrested back then," Jasmine said indignantly.

"Priests? I'm referring to the attack. I saw that boy in the infirmary. The school administration burned his clothes afterward, including his underwear. Especially his underwear."

"Attack? What attack? I'm talking about the affair between the student and the priest."

"The affair? That boy was underage, and that priest was a predator, plain and simple."

"Sorry, but this isn't making much sense to me. Sure, priests have molested young boys before—but so violently that clothes had to be burned? And a seminary student?"

"Seminary student is not a disqualifier," Fran said curtly. "Let me help you along here." Fran paused. Another revelation was in the offing. "Remember: This was the Mount Seneca Seminary at the time—a combined high school and college for young men wanting to be priests. Therefore, you had young boys in the same building, studying along with young men just under the age of twenty-one on the verge of graduating college. Their classes were on different floors, as were their dorm rooms—but they were still housed in one building, just the same."

Jasmine was on the edge of her seat and chomping at the bit to get a word in. "Which explains how a fifteen-year-old high school sophomore could have been attacked by an older boy of college age. Is that what you're trying to tell me?"

"Three older boys," Fran added. "And I mean three older seminary students."

"But why *this* boy?" Jasmine asked.

"Because they were rapists and thought they could get away with it. After all, the boy was already being abused by a priest there."

*But they didn't get away with it.* Jasmine thought again. *Or did they?*

Fran took a breath and leaned back in her chair when a knock was heard on the door. The waiter brought in their salads, sensed the heightened tension in the room, and quickly left.

"I don't remember reading about any students being arrested and prosecuted," Jasmine said.

"That's because the boy never went to the police," Fran answered.

"But what about his parents?"

"They didn't either."

"Did anyone call the police? Did someone at the school? Did you?"

"Hell, no. I was part of the cover-up—something I have had to live with for what seems like an eternity. Don't forget—I was young, and at the time, the church was my whole world. But I did have one noble moment."

"What was that?

"I called an ambulance for the boy. I denied it then, of course. I suppose something inside me was nagging at my conscience. The last thing the school wanted was the outside world to know anything about the attack. But then, after the boy was examined in emergency, someone at the hospital notified the police—and wouldn't you know it—the only honest cop on the force at the time took that call. Simultaneously, someone at the *Cartersville Gazette* got wind of it and, minutes later, both the police and a member of the press showed up. But the boy wouldn't talk—not a word. The reporter then got a hold of the boy's medical chart, got his name off it, and called the boy's father—who happened to be editor-in-chief of the paper."

"I suppose that explains the scandal." Jasmine said.

"Not really, and you're jumping ahead. I was a teenage novitiate nun at the time—stalwart in my devotion to God, the church and its teachings, even when they were tailored to suit the circumstances—like aiding in a cover-up."

Jasmine downed the balance of her wine. Since she was as much hell-bent on learning the truth as Fran was in telling it, neither woman had yet touched their food.

"The boy still refused to talk, even after his father showed up at the hospital," Fran continued. "Then the father threw everyone out of the boy's room, including the nurses and doctors. A few minutes later, the boy fessed up, but not completely."

"What do you mean?"

"It wasn't until the father searched his dorm room that he came to know the true nature of his son's relationship with the priest—no thanks to the seminary staff. By the time the father got there, all signs of the attack were gone. The original bed sheets were changed, and any and all evidence of blood was cleaned up entirely. The father, however, was far more thorough than the clergy—and more thorough than even I was."

"What do you mean—'more thorough than even you'?" Jasmine asked.

"I was one of the nuns assigned to clean up the mess." Fran said contritely.

"And so…what did the father find?"

Fran took another sip of wine. "The letters. He found the letters."

# CHAPTER 38

Stress always had the effect of raising my body temperature, as did sleep, which meant that the thick and fluffy bedspread at The Red Mill Inn was of little use to me. Halfway through my first night there, no matter how high I turned up the air-conditioning, I felt as though I were sleeping in a sauna. Fielding bits and pieces of disturbing information—rooted in both the past and the present, filtering in from a variety of different sources—left me exhausted. But most unsettling was the dark cloud of fear and acceptance that hovered over a town where children had apparently been going missing for decades.

As my eyes grew heavy with the hour approaching midnight—lying under a thin sheet, my head on a soft pillow—I wanted out of this world, at least until morning. Fate though, would have none of it. Donald Riggins was ringing my cellphone.

It was late. I was tired. Not recognizing the caller, I was about to turn the phone off, but for the fact that I had given out my number to countless residents of Cartersville that day.

I expected that Riggins, the acclaimed former FBI agent that he was, would be only too proud to tell me how he had solved the mystery of the assault on Maureen.

I was only half-right.

"I suppose Paul told you that the landlord was missing his key to Maureen's apartment," Riggins began.

"Yes, he did," I answered.

"Well, the landlord eventually remembered why."

"He remembered?" I asked sarcastically.

"He's eighty-five, Nick. He called me this afternoon and told me that the local detective on the case had just returned the key. Seems the landlord had given it to him while Maureen was in the hospital. The detective, a guy named McCormick, wanted to take another look inside."

"I met that guy. Makes sense. He's nosy, but I suppose that makes him a good detective," I said.

"Yeah, but what still doesn't make sense is how someone got in and out without breaking anything—and without being seen."

"Okay then, what's the answer? Because I'm sure you didn't call me this late to tell me you don't have one."

"That's correct, counselor. I didn't."

"Okay I'm overtired, so just tell me. Who was it that assaulted Maureen, and how did they get into the apartment to do it?"

"I went over every inch of that place—every inch of every floor, wall, and ceiling," Riggins answered. "I checked every door, window, and every possible entry and exit. I even checked for trapdoors. Nothing."

"Maybe she was hit on the head in the hall as she was going in?"

"If Paul's notes are correct, and they always are, that's not what she said. She specifically remembered *being inside* before she got struck."

"What are you saying, Don? It's late and I'm beat to shit."

"What I'm saying is…she did it to herself."

# CHAPTER 39

"They were love letters," Fran exclaimed.

"To whom and from whom?" Jasmine asked, her impatience heightening with every revelation.

"From the boy to the priest," Fran answered, in a tone that indicated surprise that Jasmine hadn't figured that out already.

But Jasmine's mind didn't work that way. She assumed nothing because assumptions can be misleading. Conclusions come from cold hard facts and nothing less. The purveyors of dark secrets love nothing more than to send their adversaries down the wrong path and further away from the truth.

"Were there any letters from the priest to the boy?" Jasmine asked.

"No," Fran replied. "The boy's letters did refer, however, to statements of affection made by the priest, but nothing that was found in writing. But here's where it gets interesting: In one of the letters, the boy wrote about being physically bullied by some of the older boys while they taunted him with homophobic slurs."

"If I understand you correctly, these letters were written while the priest was having a sexual relationship with the boy, and still nothing was done to stop the bullying?"

"No one really knows if the priest did anything to protect the boy.

Maybe he tried. Maybe he spoke to the older boys—or maybe there was some other reason for the assault."

"Something is not making sense here," Jasmine interrupted. "You said the boy's father found these letters hidden in the boy's room. If they were letters meant for the priest, what were they still doing in his room?"

"The boy wrote them, but never sent them," Fran answered. "They were found in envelopes with no addresses on them, dated only a few days apart. It was a cry for help, if you ask me, which leads me to believe that if the priest never got the letters, he might never have known about the bullying. Maybe the boy was afraid to send them, or maybe—in some therapeutic way—writing it down helped him to cope. No doubt he was suffering. The last letter was dated the day of the attack. In it, he wrote that he was considering suicide."

"I'm not surprised," Jasmine said sadly. "And the boy just left the letters in his room for anyone to find?"

"No. They were hidden in the ceiling tiles."

"And his father was the one who found the letters?" Jasmine asked skeptically.

"The father was a reporter for the *New York Daily News* for ten years before relocating to Cartersville. I guess he looked where no one else thought of looking."

"Why would someone who worked for the *Daily News* in New York City take a job in Cartersville?"

"I don't expect you to remember this note in history, but in 1950, New York City was in a financial crisis. I suppose the serene, rural landscape of Cartersville had its appeal."

Jasmine shook her head in disbelief, though she believed Fran probably had it right.

Fran continued. "He also had a son who expressed a desire to become a priest. With the Mount Seneca Seminary in town, it probably seemed like the perfect fit."

Jasmine still hadn't touched her food. "None of my research uncovered what happened to the boy afterward. The priest was reassigned to a parish in Buffalo, but that's all I could find."

Fran took another sip of wine. "After the boy got out of the hospital, he did not return to Mount Seneca. He finished at a local public high school. After graduating, he started college at Fordham University in the Bronx, but then transferred to Columbia—which doesn't make much sense, considering his grades at Fordham were poor to mediocre. But I'm leaving something out: his family's wealth—especially on his father's side. I'm talking about the Holcomb family. That was their name. It escaped me for years, but just popped back into my head like a chicken coming home to roost."

Fran picked up her glass of wine, and in one swig it was gone. She then took a breath and continued. "Though in her own right, his mother was considered well-off, the father was heir to a huge family fortune. George Holcomb was his name. The boy's name was Richard. It's all coming back to me now. No doubt Richard's transfer was on the heels of his family's influence. Fat Ivy League endowments can do that. Unfortunately, fruit from that money tree would have been better used for psychological counseling—considering the incident at Columbia that eventually resulted in the boy's dismissal. It seems young Richard had gotten himself 'a girlfriend'." Fran made quote marks with her fingers. "I suppose they were getting serious, or so she thought, which explains why she stayed over in his dorm room 'on the sneak' one night. The relationship though, was short-lived—excuse the pun. In the wee hours of that same evening, students in the adjoining rooms heard them arguing. Curiously, it was something about his manhood. Seems the young coed wasn't getting enough of the 'slap and tickle' to keep her satisfied. The next morning, she was found lying on the courtyard pavement five stories down. Afterward, Richard claimed that she had been suffering from depression and must have jumped. But when the police arrived, the sole dorm room window was not only closed, but also locked. According to Richard, when he got up that morning, he found it open, and figured it was the girlfriend's doing before she went to classes. The room would often get stuffy at night. In turn, he shut it and locked it. Since he had no reason to believe she jumped, he had no reason to call the police. The problem with his story was the time of year. It was January. Why would she leave a window open in New York in the dead of winter with her boyfriend still asleep? The other problem: It was Friday, and like most of the student population, she had no classes. Bottom line: Considering the argument they had, and that no one was able to corroborate her so-called 'depression,' Richard was charged with second-degree murder. After his father posted an exorbitant two-hundred-and-fifty-thousand-dollars bail—quite a fortune back then—Richard was released from jail. When he never returned for trial, a warrant was issued for his arrest. Richard, however, was never found."

As a postscript, Fran went on to explain that two years after the scandal at Mount Seneca, she left the order of novitiate nuns. At the young age of twenty, she had heard and witnessed enough religious hypocrisy to last a lifetime. She went on to finish college and started a career as a social worker, which eventually led to a managerial and board position at USadoptions.com.

Before their lunch meeting was over, Fran leveled one more tidbit of puzzling information at Jasmine. "By the way, I don't know if this has any importance to you, but I heard talk of a passageway—a tunnel. I'm not sure where it is—under the seminary, or the Seneca River, or somewhere under the town. Don't know if it still exists, but every time that tunnel was talked about, seriously or in jest, it seemed like something to be afraid of. If you ask me—it has its own secrets."

# PART 3

# THE CON

*Back in small-town USA again.*
*What a crock.*
*I'll take the big city any day.*
*Nothing here is what it appears to be.*
*Everyone is always smiling like they're hiding something.*
*It's too much for even Madeline to deal with.*
*That's why we have to join forces, like in <u>Star Wars</u>.*
*Got to keep Mia away from all this.*
*I just know it's going to get ugly up here.*

*Judy*

# CHAPTER 40

As I continued my conversation with Donald Riggins—while still lying in bed with my head and neck stiffening on a soft pillow—I started to wonder if I would ever be able to fall asleep again.

"What do you mean, 'did it to herself'?" I asked, as my nerves reached high alert, and the last thing I felt was tired.

"What I mean is," Riggins countered, "just like I said, she either did it to herself or someone she's in cahoots with did it to her."

"Like her ex? She can't stand him."

"It's not the ex, Nick. I can tell you that."

"He's probably still in Tennessee. She told me that he was a real chauvinist—demeaning and downright abusive—made her quit teaching to be a stay-at-home wife and mother. She had no choice, she said."

"I'm not going to mince words. Paul told me that you have feelings for this woman."

"Yeah, so?"

"I had a friend at the FBI run a check on her after I pulled her prints off the inside corner of her medicine cabinet. You would think it would be easy to find her prints all over her apartment, but no. Someone had wiped it clean, along with getting rid of all food boxes, cans, bottles, and jars in her kitchen cabinets, pantry, and refrigerator. Someone was not taking any chances of leaving a fingerprint on anything."

"Someone?" I asked. "Do you mean, her?"

"Maybe," Riggins answered. He took a breath, and I could tell he was choosing his words carefully. "Probably her."

"Just spit it out. What did your FBI connection find?"

"I assume you're sitting down."

"I'm actually lying down. I don't know where *you* are, but it's midnight here. So please...I'm sure I've heard worse."

"Well, here goes. First, there is no ex, and there is no son in the Marines or anywhere else. She did have a husband—a car dealer who died in an accident five years ago when his car ran off the side of the road and into a mountain wall on LA's Mulholland Drive. I'm sure Maureen...I'll call her that for now...was very upset upon hearing the news, only not for the reasons you may think. Turns out, according to the hubby's accountant, he was heavily in debt and left her the paltry sum of only fifty thousand dollars after he died. It was not what she bargained for, I'm sure."

"Okay, Don, what exactly are you telling me, and what the hell is her real name anyway?"

"Olga Sokolov."

"She's Russian?"

"That's right, and a Grade-A con woman with Russian mob ties to boot."

By this time, I was sitting up in bed with my head in my hands. "You had started to say that her injury was somehow self-inflicted."

"Nick, did it seem to you that the detective on the case in Franklin was kind of cool about the matter?"

"McCormick? Yes, it did, actually. At the time, I thought he just didn't give a shit. Or maybe he just didn't like me when I met him—my New York accent maybe."

"As it turns out, he didn't like her accent either—or at least the trace of it that he heard. Then there were her medical records. The lump on her head was closer to her neck. The part of her head that was the surface of her brain was untouched. But there's more. When I searched a kitchen drawer where the knives, forks, and spoons were supposed to be, I found a hammer—no utensils, just a hammer. Evidently, she was quick to put

144

it away before the police arrived. But her big slip up was...she forgot it there. She didn't forget to wipe it clean of prints though. If you ask me, she hit herself on the back of the neck with it, heard someone coming—maybe the widow upstairs, who found her—and then hurried into the kitchen where she stashed the hammer away before lying back down on the living room floor."

My mind started to drift. "So, her name is not Maureen?"

"Correct. She's Russian and a citizen of the United States via her marriage to that LA car dealer—may he rest in peace—who I suspect was probably murdered."

"Holy shit." I spoke reflexively, as it all sunk in, and I felt as if that same hammer had struck me, too.

Riggins cut in, and I welcomed the sound of his voice—anything that could interrupt the nausea I was feeling. "Let me ask you, Nick. No way she's with you now up in Cartersville, right?"

"Right."

"Good, and though I'm almost afraid to ask—where exactly is she now, if you know?"

"She's in Manhattan, staying in my daughter's apartment in Riverside Towers."

To which Riggins responded: "You're kidding, right?"

# CHAPTER 41

After my call with Riggins ended, it took me two hours to fall asleep—although I'm not sure I ever did, completely. I couldn't help but wonder exactly why Maureen—the only name I knew her by—was conning me. And what an elaborate con it was.

She started working at the diner on Main Street in Franklin sometime after Eleanor's passing. Exactly when, I can't be sure. She was friendly. She was attractive. I was lonely. No doubt she knew everything about me. My Google history alone would have disclosed the Jones Beach serial killer investigation and the building of the Veterans' Center in Manhattan. She would have known I was wealthy. She would have known that my rich wife had died and that I was alone. But knocking herself on the head with a hammer to get me back to Tennessee? That was extreme, which made the con, in retrospect, even more unnerving. But that's what a good con does. It defies logic, catches you by surprise, is unpredictable, convincing, and therefore, very dangerous. Regardless, one thing was for certain: Up until the call I got from Donald Riggins, I was clueless, definitely being conned, and so were my kids.

Come morning, I called Charlotte. It was Friday, and the time was 8:00 a.m. She would be at her desk in the corner office of her grandfather's hedge fund, probably trading bonds before the equity markets opened at 9:30. When she picked up the phone, I immediately asked about Maureen.

"She's gone, Dad. Left yesterday." Charlotte didn't sound at all disappointed. "Didn't she tell you? Said she was meeting up with a girlfriend of hers who happened to be in New York. She sure did ask a lot of questions about you while she was here, though. Tried to hide them in conversation about one thing or another."

"Where are you now?" I asked casually, as I tried to conceal my concern.

"Where else? It's 8:02. I'm in my office and trying to convince a few billionaires to stay away from long-term bonds." She sounded tired and exasperated.

"If you hear from Maureen, let me know." I hesitated. "And by no means let her stay in your apartment again."

"Finally realized she's a gold digger, huh? John and I could've told you that. John had that gal figured out the first time he met her."

"Thanks for letting me know," I said sarcastically.

"C'mon, Dad. You were smitten, and I liked seeing you happy again. Besides, John and I knew you were too smart to let her take advantage of you. After all, we only suspected. It's not like we knew for sure. We were also willing to give her a chance for your sake. But I am sorry. Are you okay?"

"Yes. I suppose."

"And are you sure she's from Tennessee? I listened to Mom's Southern accent my whole life. Maureen's didn't exactly sound authentic."

"It wasn't, and her name is not Maureen. It's Olga, Olga Sokolov."

"Holy crap! What is that? Russian?"

"Apparently."

"I don't like this one bit. Have you tried calling her?"

"It just rings and goes dead."

"Have you tried her at your apartment?"

"There's no landline there."

"To hell with that. I'm taking one of our security guards and heading over." As smart and as tough as her mother, Charlotte was wholly proactive, as I knew she would be. None of what I was hearing from her surprised me.

"Okay, but please be careful. You still have the key your mother gave you?"

"Yes, and if I catch her there, fake Maureen is the one who'd better be careful."

"Charlotte, please don't make me crazier than I am right now. And bring two security guards."

"If she knows what's good for her, she'd better leave the country."

"And you wonder why I'm worried about you going to the apartment."

But what really made me nervous was Maureen's likeness to Eleanor. It made me wonder whether she acted alone, and to what lengths she, and whomever else she was working with were willing to go to achieve their ultimate goal—whatever that was.

# CHAPTER 42

Since Paul had scheduled our breakfast meeting for 9:30 a.m., I was looking forward to drowning myself in a long hot shower before further discussions about missing children and God knows what else. Then my cellphone rang.

The caller ID read: MAUREEN.

"No, it's not your long-lost love," Riggins blurted as soon as I picked up.

"Very funny," I answered.

"Guess where I found her phone?"

"I am apparently no longer qualified to answer any questions where Maureen—or should I say, Olga—is concerned."

"Seems Detective McCormick had it."

"Are you about to tell me that he stole her phone?"

"In the process of gathering evidence, yes."

"And did he gather any?"

"After a little help from yours truly and a call I made to Quantico, we got in."

"Got in?"

"We were able to access her cellphone history and contacts—at least those she hadn't deleted. It will take a while to get the full history."

It didn't sound like Riggins was waiting to get a warrant. No surprise there, though I doubted he'd even be able to get one if he tried. After all, what crime had Maureen committed thus far? As yet, I hadn't been defrauded of anything—unless hurt feelings and embarrassment count for something.

Riggins continued. "Seems your Maureen hadn't counted on McCormick lifting her phone, but he sensed something wasn't right about her. Unfortunately, there were no texts on the phone that we could find, and no contacts either. She erased them. All we came up with was a brief, recent call history she had yet to delete. Three calls to be exact, and all made by her."

"Were any of those calls to me?"

"No. All three went to prepaid cellphones. One was purchased in Brighton Beach, Brooklyn—big Russian population there, you know. The second was bought in the Bronx. The third—which might concern you the most—was purchased in Nashville, Tennessee."

"You mean there was someone local she was secretly contacting?"

"While she was conning you, yes. That's about the size of it."

"I had a feeling once that we were being followed."

"That was no feeling. I'm sure you were. And one more thing: You two ever talk marriage?"

"No," I answered tersely.

"Were you two living together?"

"No, but she slept over at my house quite a few times."

"Hmm."

"What? What is it, Don? What's with the 'hmm'?"

"You know, people con people all the time. And it's always for money. I just haven't figured out exactly what her angle was yet." I waited for what Riggins would say next, but all I could hear over the phone was heavy breathing, until he uttered with a calm sense of confidence that both comforted and frightened me. "Don't worry," he said. "I'll figure it out."

"You got any other good news for me?"

"Yeah…be thankful you're still alive. I got a bad feeling about this gal—Russian connections and all."

# CHAPTER 43

W e met for breakfast at a local diner, where Paul brought us up to speed on Jasmine's lunch meeting with Fran Manz. Charlie then asked if Jasmine knew the exact year the assault took place on the high school sophomore. Paul was fairly certain it was 1953.

"Ancient history," I said, not in the best of moods. "What the hell can we learn from ancient history?"

"A lot," Lauren answered. "That seminary, which became an orphanage and then a group-home, keeps coming up in our investigation. It's like a haunted house with ghosts trying to tell us something."

"I don't know if it's my mind playing tricks on me," Charlie said. "But even from the photos of it, it looks like one hell of a creepy place."

"It's not really, once you get up close," Paul said. "There's a playground and a basketball court behind the main building, and further back, a Little League baseball field."

"And this kid who got assaulted...what was his name again?" Charlie asked.

"Jasmine said his name was Holcomb, Richard Holcomb," Paul answered.

"I don't remember growing up with anyone with that name," Charlie said. "If I did, I would have remembered him."

"First of all, if my math is correct, the assault took place when you were only four years old," Paul responded. "And by the time you were old enough to know what was going on, Mr. Holcomb was a fugitive from justice wanted for murder, so I doubt he was showing his face anywhere."

"What about this talk of a tunnel?" Charlie asked. "Seems like a great place to hide and travel through undetected. Could this be something worth looking into?"

"I doubt it's a tunnel," Paul answered. "Stories, over time, tend to take on a life of their own—like small-town folklore. I also did some digging, too. The Chamber of Commerce gave me the names of the local storeowners dating back to the 1950s and 1960s. Some of them are still alive. Early this morning, I took a drive and went to see one old man who's convalescing in a nursing home in nearby Phoenix. He had a diner, smack in the middle of town from 1950 to 1990. The old guy was happy as all hell to have a visitor, and more than happy to reminisce about old times. He claimed to have the memory of an elephant, and proudly recited every Brooklyn Dodger on the 1957 team that left for Los Angeles. He also remembered Richard Holcomb and knew about him jumping bail in New York City. He told me that there were several witnesses, including a shop owner or two, who swore they saw Holcomb get off a bus in Cartersville's center of town, and walk into the corner sewing shop. Apparently, the local police couldn't have cared less about Holcomb's 'wanted' status. They didn't even bother to follow up on the tip. The old man also said that over time word on the sighting changed from Holcomb going into the sewing shop, to him walking into the woods behind it. Either way, after that, Holcomb was never seen nor heard from again. This may be where the myth of the tunnel started. After fifty years, who knows what really happened?"

"Aren't there a lot of underground caves in upstate New York?" Lauren asked.

"Definitely," Charlie answered. "But before we go there, I want to know more about this sewing shop. I often wondered what happened to the woman who owned it when me and my family lived here."

"Couldn't say," Paul answered. "I doubt she is still alive though."

"This is the woman who claimed that she was the last one to see my sister alive—or should I say—the next-to-the-last one," Charlie said sadly. "She told the police that she saw Peggy chasing after an outbound bus on the same day she went missing. That never made any sense to me, especially since my sister's body was found right here in Cartersville."

"But why would the woman lie?" Paul asked.

"You tell me," Charlie said. "It's something that has always been gnawing at me."

"I just wonder how much going back to the 1950s can help us in 2018," I said. "I don't know—maybe I'm just losing my patience with this investigation."

"You're not expected to have patience, at least not now," Paul said. "Besides, you said the same thing on Long Island in 2010 when it was just the two of us working the case. I told you to have patience then, and I'm saying the same thing now. We work tirelessly. We eliminate false leads. We try different avenues of investigation, hoping to find the right one. We're not here because it's easy. We're here because children have been going missing, and it doesn't seem that law enforcement ever has or ever will do anything about it."

"You call this law enforcement?" Charlie asked, with biting sarcasm.

"If law enforcement up here is as phony and corrupt as I think it is, then that only makes our job even harder—and this investigation all the more dangerous," Paul said definitively.

"Another thing," I added ominously. "Donald Riggins got back to me. Seems my girlfriend of late was an elaborate con artist."

"What?" Charlie interrupted. "You mean she gets assaulted in her apartment while she's conning you? I'm sorry, that's too much of a coincidence, if you ask me."

"That's because it's not a coincidence. She did it to herself to get me back to Franklin."

"I'm sorry, Nick," Lauren said in a tone that was both curious and sympathetic.

My cellphone's *Moon River* melody interrupted my train of thought. It was Charlotte.

"The apartment is untouched. I don't think she returned," she said anxiously.

"Did you go with security?" I asked.

"Yes, but I brought only one guard, not two."

"Where are you now?"

"Headed back to the office."

"Charlotte, until we get this sorted out, I want you to have eyes in the back of your head. Understand?"

"Yes, but there's more, Dad. Olga, alias Maureen, left a note."

"I thought you said the apartment was untouched."

"It was. The doorman confirmed that she never returned. That's when he handed me the note she gave him. Seems she ran into the lobby, handed it off, and then hurried out. It was in a sealed envelope with your name on it."

"Read it to me."

All eyes around the breakfast table were fixed on me, and listening. Hearing my end of the call, Paul, Lauren, and Charlie could easily decipher the other.

"*You are in great danger. I had no choice in this.*" Fear and concern were evident in Charlotte's voice.

"How did she sign it?" I asked.

"She didn't. But damn it, Dad, I—"

"Just destroy the note," I said. "And don't worry. It's probably as phony as she is."

"I know you're with Paul, but please be careful, okay? Dad, you will listen to me this time, right?"

"Yes, and don't worry." I answered as convincingly as I could.

# CHAPTER 44

E vidently, Paul had heard enough about my forlorn self and my phony girlfriend. "Meanwhile, we've got a missing kid out there who may or may not still be alive," he said.

"Let's hope he still is," Lauren added.

"Enough canvassing. We've got to get in those woods, starting where the boy's bicycle was found," Paul insisted. "The sheriff's department claims they combed the area and came up empty, which doesn't count for shit. For all we know, all they did was shine a flashlight through the trees. Besides, it's entirely possible that the kid was dragged into a vehicle." Paul turned to me. "And one that had a tire with a bulge in it."

I nodded.

"Of course, that tread could also be from any random car that just pulled over onto the shoulder." Paul said, and then thought again. "But I don't buy it. That's why we've got to get into those woods and check for ourselves."

When I got back to my room, I called Jasmine. She put me on hold. She was on the phone with Paul, while at the same time trolling the dark web on a new computer—which seemed wholly unnecessary since the whole point of the dark web was to provide its users with complete anonymity. But Jasmine was taking no chances. Paul wanted a complete breakdown of the topography of the wooded area next to the roadway where Billy's bicycle was found. To get it, Jasmine moved from her store-bought computer to her office Mac, then right to Google Earth to get the best assessment of the terrain.

Paul later told me that Jasmine was not in the best of moods that day. She was disgusted with having to search for child molesters in chat rooms and on child porn sites, while hoping to find something—anything—that might provide a lead.

"I know how important this investigation is," she told Paul. "I also have a pretty good stomach. But I have already thrown up in my mouth twice, and I just don't know how much more of this I can take."

Paul simply responded: "Then take a break, remember why we're doing this, and get back to it."

Regretfully, Paul was right. A ten-year old boy was still missing, which meant that all avenues—however dark and disturbing—had to be explored.

After they hung up, Jasmine was only too happy to talk to me—another reprieve from scouring the underbelly of the internet.

If this were Metropolitan New York, or an affluent suburb of Long Island, this ten-year-old boy would probably have had a cellphone with location tracking. Billy didn't. But it occurred to me that perhaps we could track Billy's location by using the IP address on the kidnapper's computer. In a small town like Cartersville everyone knows everyone else, which is why I believed that the children were not held captive in some neighbor's home, but in a secluded cabin, barn, or house—of which there were many in the area.

I asked Jasmine to employ her hacking skills and get information on all cellphone transmissions and IP addresses traceable to secluded locations in and around Cartersville. In turn, she was only too happy to comply, especially since it meant that she had to cease plodding through the dark web to do so.

In 2010, Jasmine's hacking skills had helped narrow down the possible places the Jones Beach killer was keeping his victims, both dead and alive. Though the terrain in Upstate New York was nothing like that of Long Island, I was still hoping her genius and talents at punching the right computer keys would pay off as it had before.

Paul wasn't so optimistic, which is why he wanted us on foot and tracking through several square miles of forest in and around Cartersville.

# CHAPTER 45

The Cartersville daily paper had published an article that included an interview with Deputy Carter outside the police station—an unusual act by a local paper that had thus far given little-to-no coverage to missing boys over the last fifty years. I could only figure that this departure was either because this boy, unlike the others, was from a middle-class household, or because our investigative team had stirred things up by our door-to-door campaign. Either way, the deputy was undeterred.

"Billy might've run away," he said. "It's a possibility we are considering."

"And leave his bicycle?" the reporter asked.

"It was just a bicycle. Could be his real father took him. I heard his stepfather was a bit rough."

If we needed any reassurance that law enforcement had no intention of seriously investigating the boy's disappearance, we got it. The local police weren't just moving at a snail's pace; they weren't moving at all. Besides, Billy's home was in the section of town Lauren had been canvasing. She reported back that she would have approached the house and knocked on the door, but there was still a reporter or two hanging around outside. No way anyone was going to answer. So, she telephoned later that day and the stepfather picked up the phone. When she told him she worked for CNN, he didn't hang up.

"This man had nothing to do with his stepson's disappearance," Lauren told us. "He cried over the phone. Said his wife is in pieces. I also spoke face-to face with a woman who lives next door. She told me that Billy's stepdad even coached the boy in Little League. They were very close, she said. 'Billy adored him' were her exact words. No way this man would have hurt that boy."

Lauren was resolute. Forget the local police. We were Billy's only hope.

When we met again in the hotel lobby, Lauren had some disappointing news for us. Her program head had summoned her back to CNN head-quarters in New York City. She had "*done enough out of town,*" the email directive began. "*You can keep in touch with your contacts just as well from the home office.*"

A big part of me took comfort in the fact that Lauren would be safer farther away from this town, especially as we escalated our efforts to find the criminal—or criminals—behind the kidnapping of Billy, and what seemed like countless others. Otherwise, I would miss her perspective on things. She was smart, caring, and rational. I also took comfort in the fact that she was no longer halfway around the world, but only a short flight away.

She also provided a degree of protection that came with her media mantle—a reason I wanted her to stay. Paul, Charlie and I were dispos-able—a crew of PIs who'd stuck their noses where they didn't belong and suffered the consequences. Maybe our bodies would be found. Maybe they wouldn't. But a missing and murdered CNN reporter and broad-caster? That would get national attention that wouldn't go away. I may have been wrong, but I believed we were untouchable as long as Lauren was with us. We certainly couldn't depend on police protection.

Whether I had mixed feelings or not about her departure, it was for the best. In New York City, Lauren was safer, while the more our purpose in Cartersville became known, the more Paul, Charlie, and I weren't.

Charlie must have been watching his language around Lauren, because no sooner did she leave for the airport then he let the expletives fly over Paul's proposal that we scour the woods on foot. Whether it was born from his frustration over his obvious inability to participate or not, "plain fucking dumb" is what he called it.

In a wheelchair or not, Charlie was a force to be reckoned with.

In contrast, Paul could be very cool in the face of outrage and aggression. I speak from experience. So, when Charlie ran off at the mouth, Paul simply responded with: "You may be right, which is why I'm going to fly a drone over the area first, to see what I can find."

"Exactly," Charlie said brashly.

Paul closed with: "See you guys later," then left the hotel and drove off in his rented SUV, a laptop and drone on his front seat. He was headed to the exact spot along the road where Billy's bicycle was found, while Charlie and I remained in the lobby of The Red Mill Inn, wondering what the hell to do with ourselves until he returned.

"Do you want to see where I grew up?" Charlie asked, in a tone that was laced with uncertainty and out-of-character humility.

I could hear the loneliness and yearning in his voice. Since I didn't have the heart to say no, I answered: "Why not?" And it wasn't because I felt sorry for Charlie. He had become a friend. And who knew when he would get back to Upstate New York again? We had the time. I welcomed the distraction. It was the least I could do. This cantankerous disabled veteran—who had volunteered to serve his (and my) country—deserved an afternoon of my time. But there was only one problem: With Lauren gone, and Paul out with his drone and laptop, we had no means of transportation.

"You're rich," Charlie barked. "Tell the front desk to put it on your bill and they'll have a car here in ten minutes."

I smiled and did just that.

No sooner did I sit back down on the lobby couch and wait for the arrival of my rental, then my phone rang. It was Charlotte again. I was about to say something polite to Charlie like, 'sorry, I have to take this,' but he was already immersed in his own cellphone, playing Angry Birds.

"You okay, Dad?"

"Sure. Is that why you called?"

In the seconds before she spoke, I thought back to how difficult and bratty she was as a teenager, and how proud I had become of the responsible and accomplished woman she had turned out to be.

"When are you coming back to the city?" she asked. "When are you coming home? I know this Maureen thing did a number on you, and I'm worried about you."

"I'm sorry about Maureen," I said. "Sorry you got roped into the charade."

"Forget it, Dad. She may have broken your heart, but she didn't break your bank. You are too smart for that one."

"Don't be so sure."

"I'm sure, alright. Now promise me you'll be careful with whatever you're doing up there. Promise me."

"I promise," I said, touched by her concern.

"Now, I want to know: When are you coming home?"

"Home? Frankly Charlotte, I'm not sure where home is anymore."

"Yes, you do. Home is where there is someone who loves you. Home is here in Manhattan with John and me."

I gulped before I spoke for fear my voice would crack. "I hope to be back soon." I could barely get my words out after hearing my daughter speak such a beautiful and blessed truth to me.

# CHAPTER 46

Before the rental car arrived, I had at least ten minutes that I was determined not to waste. I knew Charlie was quite observant and sensitive to his surroundings because he had to be, but he barely moved a muscle while focused on his phone game—even when I choked up while talking to Charlotte. No apology seemed needed for ignoring him, so I called Donald Riggins.

"I love Denny's," Riggins said heartily. "And you're disturbing my lunch."

Not knowing Riggins that well, I wasn't sure if he was serious or not. "A little early for lunch, isn't it?"

"Like I said, I love Denny's. Call it a late breakfast."

"Do you want to call me back?"

"Nah, I'm almost done."

"Good, because I was just being polite. You're on my payroll, you know."

"Gee, and I thought I was doing this for truth, justice, and the American way."

"You are. Now tell me: Anything new to report?"

"I gotta tell ya—meticulous is how you've got to be to get anywhere in this business."

Riggins probably just wanted to talk into a friendly ear about anything but business for a change, which was fine with me, except for the fact that my rental car would be arriving soon. I was also beginning to assume that he had nothing to report; otherwise, I wouldn't be competing with a hamburger, or whatever the hell else he was eating.

"Yes, meticulous." I tried not to sound patronizing. "Paul thinks highly of you, Don. So, please tell me: What, if anything, did you find out?"

"Since I didn't want to ask you until I knew more, Paul's gal, Jasmine, hacked me a copy of the camera footage around your home the week before your gal's so-called attack. As you know, the system films and records whenever there is movement. So...guess what? I checked the footage recorded a mere twenty-four hours before your girlfriend goes into the hospital over her fake assault. And surprise, surprise—I see the figure of a tall, thin man in a hooded sweatshirt casing the place. A minute later, he goes inside."

"Goes inside? But what about the alarm? I always had it on."

"And I'm sure you did this time, but did you ever give your alarm code to your girlfriend?"

"No, but I never hid it from her either. She was always with me when we walked in the house together. She could have picked it up then."

"Or even recorded it on her phone when you had your back to her."

"I suppose."

"Either way, I have no doubt that this guy was working with her."

"Okay, but I never kept cash in the house. And whatever jewelry my wife had that isn't still in a safety deposit box, I gave to my daughter."

"Did you ever notice anything missing?"

"No."

"I don't think this guy who went in stole anything from you either. But he sure did stay inside a while—a little over twenty minutes. And when he came out, he came out empty-handed."

"Well, is that a good thing or not?"

"Not really. It means he was there for another reason."

"Like what?"

"Give me your alarm code. Let me get in and see what I can find out."

I gave Riggins the code. "But you don't have a key."

"Don't need one. And don't worry about the locks on your doors. They will be as pristine as when you last saw them."

"What exactly will you be looking for?"
"Let me get back to you on that. My coffee is getting cold."
"No, Don, I want to know now. What is it you're looking for?"
He didn't answer and hung up.

# CHAPTER 47

After my call with Riggins ended, I turned to Charlie. He had stopped playing games on his phone and was staring at me. "You look like death warmed over," he said.

"Now there's an expression I haven't heard since my mother passed." I stood up to clear my head then looked down at him. "You get any of that conversation or was Angry Birds all-consuming?"

"I heard enough to figure out that the problem with your girlfriend just got worse."

"I wish everyone would stop calling her my girlfriend."

"What should we call her? Maureen? Olga? Mata Hari?"

"And I thought Franklin, Tennessee was a safe place to live."

"It is, except when someone's out to steal your money—and from what I heard, maybe a whole lot more."

"It may not be safe to be around me, you know," I said with a smile. "You sure you want to hang out today?"

"Hell, I'm sure. Bring it on. I'll cut the balls off the first asshole that shows his face." Charlie then pulled up his left pant leg, cut above the knee, to expose a serrated hunting knife strapped to his thigh. It reminded me of the one the Jones Beach killer used that cost me two kidneys, a transplant, and a slight limp I try to hide—but not always successfully.

Oddly, I felt a sudden kinship with Charlie that I hadn't before. Unfortunately, he wasn't done with his weaponry revelations. "I'm packing heat as well," he added, with an air of bravado that both infuriated and scared the crap out of me.

"No way, Charlie. That's not the deal."

"Mia has been trying to tell us something about this place," Charlie said. "That's why we're here, and if you think I'm going to confront animals—the like of which have been killing little boys—with only my dick in my hand, you're out of your mind."

"Nice *Godfather* reference. Now where's the gun, Charlie? I want to see it."

"I don't think so. All you need to know is that I've got it, and you can bet your ass I know how to use it."

"Paul is not going to like this."

"I don't give a damn what Paul likes. I gave my legs for this country. No one is taking my gun away."

"Do not tell me you kept this gun in the Veterans' Center."

"Of course not."

"Then where did you get it?"

"That's my business."

"And how did you get it on the plane?"

"I didn't. That should ease your mind a bit, along with the fact that I don't plan on taking it home with me either."

"So, you got it up here?"

Looking rather smug, he didn't answer.

"As long as you bury that gun somewhere in this godforsaken town before we get back on a plane to New York—"

"You have my word. Cross my heart and hope to die." As he spoke, he crisscrossed his right index finger over the left side of his chest then raised his palm in the air.

I was about to rail at him once more when an attendant from the rental car company came walking into the lobby with a set of keys in his hand. We followed him outside. The car was a Nissan Altima, which was the perfect midsize vehicle for Charlie to climb in and out of with only the use of his arms. I wheeled him over to the front passenger door, and without thinking, offered to help him in. "If you want me to crack you one, just try," he answered, not exactly appreciating my kind gesture.

"Fine, I forgot. You see, kindness comes naturally to me." I then stepped back, whereupon he lifted himself off the chair and climbed onto the passenger door.

"Now just close it a bit, so I can get my ass on the seat," he bellowed harshly.

With hands gripping the doorframe and veins bulging grotesquely from his arms, he hung on as I slowly and carefully closed the door until he dropped himself on to the front seat of the car. Once I saw he was safely in, I shut the door completely, and placed his wheelchair in the trunk.

"You just wanted to help me so you could feel for my gun," he barked, as I opened the driver's side door and got behind the wheel.

"Right, Charlie. Groping an old man in a wheelchair is a real thrill for me."

He smiled slyly. "Whatever turns you on, though you might have come up empty. I may not have the gun on me now."

"Enough about your gun. Now just tell me exactly where we're going. I just can't wait to see where you grew up."

"Did I catch a trace of sarcasm?" he asked.

"No," I said, lying through my teeth.

"I definitely think I heard sarcasm in your voice," he said, more seriously than before.

Feeling like I might have hurt his feelings in some odd way, I reconsidered and answered, "I'm not being sarcastic, okay? Now where are we going?"

He turned to me with a Cheshire grin on his face. "Want to see where I lost my cherry?"

"Absolutely not."

"We would have to go back to Nam for that one."

# CHAPTER 48

While Charlie and I were headed to his childhood home, Paul was flying a drone over dozens of acres of dense woodland from the same spot by the side of the road where little Billy's bicycle had been found. It was the end of May, and the trees were nearly in full bloom. Aside from a culvert or two, where dried-up streams appeared to begin and end, Paul's computer screen was a sea of leafy green treetops, and he was hardly able to tell one stretch of woods from another. The only interesting part of his afternoon came when Deputy Carter arrived in obnoxious fashion by slamming on the brakes of his patrol car and skidding to a stop only inches away from Paul's rented SUV.

"You don't need to be doing that," Carter squawked. "We had a bunch of volunteers comb these woods the night the boy went missing, and the day after as well."

"You find anything?" Paul asked, his laptop perched on the hood of his rental, his eyes riveted on the screen as he maneuvered the drone by remote control, with its camera instantly transmitting footage.

"Like what?" Carter asked.

Paul eyes remained fixed on his computer. "Any indication that the boy was dragged into the woods?"

"No. Like I said to the press, this boy may have run away, and I wouldn't blame him if he did. He had a stepfather, you know."

Paul glanced over at Carter. "Why? Did his stepfather beat him?"

"Maybe," Carter said.

Paul thought to himself that this was either the laziest law enforcement officer he'd ever met, or one who was just completely full of shit. Either way, Paul wasn't buying a damn thing that came out of Carter's mouth, but he didn't let on. "Thank you, Deputy. I'm going to wrap up in a few minutes if you don't mind."

"Knock yourself out," Carter said, before he sped away, leaving a cloud of dust in Paul's wake.


Jasmine, on the other hand, had been up all night trying to track down the locations of cellphones and computers that might be operating in the thick woodland in and around Cartersville. Evidently, for someone like her, this was not hard to do. You just need the user's iCloud details. If you don't have them, you have to get them. That's where the sophisticated hacking comes in. But to see what the user was doing, she would have to hack sharing capability, which she was perfectly capable of doing, except where the dark web was concerned. No one has yet been able to crack the dark web.

As far as other internet users operating in desolate or secluded areas in and around Cartersville, Jasmine couldn't find even one.

# CHAPTER 49

C harlie directed me to the northernmost part of Cartersville that bor-
dered Phoenix, a town also cut in two by the Oswego River. Though
his childhood home did not border any waterways, as he remembered it,
you could see the Oswego and Seneca Rivers from his backyard. Since
that was over fifty years ago, I doubted it was still true, and told him so.
Surprisingly, the cantankerous and outspoken veteran remained silent in
response, and for the remaining twenty-minute drive said nothing. After
I turned onto his street, I asked him if he was okay. He responded with a
"yeah," and shrugged me off. He wasn't okay, and as I was about to turn
up the long driveway that led to his childhood home, he abruptly stopped
me. "Hold it," he said, then gripped my upper arm painfully tight. He was
staring straight ahead, his face beet red.

"Are you sure you're alright?" I asked.

"Just give me a minute." His voice was gravelly and hollow. He dropped
his head. Eyes open, he was looking down at what remained of his legs. "I
don't know if I can go any further," he said hoarsely.

"Okay," I said. "Whatever you want. Can you just loosen your grip on
my arm? It's getting numb."

Charlie turned and looked at me intensely. His eyes were red and watery. "Thank you," he said. "Thank you for bringing me here." He turned

toward the house. It was sitting on a slight hill. A small first floor lay beneath an even smaller second. There were curtains in the windows behind light blue shutters and yellow siding. "I mean it," Charlie continued. "You know...when my mother died in Florida ten years ago, I didn't... couldn't...go to her funeral. What was the point anyway? She was gone." He turned to me again. "So, I want to thank you for everything—for flying me up here and introducing me to Paul and Lauren. They're good people, and I feel like what we're trying to do—as tragic as it all is—working together—has breathed new life into me."

"That's good, Charlie. I'm glad to hear that," I said gently.

"And thank you for my home in the city. It's immaculate and run by wonderful people." He paused to swallow, then looked back at the house. "You're a good man. It's a gift to have met you. Really."

"Are you're trying to make me cry, Charlie? If so, cut it out." I turned to him and smiled warmly. "Now, you'd better be done, because any more of this, and I may just drive into the nearest tree trunk to get you to stop."

Charlie let go of my arm then smacked it affectionately, which was almost as painful as the squeeze he had given it in exactly the same spot.

"Now, are we going up this driveway, or not?" I asked. "This is a once-in-a-lifetime. You may never be coming back here again."

Charlie pointed straight ahead. "See that garden beside the driveway?"

"Yes, I do."

"That's where I last saw my mother happy. She was planting flowers the day that Peggy went missing. When I got the call from Howard, the not-so-secret boyfriend and prom date, to tell me that she hadn't shown up at his house, I yelled out to my mother from my bedroom window on the second floor. I remember it like it was yesterday—my mom looking up, squinting in the sunlight, brushing her hair off her forehead with her gloved hand. She looked so pretty then...because she was pretty."

Charlie began to cry. One of the toughest men I had ever met in my life was sobbing next to me like a child.

I put my hand on his shoulder. "I think of my own mother every day, Charlie...every day. That you love your mother is a beautiful thing."

"It's also fucking sad." He spoke through his tears.

"I know. Sometimes I think that there can be no love without sadness."

"Damn you. Give me a break. You're a fucking poet now, too?"

Whereupon Charlie began to laugh and sob at the same time. And when the laughter surpassed the tears, I joined in until we eventually gained our composure, shook it off, and sighed.

"Oh my God," Charlie said. "We had a moment there, didn't we?"

"Yes, we did," I answered—a moment neither of us would ever forget. I took a deep breath. "Okay, now are we going up to that house, or not?"

"Fuckin' A, Captain. Let's do it," Charlie howled, his voice cracking with every syllable.

I then proceeded to coast up the long driveway—my speed of approach a signal to all inhabitants that we came as friendly visitors. *We don't wish to startle you.*

We pulled in front of a pair of garage doors, beyond which a rolling hill of green grass swept down until it met the woods about a hundred yards away. A break in the trees on the north side provided a distant view of the Oswego River. A break in the south revealed a similar peek at the Seneca. *Son of a bitch*, I said to myself. *The views he spoke of are still here.*

Charlie and I had yet to exit the car when one of the garage doors opened and an elderly woman walked out in a housedress and slippers. "How we doin', boys?" She looked as friendly as she sounded.

"My friend here grew up in this house a long time ago, ma'am."

"Really," she said, with a higher pitch in her voice.

She walked over to the passenger side of the car to get a closer look at Charlie. "You want to come in, fella? Before my husband died, he was in a wheelchair too. There's a ramp around back."

I pulled the chair out of the trunk then wheeled it around to Charlie, who had already opened the car door. To avoid being reprimanded, I let him maneuver himself into the chair, which he did with ease.

The elderly woman, no bigger than five feet, and with a wide enough girth to fill her house dress, introduced herself as Hilda. She then stepped in front of me. "Let me help you there," she said to Charlie and grabbed him under the armpits from behind and adjusted his seating position. "I helped my husband in and out of his wheelchair for almost five years."

I held my breath, as I feared Charlie's pride would get the better of him and he would react poorly to the kindness of one sweet elderly woman—kiss the visit to his childhood home goodbye. But I was happy to see that he rose to the occasion and accepted Hilda's help graciously.

"My name is Nick, by the way, and this is Charlie."

"Nice to meet you boys." She looked down at Charlie. "Let's get you inside." Hilda took the chair by the handgrips and pushed Charlie around to the back of the house, up the incline, and into the rear porch.

"This wasn't here," Charlie said.

"My husband built it. He was very handy—God bless him." Hilda then left us both alone and hurried into the kitchen. "You boys go wherever you want. I've got a pie in the oven and a book club meeting down the road."

"Thank you," I shouted. "We'll only be a few minutes." I turned to Charlie. "You okay?"

"Yeah," he said. "This backyard..." He pointed out the rear porch window. "It's smaller."

"Everything seems bigger when you're a kid," I said.

"Not this time. The woods were only about fifty feet from the house, and I wasn't a kid when I last saw it. I was nineteen."

"Either way...nice memories?" I asked.

"My father committed suicide in that backyard."

"God, Charlie. I forgot. I'm sorry. And because of your sister."

Charlie nodded.

Hilda called in from the kitchen. "There's a chairlift if you two want to go upstairs."

I looked down at Charlie.

"I got this," he said, then wheeled himself over to the stairs and swiveled onto the lift with just the use of his arms. Sunlight beaming through the porch windows acted like a stage light as he strapped himself in. All it took thereafter was a finger on the armrest's toggle switch, and up he went. "This is the closest I'm getting to a ride at Disney World, so I better enjoy it," he said cheerfully.

I was happy to see Charlie in better spirits. "We solve this thing up here and we might just get there," I said, while relishing in the pleasant distraction that thoughts of Mickey, Minnie, and the Magic Kingdom conjured up in me. Meanwhile, I feared he would break down again. His PTSD was also a concern of mine, as I followed behind him carrying the wheelchair.

When we got to the top of the stairs, Charlie easily angled his way back on to it. "Now, what?" I asked.

The second floor of Hilda's home looked like it hadn't been occupied in years. A film of dust coated a long thin table against the hallway wall cluttered with framed photos, snow globes, and tiny souvenirs from different parts of the country. I waited with Charlie as he soaked in his surroundings before he spun his chair to face north.

"That was my room," he said. I then wheeled him over to the bedroom doorway. "It looks so much smaller than I remember."

"It always does," I added, and then at his direction, I turned the chair around and wheeled it over to the opposite doorway that led to what was once Peggy's bedroom.

Charlie sat silently for a moment, then gestured toward the window on the opposite wall. "There was a hope chest there," he remarked heartily. "Peggy would sit on it and look outside for hours. I always wondered what she was thinking."

"Well, it's a pretty sight. Rolling green lawns, the river in the distance, the treetops…"

Charlie rolled himself halfway into the room. "I don't remember those trees," he muttered.

"That's because they probably weren't there," I said.

"They definitely weren't there," he answered, then pointed out the window. "See that widow's walk, and that steeple over the treetops?"

I bent, looked out, and squinted. I could see the copper cap of the steeple he was referring to. It had a landing below it, and a black railing, which made for the perfect widow's walk.

"Looks like some big house over there," I said. "What is it…maybe three-hundred feet away?"

"Fifty years ago, you could see the entire house from here, and if the lights were on, you could see right into their windows, clear as day." Charlie's tone was somber.

"Which means they could see into your windows, too. Peggy's included." I answered.

Charlie muttered that he had seen enough, and we went back downstairs.

Before leaving, we thanked Hilda and returned to the Altima. I used my cellphone to Google the address of the large home behind the trees, and as we drove back to town, I called Jasmine and asked her to find out who the owner was back in the early 1960s. When she got back to me five minutes later, I put my cell on speaker phone. "From 1954 to 1970, there was only one pair of owners, Frank L. Norris and Clarice Norris."

"And before 1954?" I asked.

She took a few seconds to answer. I could hear her fingers tapping the computer keys. "You won't believe it. George Holcomb," she answered. "Seems he sold the house…No, he gifted the house to Clarice Norris, his sister, and her husband, Frank."

"Are you telling me this is the same George Holcomb who was the father of Richard Holcomb?"

"And editor-in-chief of the *Cartersville Gazette*. Absolutely," Jasmine said. "And I wouldn't be surprised if that house gift was payback to his sister, Clarice, and her husband, Frank, for hiding his son, Richard, after he jumped bail on that murder charge in New York City. After all, he was last seen getting off a bus in Cartersville."

"And walking toward a sewing shop!" Charlie yelled. "The same sewing shop whose owner claimed that she saw my sister, Peggy, running to catch a bus on the day she went missing. Could there be a connection between the sewing shop and the Holcomb family?"

"There is," Jasmine said definitively. "There's only been one sewing shop in Cartersville, and the record owner—you won't believe it— is still none other than Clarice Norris, Richard Holcomb's aunt."

After I hung up with Jasmine, it was all Charlie could do to contain himself. "Damn…it's all starting to make sense to me now. With an evil murderer in town and living next door, my little sister didn't stand a chance."

"We don't know that, Charlie. There's no reason to believe Holcomb had anything to do with your sister's murder." I thought again. "I have to admit, though…I do recall Lauren telling me, early on, that her research revealed that young boys started to go missing around here sometime in the mid 1950s—which would be about the same time Richard Holcomb was seen returning."

Charlie responded as if he hadn't heard a thing I said. "Do you think this Clarice Norris still runs the shop?"

"She would have to be a hundred years old by now."

"Either way, c'mon—what do you say we go check it out?"

Considering the emotional roller coaster Charlie was riding that day, I just couldn't say no. "If you want," I answered. "We're headed that way, anyway."

"And you thought you'd be bored to death running around with me today."

"I never said that."

"But you were thinking it."

# CHAPTER 50

Weed-covered tracks of an abandoned railroad crossing outlined the northern end of the Cartersville business district, where half the storefronts were closed, boarded up, or had whitewashed windows. From the look on Charlie's face, he was saddened by what had become of his town, and—despite the bright sunny day—the streets we drove past had a creepy feel to them. Deserted property can do that—spurring thoughts of a backstory filled with dark secrets.

"I think you made the right move getting the hell out of here," I said.

"It didn't always look like this," he answered, and I tried to imagine the same town filled with pedestrians and bustling with economic fervor. Then, like a lone black crow swooping down from the sky, I envisioned a young Richard Holcomb lurking along the same streets and sidewalks—expelled from college, charged with murder—dark thoughts swirling around in his head as he trekked to his aunt's sewing shop on the far edge of town.

After we passed a gas station that looked like it was built in the 1960s and a shuttered drive-in burger stop called Louie's Beefy Burgers, we spotted the shop. I pulled over and parked a block away. Since I had no idea who, if anyone, was inside, I didn't want to telegraph our approach.

After I retrieved the wheelchair from the trunk of the car, as usual, Charlie got himself into it. He insisted upon wheeling himself as we headed across the street and toward the corner entrance, but the closer we got, the more the shop appeared to be closed.

But it wasn't.

I opened the wood framed entrance door comprised mostly of a large thin pane of glass. *Not exactly burglar-proof*, I thought to myself, as I wondered how many generations of secrets this shop must be hiding. But even as hope that our investigation might be getting somewhere dangled in front of us, the truth seemed to be buried so far back in time, I started to believe we would never find it. And this relic of a shop did not make me feel any better about our prospects. I let Charlie wheel himself over the saddle bump, then followed him in.

Though the store was dead quiet (even its shades were drawn), and there was no buzzer or overhanging cow bell to announce our entrance, I still expected someone to pop up from behind a counter or hurry in from the back. But there were no comers—at first.

We waited a bit longer amid an array of displayed fabrics, spools of thread, and mannequin torsos modeling a variety of dowdy skirts and blouses. A waist-high display counter marked the rear of the shop. An open doorway was behind it. Green shag carpet covered the floor. Inside the storefront windows that wrapped around the corner were more dressed up mannequin torsos—their clothes old and faded.

Suddenly, a voice rang out that startled us both.

"What can I do for you fellas?" A woman in her late forties entered from the rear of the shop and looking like she had just popped out of a nineteenth century time capsule. Wearing a laced gingham dress down to her ankles, her hair in a bun, her eyes immediately dropped down to Charlie. I could sense a note of discomfort in them that I couldn't quite calculate the import of. She smiled and extended her hand. "I'm Johanna Ferrigno. Looking for something for the missus, fellas?" Between the gingham dress, the 'missus' remark, and the look of wheelchair discomfort, I was afraid that I had stepped back into a time and place where provincial mores presided over kindness and common sense. But I was wrong to jump to conclusions, as I quickly found out when Johanna explained the dress. "My book club is meeting in half-an-hour," she chuckled. "This get-up is in celebration of *Pride and Prejudice*—our book of the month. We do this sometimes."

"Is there a Hilda in your club?" I asked.

Her eyes lit up. "Oh, yes. You know Hilda?"

"Charlie and I just paid her a visit. Charlie used to live in her house."

"Why, that's great," she said cheerfully. "Hilda is such a wonderful woman. Sad that she is a widow and all."

"Yes, it is," I said.

"Well then, if you're a friend of Hilda's, you're a friend of mine. What can I do for you?"

"Frankly, we're a couple of history buffs, you might say. Small-town history buffs...and, driving by your shop...we just had to stop in. It has such a charming, old-world quality."

She looked around. "It does, doesn't it? And if all you want to do is explore, by all means, go ahead. I only bought this place a few years back."

"Why thank you," I answered.

"But I am also sorry to tell you that I have to go," she said apologetically. And as she did, a tall, curly-haired teenage boy of college age entered the shop wearing a Mötley Crüe T-shirt and jeans that looked like they passed through a woodchipper. He was donning earbuds and bobbing his head to music that was mercifully his alone to hear. "This is my nephew, Garth," Johanna announced, as she headed toward the door. Garth glanced at us and nodded rhythmically in affirmation. "These men are history buffs and will be looking around the shop!" She had to shout to be heard her over the earbuds.

Garth's eyes widened, more in pretense than as indication that he had heard anything she said. Fortunately, Johanna gestured to us as she spoke, which I figured was enough for Garth, because he responded by smiling in our direction and waving us off in a 'no problem' fashion.

"Good," Johanna said agreeably as she turned again to Charlie and me. "And you boys feel free to go in the back. There's *real* history there. When I bought this place, I promised to leave it the way I found it. I believe the old woman who had it before me slept here sometimes, which explains the makeshift apartment back there. A relative was supposed to pick up her stuff, but never did...and, frankly...I just haven't gotten to it myself."

I couldn't believe she was leaving two strangers like us in the store with Garth, earbuds, and all, but before I could say another word, Johanna and her gingham dress were gone.

"I guess Hilda carries a lot of weight in these parts," Charlie said.

"Yeah, either that, or she's just the trusting type." I tilted my head in nephew's direction.

Charlie huffed, as Garth—with eyes closed—adjusted his earbuds and slouched back in a chair behind the front counter. "Shut-eye—instead of watching the store—seems to be on the menu this afternoon," Charlie added. "Not that a store around here needs watching."

"Believe it or not, there are towns in this country where people don't even lock their doors," I said.

"I know. Hard to believe, living in New York," Charlie answered. "Did people lock their doors in Franklin?"

"I think so. I know I did. Put the alarm on, too. A lot of good that did me."

Charlie suddenly became both bored and anxious. "Let's get to that backroom before sleepy-time Garth over there comes out of his coma," he said. "I'm curious as all hell to see just what Holcomb's old aunt left behind."

# CHAPTER 51

Charlie and I took one more look out the front door of the shop, thinking that perhaps Johanna would change her mind about both Garth's presence and ours, and turn right around. But she was gone, having sped away in a station wagon. I walked toward the rear of the shop, and after I passed through the opening between the glass display counter and the side wall, I heard Charlie bellow: "Shit!"

His frustration was justified. His wheelchair was too wide to get through.

"Hold on," I answered calmly.

Behind the counter and just beyond the doorway was a makeshift office with a desk, a phone, and the target of my search—a chair on wheels.

After I pushed it over to the counter, I discovered that it too was wider than the opening. After Charlie barked 'shit' a few more times, I laid down the bare necessity of our situation. "I've just got to get you onto this office chair and then I can easily push you around back here. Since the counter is too high and deep for you to get over it yourself, somehow I will have to carry you a few short feet from one chair to another to make this happen."

"Shit," was evidently the word of the hour, and he repeated it a few more times.

"I'll pick you up under your arms from behind. I figure that's the best way to do it."

"No fucking way," he squawked. "You drop me, and I'll crack my coccyx. I'm getting on your back."

"My back? How much do you weigh anyway?"

"Without legs, about a hundred and ten pounds or so."

"It's the 'or so' that I'm worried about." Truth is, I just wasn't sure I could do it, i.e., the random bouts of pain running down my left side which caused my occasional limp.

"C'mon," Charlie said. "You're stronger than you think. Turn around, bend down a little, and I'll climb on to your back. It's that simple. Then all you have to do is turn around, back up against the chair, and I'll do the rest."

We pulled it off. Charlie was even heavier than I thought, and I was even stronger than I thought. Since there was no way Charlie could maneuver himself in a chair without a push ring, it was up to me to do it for him. But before moving another inch, I turned to check on Garth. He hadn't budged an inch, and I do believe I heard him snoring.

Gripping the back of the chair, I pushed Charlie through the makeshift office, and then into a storage room full of boxes, before we came to our first closed door. It was made of steel, much like the apartment doors in New York City, which made it seem all the more out-of-place in this small-town sewing shop.

I tried the knob. It was locked, which would have been a problem except for the fact that the key was taped to the door.

"Why lock the door if you're going to tape the key to it?" Charlie asked.

Like many questions about this town, and this shop, I had no answer.

The door opened into a dark and musty hallway. After I flicked on a light switch, everything about it—the wallpaper, the ornate ceiling, the thick wood molding, the feeling of confinement and isolation as you stepped through it reminded me of the hallway outside my grandmother's third-floor walk-up in Bensonhurst, Brooklyn. It had a natural 1950s feel to it, because that was probably exactly when it was built and decorated.

When I closed the door behind us, I noticed there was a key tumbler on the other side as well, which meant that if the door was locked, you couldn't get in without a key, and you couldn't get out without one either.

As I rolled Charlie toward the end of the hall, I asked how he was doing.

"How do you think I'm doing? I'm being rolled around in a desk chair."

"See another light switch?" I asked. The more we moved forward, the darker it became.

Charlie turned on his cellphone's flashlight. "You'd think one of us would've thought of this sooner," he said, as another switch came into view, which I immediately flipped on.

An open doorway appeared at the end of the hall. We quickly moved toward it and into a small, sixty-plus-year-old kitchen that included an old Frigidaire refrigerator and a Welbilt stove. Once an overhead light brightened the room, a metal trashcan with a foot pedal lid came into view, along with a chrome-rimmed red-and-white Formica kitchen table with matching stuffed vinyl chairs. All were resting in peace on a linoleum floor.

"Wow, now this takes me back," Charlie said.

"Me too," I added, then rolled Charlie through the kitchen and into a small parlor, where I flipped on another light switch. There, surrounded by wallpaper patterned in vines and faded pink strawberries, was a vintage thirteen-inch Philco television set on a rolling TV stand. It was positioned in front of a green velvet loveseat. A shag carpet covered the floor, similar to one in the shop. Most interesting and unusual though, were the framed vintage movie posters that hung on each wall: *The Pleasure Garden*, *Blackmail*, *The Lodger*, and *The 39 Steps*. More framed posters were stacked upright against the back wall. *The Lady Vanishes* was facing front. All were films directed by Hollywood's 'Master of Suspense,' Alfred Hitchcock.

We moved straight ahead, over to another door that had glass panes on its upper half, and lead to what Charlie called a mudroom.

"What exactly is a mudroom, anyway?" I asked, not entirely sure of its purpose.

"It's a foyer where you hang up your coat and leave you dirty shoes or boots before you go in the house," he answered.

"Then why is this one in the back?"

"I suppose the old lady who had this place came in through the back sometimes. What the hell do I know? Everything about this place is strange."

On the other side of the mudroom was an exterior steel door with two double bolts on it. A shovel was leaning against the wall next to it.

"What do you think is back there?" I asked.

"Can only be woods," Charlie answered.

Inside the parlor and just beside the door that led to the mudroom, was another interior door with three deadbolts on it. It, too, was made of solid steel.

Charlie and I looked at each other.

"Could this lead to the old lady's bedroom?" I asked.

"Nah," Charlie said. "This loveseat in the parlor here opens into a bed, like an old Castro Convertible. Remember those?"

"I'm afraid so."

"Three deadbolts," Charlie mused. "But where are the keys? Got to be somewhere around here. Nobody's carrying three deadbolt keys around with them. Try this room first."

"There aren't too many hiding places in here," I answered as I checked the drawer of a small table beside the TV stand. I then looked behind the framed movie posters, under the loveseat, and behind it.

"Flip up the cushions," Charlie commanded.

I did but found nothing.

"I heard something—like a clink," he said. He pointed to the loveseat. "Take that left cushion away."

When I did, a ring holding three keys came into view. Taking a closer look, I also confirmed that the loveseat was a pullout twin bed.

Opening the deadbolts, though, took some doing. The locks were as old as the keys. Once I got all three turned and released from their casing, I pulled the door open by a handle that was large enough to fit both my hands around. It took two pulls to free the door from its frame. When I hit the light switch on an inside wall, I looked down a long steep stairway, the bottom half of which was engulfed in darkness.

"Maybe we'll find Jimmy Hoffa down there," Charlie joked.

As he leaned over to look, I grabbed the inside handrail and stepped down onto the first step.

"Where the hell do you think you're going?" Charlie asked indignantly.

"You're kidding me, right?"

"I got on your back once, I can do it again." Charlie was adamant, and inasmuch as I wanted to tell him to go to hell, when I looked down at him in that office chair, I just couldn't.

"Fine, but if we fall down these steps, know this: We're never getting out."

"You're stronger than you think. Now, c'mon."

I reluctantly stepped back through the doorway, turned my back to Charlie, and crouched down. And just as he had done before, he put his arms around my shoulders and pulled himself on to my back.

Taking it slow and steady, I stood back up, stepped through the doorway, then down into the stairwell while firmly gripping onto the handrail for dear life.

# CHAPTER 52

What remained of Charlie's legs, amputated above the knee, were straddling my waist, which took some of the pressure off the hold his arms had around my neck. I was managing the carry, but it was no easy task stepping down a staircase with a seventy-two-year-old veteran on my back. Maybe I should have insisted he remain in the parlor, but the truth was, I wanted his company. I didn't want to go down into that basement alone.

"Now tell me," I said to Charlie. "Are you carrying the pistol on you or not, because if you are, I can't tell." While descending into the dimly lit stairwell, dampness and mustiness filling my lungs, I was actually hoping he was.

"I'm not," he said. "But even if I was, you still wouldn't be able to tell. And stop worrying so much. I can feel your heart racing. What are you worried about anyway? You're the one who can run the hell out of here if you need to."

"Like I would leave you down here."

"Enough already. It's a basement, plain and simple. What's there to worry about?"

"Really? Last time I went into a basement like this, I barely made it out alive."

"Then get some therapy, but for now, keep moving. This is starting to get uncomfortable for me too, you know."

"The conversation, or riding me like a mule?"

"Both. I'm trying hard to keep a tight grip around you with my legs, so I don't drop down and choke hold you to death."

"And I am oh so grateful for that," I said sarcastically, as I wondered if this staircase was ever going to come to an end.

"Can you see anything?" he asked.

"Not anymore."

"Use your cellphone."

"Right," I said. I let go of the handrail with one hand while steadying myself on the wall with the other.

After using my thumb to turn on the phone and its flashlight feature, I gasped as the light brightened up a dozen more steps before we would reach bottom and a hard dirt floor.

"You okay?" Charlie asked.

"I've got a bad feeling about this place, that's all."

"It's a dark and musty basement. You're not supposed to get a good feeling."

Charlie adjusted his position on my back, which I was grateful for. I was getting sore from his legs clinching against the same pressure points.

"We're almost there," I said, breathlessly.

"Just keep moving," Charlie answered, true to form.

As we got closer to the bottom, the area around us was looking more like a cave than any basement I had ever seen. The first thing I did when my feet finally hit the dirt floor was look around for another light switch. I immediately noticed a string dangling in midair, several feet away. With Charlie still on my back, I walked over and pulled it. A bulb lit directly above my head. I then knelt down and let Charlie slide off. Surprisingly, I felt fine when I stood up, except for that recurring pain in my left leg. As I waited for it to pass, I took in my surroundings.

I estimated the area around us to be about twelve-by-twelve inside walls made of large cut stones and a ceiling comprised of thick wood joists held up by even thicker beams buried into the floor.

"There's nothing here," Charlie said. "It's just a hole in the ground."

"Deep in the ground," I added. "So deep, who would want to store anything down here in the first place?"

"Well, somebody used it for something. Otherwise, why the three deadbolts on the upstairs door?"

I hadn't turned off my cellphone's flashlight yet, so I used it to enhance my view of the dirt floor and stone walls. There was nothing I could see that gave this basement—or hole in the ground, or whatever the hell it was—any purpose.

Charlie then turned on his own cellphone's light and put it in his mouth. Pivoting off his hands, he moved himself about.

"Wait a minute," he said. "Why is it cold over there, and there?" He pointed as he spoke. "But warm over here where I'm sitting now?"

"I don't know what you're talking about," I said.

"Of course, you don't. You've got shoes on, while I've got my ass on the floor."

I put my bare hands on the areas that Charlie had pointed to. He was right. Almost the entire floor was as cold as you would expect a basement floor to be, but where he was sitting, the area was warm.

We proceeded to push aside the dirt next to him with our hands until a steel plate appeared. I could feel its ridges and its hard surface, along with its ring handle.

"Remember that shovel against the wall in the mudroom?" Charlie asked. "You noticed it too, right?"

"Yes, I did."

"Maybe this is what it's used for—to get to this plate."

After we finished moving most of the dirt away, I stepped to the side of what was apparently a hidden door hatch in the floor. Charlie and I looked at each other quizzically. Without saying another word, I reached down and pulled the door up by its handle.

A thin cloud of dirt and dust wafted into the air, and the wider I opened the hatch, the more light filtered up into the basement from below. When the air around us cleared, and we looked down, a ladder beneath the opening in the dirt floor came into view.

# CHAPTER 53

It was a much shorter set of steps.

I counted seven rungs to the floor on what appeared to be an iron ladder bolted to the wall of a tunnel, big enough to stand in.

"I'm going down to take a look," I said, as I shut the light on my phone and slipped it into my pants pocket. "Seems bright enough down there to begin with."

Charlie dropped to his belly, stuck his head in the hole, and looked down the tunnel. "No way you're leaving me here," he said curtly.

"I'm not going anywhere beyond the bottom of this ladder. You won't lose sight of me."

"I'd better not, or I swear I'll crack my head open coming after you and you'll have one bloody mess on your hands."

After Charlie sat back up, I slowly and carefully lowered myself into the hatch opening and down the ladder. When I reached the bottom, I was standing between arched walls in a bowl depression for the passage of water or waste.

"It's a sewer!" Charlie shouted.

"I'm right here. You don't have to yell. The echo down here is deafening."

"Looks dry as a bone. Must be abandoned," he added.

"Then why is it so warm. And why are there working ceiling lights every thirty feet or so?"

"How far can you see down the tunnel?" he asked.

"Only about a hundred feet, and then it turns."

"What about the other direction?"

"There are no lights on in the other direction." I took out my cell-phone again and turned on its flashlight to get a better look. "It's been filled in, Charlie. About ten feet in front of me is a heap of rock, sand, dirt, you name it. The tunnel is closed off on one side." I turned to look back in the other direction. The ceiling lights were set inside little cages that were probably as old as the abandoned tunnel. Their bleak light against the curved, dingy tile walls appeared to cast a green hue. "I've seen enough," I said. "I'm coming up."

After I picked myself up out of the hatch opening, I slowly lowered the plate cover onto the basement floor. Charlie and I then used our hands to cover it back up with the dirt we had pushed aside.

Before we ventured up the long flight of stairs and back into the apart-ment behind the sewing shop, we each slapped our hands together a few times to rid them of excess dirt. Having laid on his belly to see into the tunnel, Charlie also repeatedly patted his clothes.

It was hard to believe but going up was easier than going down—prob-ably because I knew the staircase would hold us and I climbed faster as a result. Of course, by the time we got to the top, my left leg was aching again, and my slight limp was more pronounced than ever. Once back in the parlor, I lowered Charlie gently back on to the office chair we had left there.

"You okay?" he asked.

"I'll be fine," I said. "A hot shower and a soak, and I'll be fine."

"I could use a shower myself," Charlie muttered under his breath.

"No shit," I snapped back.

I locked the steel door behind us, three deadbolts and all, then put the keys back under the left cushion of the loveseat.

Once we returned to the shop, I managed to get Charlie back in his chair. As expected, Garth was out cold—face down—his chin in his chest. Though we didn't think a marching band could wake him, we left quietly anyway.

As we crossed the street to our car, with Charlie moving in his wheel-chair quite capably on his own, a man of average build with short blond hair, thick glasses, and carrying a small paper bag was headed toward us. He smiled as he passed.

He seemed friendly and unassuming, so I paid him no mind.

But I should have.

# CHAPTER 54

Before we got back to The Red Mill Inn, Charlie and I stopped at the first gas station we saw. We needed to wash our hands and didn't think it polite to dirty the apartment sink behind Johanna's shop, not to mention the towels that were hanging nearby. I also thought it best to keep our underground adventure to ourselves. After all, I had no idea where that tunnel led.

I went into the station's convenience store and bought us each a sandwich and soda, which we ate in the car. When we were done, I surprised Charlie with a package of Hostess cupcakes, but before either of us could take a bite, *Moon River's* symphonic strings beckoned me once again.

According to the screen on my cellphone, it was Mia calling.

"Are you Nick?" The voice was female and except for the trace of uncertainty in it, sounded far too mature to be a teenager's.

"This is Nick. Is this Mia?"

"Hell, no."

"Can you put Mia on the phone, please?" I looked over at Charlie. He was listening and hanging on every word, while quietly downing his cupcake.

"That's not possible," the female on the phone responded.

"Why not?"

"Because if I'm here, Mia can't be."

"How old *are* you anyway, if you don't mind me asking?"

"Twenty-four, but what does that have to do with anything?"

"I don't know that it does. I'm just trying to understand who you are exactly."

"If you want to see who I am then FaceTime me," she said matter-of-factly.

"That's a great idea. I'll call you right back." I turned to Charlie nervously. "Shit, how do I FaceTime again?"

"You may be 'technology-illiterate,' you know that?" Charlie grabbed the phone from my hand, hit a button or two with his thumbs, then handed it back to me.

The face that popped up on the screen was Mia's, but with a few changes. Her hair was up, and she was wearing makeup that included both lipstick and eye shadow.

I was talking to one of her alters.

"What's your name?" I asked.

"Marnie," she said proudly.

Charlie tapped me on the arm, and mouthed: "Marnie?" He had a look of astonishment that was lost on me. I turned my attention back to the screen. "Where are you calling from?"

"My bedroom—Mia's bedroom."

"And where is that?" Though I knew, I asked anyway.

"We live in Manhattan, on Park Avenue. I'm alone in the apartment right now. Her mom went out, which is why I called. I don't want to upset her by talking to you. And I don't want Mia to know about this call either. She has tried many times to block me out of her memory, along with everything I've seen and everything that I know happened to her, which by the way, is very different from what she told you."

Charlie mouthed the words: *"Holy shit."*

"But I'm not going to tell you anything more on FaceTime," Marnie continued. "It's too important. If I can't tell you in person, forget it."

"I'm kind of stuck here in Upstate New York right now. Will you talk to someone else—someone who is working closely with me? She's a woman, only a little older than you. You'll like her, and she can definitely be trusted. I promise you that. Her name is Lauren."

192

"Since Mia trusts you, I trust you. But the one who she trusts more than anyone is Charlie."

I gave Charlie the phone. "Hey sweetie, I'm here," he said warmly, and in a manner befitting the softer side of an otherwise crusty old man.

"I see you, Charlie," she said. "Are you okay with me talking to this person, Lauren?"

"Absolutely. Lauren is good people."

"I don't want her judging Mia," Marnie said. "I don't want anyone judging Mia. She was just a little girl when all this happened."

Charlie thought of his own sister and began to tear up. "No one is going to judge her on anything. We're up here trying to find out what happened to her, and to stop it from happening to any other children."

"Please give the phone back to Nick," she said softly.

Charlie passed me my cell. "Is there anything you can tell us now?" I asked. "Any new information could be a big help while we're still up here."

I watched as Marnie swallowed hard, looked away, then back into her phone. "Mia wasn't supposed to go in the box."

I was then the one swallowing hard as I tensed up in anxious anticipation.

"Mia was the lure," she said regretfully.

# CHAPTER 55

I immediately called Lauren to set up the meeting, while worrying that by the time it took place, Marnie would be gone—off to wherever alters went when not inhabiting Mia's mind and body. Since Lauren was tied up at work until five, I set up the meeting for 5:30 p.m. at her office at CNN. Mia had seemed to enjoy going there. I hoped Marnie would too.

Before I hung up with Lauren, she told me that she had to hire a lawyer to represent Mia. "After the doctor/patient waiver was served on Dr. Field for the production of her notes and records, she refused to comply," she said. "Mia's lawyer is now going to court to get an order, directing the doctor to turn them over."

"Did the doctor give any reason why?" I asked.

"Yes," Lauren answered. "She's taking the position that Mia is still incompetent due to her multiple personality disorder."

"What a crock, not to mention how hurtful and insulting that is to Mia," I said.

"And should Mia be ruled incompetent, I don't have to tell you that her adoptive mother, Beatrice Langley, will be calling the shots. And, if given the chance, she won't be consenting to anything."

"Maybe we'll find out that the former Secretary of the Treasury of the

United States was no deer hunter, but, in fact, a pedophile involved in an Upstate kidnapping ring."

"If the truth is in the records, we'll find it. It's just a matter of time," Lauren said.

"Either way, good work—and good luck at the meeting with Marnie. I'll wire that lawyer of yours his retainer as soon as I get back to the hotel."

"Thanks, Nick. I was just about to ask."

I then cautioned Lauren that there was no guarantee that it would be Marnie who showed up at the meeting, or that she would even stay once the meeting began. When I called Marnie back, I was pleased to hear that she was the one who answered.

As I drove toward The Red Mill Inn making my calls, Charlie listened in but remained unusually quiet. After I hung up, about ten minutes passed before either of us said a word, which surprised me. Something was bothering Charlie.

"I hope when this is all over that you're not disappointed in me," he said.

"What? Why would I be?"

He didn't answer.

I glanced over at him. "Charlie? Why would I be disappointed in you? Is there something you're not telling me?"

He crumpled the paper bag our lunch came in and dropped it to the floor of the car. "I know…I know carrying me…I know I can be a liability."

"Okay, now I know there's something you're not telling me. So, what is it? You know better than anyone that you're not a liability, so why would I be disappointed in you?"

"Inasmuch as I care about these missing kids, and you know I do, I am more determined than anything to find out what happened to my sister." Though I was in the midst of getting a crash course on the unmistakable Charlie Malone, this was a side of him I had never seen before. He was both contrite and humble. "When I was young, and my sister was murdered, I went halfway across the world looking for answers—and came back a cripple. I need to know what really happened to her. I need to know that I lost my legs for something more than a winless war. Over the years—and I mean years—I've been researching missing children in Upstate New York. I looked for clues, answers. The police have been useless, and still are, but someone like you, who built that Veterans' Center and caught the Jones Beach killer—only someone like you, who could sponsor the right kind of investigation, can find out the truth."

"So, what you're saying is that you weren't entirely sincere with me regarding your motivations."

"Yeah, I guess you could say that."

"Then you're either the most honest man I have ever met, or the most foolish to think that even for a second I was under a misconception about how much the truth behind your missing sister meant to you. So, forget it," I said firmly. "We are here now. We're invested in this, and that means you, too."

"Really? I mean...so we're good?"

"Yes...we're good—two good guys. That's all that matters." The relief that poured over Charlie was palpable. "Anything else you may want to tell me?" I asked, halfheartedly.

"Yeah...I've got to take a leak. Can you step on it?"

# CHAPTER 56

As we pulled up to The Red Mill Inn, we saw Paul's rented SUV parked outside. With no sign of him in the lobby, we went up to his room and found him sitting at a desk by his bed, pouring over the drone footage on his computer.

"What's with these dried-up ravines?" he asked, as he pointed at the screen.

Charlie, who had to go to the bathroom in such a rush that he didn't even close the door, overheard Paul and answered: "Those were creeks. They used to help with the river runoff."

"Well, the river is still there. So why no water in the creeks?" Paul asked.

Charlie wheeled himself out of the bathroom. "In somewhat better days up here, there was talk of a plan to put up homes in those woods—a whole housing development," Charlie added. "When I was in Vietnam, I heard that it was green-lighted. Zoning hearings were held, and permits were issued. The only problem—those creeks were in the way. So, as a trade-off for all the real estate revenue the town would receive from the project, the local board of trustees voted to bear the expense of eliminating the creeks and diverting the runoff from the river into an underground sewer system. This sewer system would also help with the heavy accumulation of rain and snow, which we get plenty of up here. Problem was, the economy turned, and the developer abandoned the project; only the idiot town elders—instead of waiting for a surety bond to cover the cost of the sewer system if the builder walked—had already gone ahead and completed it." Charlie turned to me. "This might explain what we saw down there."

"And how the hell do you know all this?" Paul asked.

"Over the years, I kept in touch with a friend up here. He even went to Nam with me; only difference—he made it out in one piece."

"So, I'm guessing he's your gun connection," I said.

"Could be," Charlie answered coyly.

"And what do you mean by 'what we saw down there'?" Paul asked.

I instantly filled Paul in on the details of our journey into the bowels of Cartersville.

"And Charlie went with you?"

"On his back," Charlie added blithely.

"And there was a tunnel," I interrupted. "It was dry as a bone, but with ceiling lights that actually worked."

"And where does this tunnel lead to?" Paul asked.

"I don't know," I said. "I didn't want to leave Charlie alone to explore, and even if I got him down there, it seemed like too long a trek to take with him on my back."

"Strange," Paul said pensively. "That rear apartment, the three dead-bolts, the hatch in the dirt floor leading to the tunnel?"

"Tell me about it," I said.

Paul resumed scanning on his laptop. "Maybe we can find the sewing shop on the drone footage," he said.

Charlie wheeled himself over to the computer screen where the woods were shown from a height of about five hundred feet. "You have to go farther south," Charlie said. "To the edge of town, past the abandoned railroad line."

Paul jostled his mouse until he saw the stretch of tracks.

"More south," Charlie said. Paul moved his mouse accordingly. "There it is!" Charlie shouted.

The edge of town, the tracks, the roof of the sewing shop, the dead-end street that led into the woods—all were clearly visible.

"That shop appears to be inside a freestanding building," Paul said.

"Right," Charlie answered. "And look…in the woods. There's one of those dried-up creeks not far from it. See the culvert?"

Paul sat back in his chair. "I still don't get why there's electricity down in that abandoned sewer tunnel." He paused to give it more thought. "I bet when it was built, it ran under the town, which means it's probably still running off the Cartersville electric grid. That would explain the lights."

"But the sewer doesn't run under the town anymore," I responded. "That part of the tunnel has been completely closed off like a cave collapse. And it looked to me like it was done intentionally."

# CHAPTER 57

B y the time Lauren called, it was too late.
Marnie was gone and another alter, Madeline, answered. She seemed friendly enough and had a succinct way of speaking—no mincing of words. Lauren asked to meet her instead, and Madeline readily agreed.

When I filled Paul in on the upcoming meeting, he just shook his head. "How many personalities is it now?"

"Two personalities have spoken to me—Mia and Marnie," I answered. "Another alter, Melanie, had spoken to Charlie once, and now Madeline has spoken to Lauren."

"What does Lauren hope to accomplish anyway?" he asked. "It was Marnie who had something to tell us."

"At this point we have no choice," I said. "It's Madeline or nothing, and if an alter is willing to talk, we should listen."

"I suppose you're right," Paul said. "After all, these personalities are swirling around in the same mind and body."

While I was listening to Paul, I couldn't help but wonder what it was that made one alter leave and another appear. I figured there had to be at least one dominant personality that pulled all the strings. Putting aside another *Godfather* reference, I resigned myself to the simple truth: I knew little-to-nothing about multiple personality disorder.

Paul continued. "I worked a case once, about ten years ago, where a key witness had multiple personalities. So, I came to know a little bit about it—but I also learned that every case is different, which makes the disorder somewhat unpredictable. I think that if we ever do get to speak to Marnie, we should be upfront with her about the meeting with Madeline."

"For all we know, Marnie will be the one to show up anyway," I said.

I purposely kept Marnie's claim—that *"Mia was the lure"*—from Paul. I just didn't know what to make of it at the time. It was such a strange thing to say, and I also thought I might have misheard her. Either way, whether it was with Marnie or Madeline, the meeting was at 5:30 p.m., and when the time came for Lauren to report back, Paul, Charlie, and I would be huddled together, anxiously waiting.

# CHAPTER 58

Bookish—with eyeglasses, and smartly dressed—Madeline was polite and serious. Holding a small handbag, she seemed unfazed as Lauren escorted her through the elaborate corporate offices of CNN to a conference room she'd especially reserved for the meeting.

Before sitting down, Madeline greeted Lauren with a "wonderful to meet you," and the two shook hands.

Lauren spoke in a soft and gentle manner. "So how are you doing today, Madeline? Did you get here okay?"

"I took a cab, and I'm fine, thank you." Madeline fiddled with her glasses, while gripping her bag so tightly that the tips of her fingers had turned pink.

"Glad you were able to come," Lauren added.

"I go where I'm needed, when I'm needed. It was either me or Judy. So…here I am."

"Judy?"

"I'm closest with Judy, though she's been pretty quiet for a while. As for me, it's nice to get out—even though the city makes me nervous."

Though Lauren suspected that Judy was an alter, she had to make sure. "Do you two often travel together?"

"You mean out of the city?"

"Anywhere?"

"No. We're only together in the playground—Judy, me, and the others."

"The others?" Lauren asked.

"Yes, the others." Madeline seemed to grow more comfortable—Lauren's kind demeanor a contributing factor.

"Can you tell me more about the others?" Lauren asked.

"I can only tell you what my psychiatrist, Dr. Field, told me," Madeline answered.

"Dr. Field?" Lauren asked, pretending to know less than she did.

"My psychiatrist—and the psychiatrist of the others as well."

"Oh, of course."

"In the playground, we don't talk, and we don't call each other by name. Somehow, we just know who we are. Dr. Field is the one who told me about Judy. Judy is the one who replaces me the most—whether I'm out in the real world, or just talking to Dr. Field."

"But do you know the names of the others?" Lauren had a slight uncertainty in her voice.

"I'm not sure. I only know...who I know." Madeline seemed rattled by the question—not Lauren's intention. "There may be others in the playground when I'm not there. I'm not there all the time. It depends, you know."

"On what?" Lauren asked.

"We are here for Mia when she needs us." Madeline hesitated then looked down at her fingernails, which were painted a dark green. She appeared to be scrutinizing them, while biding her time and searching for the right words. "We're all stronger than Mia, but she is getting stronger, which is why we don't get out as much as we used to." Madeline giggled nervously, then did little to mask a momentary sadness.

It was a bittersweet declaration that recognized the temporary life that each alter had. The stronger Mia became, the less she would need them. When the day came that she would be able to fully cope with the horrors she had witnessed as a child and lead a long and healthy life, her best friends—her protectors—her alters—would be gone.

"Can you tell me the names of the alters that you do know of?" Lauren was giving the question another try—her empathy evident in her tone.

Madeline looked up at the ceiling. "There's me, Madeline, and of course, there's Judy...then there's Marnie. She is the one to talk to if you really want to know what happened to Mia, though Mia is afraid of her—afraid that if Marnie tells the whole truth, Mia might not recover from it. That may be why I am here and not Marnie."

"I'm glad you came, though," Lauren said sweetly.

Madeline looked at her and smiled, then adjusted her glasses again. "There's also Marion and Melanie, and Lisa, though I don't think Lisa has been around for quite some time, either." Madeline nodded her head in affirmation, then repeated: "Yes, I'm pretty sure that Lisa hasn't been around in a while."

"Is that it?" Lauren asked.

"As far as I know, yes. Mia has no brothers or sisters—only Beatrice and the rest of us."

"How has Beatrice been treating Mia lately?"

"They're not talking. She's mad at her because of the court matter—something to do with Dr. Field."

Lauren felt it was time to ratchet up the questions and take the dangerous but necessary leap into the past.

# CHAPTER 59

As we sat around Paul's hotel room, waiting for Lauren's call and what, if anything, would be learned from the meeting with Madeline, I was reminded of a similar point in time during the Jones Beach investigation—a break in the action when we reassessed all we had learned and where it might take us.

Paul was making notes on a legal pad when I asked: "Why don't we discuss what we've got so far? Who knows when Lauren will call?"

"My thoughts exactly," he said.

"Yeah," Charlie added. "Makes sense."

Paul continued to look down at his pad as he spoke. "Let's start with a couple of plain truths that are both consistent and inconsistent at the same time—so much so that I actually lost sleep over them. And I don't lose sleep often." Paul looked up and eyed us both intently. "One... young boys started going missing in and around Cartersville after Richard Holcomb was seen getting off a bus in town and walking toward his aunt's sewing shop. Two...young boys continue to go missing to this very day."

"You think Holcomb could still be the one responsible?" Charlie asked in disbelief.

"Doubtful," Paul said. "If he was about fifteen while attending Mount Seneca Seminary in 1950, that would make him 83 years old today...

assuming he's still alive. No… at some point in time, someone took over where he left off." Paul then stood up, the pad still in his hand. "Now let's break it all down. First…we have Holcomb at Mount Seneca, having underage sex with a priest and getting assaulted by three older students. By the way, I had Jasmine find out who those students actually were, and here's an interesting postscript. As grown men, each died of unnatural causes: One in a car accident when his brakes gave way; a second drowned; and the third supposedly committed suicide by jumping off the terrace of a high-rise apartment building in Rego Park, Queens. None of the three ever made it to the age of forty."

"Holy shit," Charlie blurted.

"Now, let's go over what else we know about young Richard Holcomb," Paul continued. "After the priest affair and the assault, Holcomb leaves Mount Seneca, graduates from a local public high school, and then heads off to Fordham University in the Bronx. After a freshman year of poor-to-mediocre grades, he transfers to Columbia University in New York City on his rich family's dime and influence. While a student there, he gets charged with murdering his girlfriend." Paul looked down at his notes again. "Holcomb then skips bail and is next seen walking toward a sewing shop in Downtown Cartersville. We estimate this to be around the year 1955, when young boys started to go missing in the area." Paul took a breath, followed by a few gulps of bottled water. "Maybe that apartment behind the shop was for him. Maybe that's where he was hiding out. Maybe that explains all the locks on the doors." Paul thought again. "Maybe…and let's not forget that Holcomb's aunt lived just down the road from Charlie, when his sister, Peggy, went missing."

Paul was theorizing and sounding much too sure of himself for my liking. "We can't be certain of any of this," I was quick to point out. "What about his uncle by marriage, Frank Norris? You mean to tell me that he assisted in harboring a fugitive for murder, too, risking serious jail time himself? That just doesn't make sense to me."

Paul answered in kind. "Me neither, except for the fact that Holcomb's father gifted his sister, Clarice Norris, and her husband, Frank, the house. Maybe that bought him off. Either that, or maybe Frank never did agree to help his nephew—which may explain why he just happened to die of food poisoning at the age of forty-one, shortly after Holcomb was seen returning to Cartersville. According to Jasmine's research, the coroner's report stated that Uncle Frank's death was the result of bad squid he had caught and eaten after he had gone deep-sea fishing off the coast of Rhode Island. Curiously, no autopsy was ever performed."

Charlie interrupted. "So, you're suggesting that the uncle was done away with so Holcomb could hide out up here and murder my sister, Peggy…not to mention countless young boys."

"There is no proof he killed Peggy, but he's certainly a person of interest as far as I'm concerned," Paul said. "Now…back to Uncle Frank: According to Jasmine's research, write-ups on Frank Norris depicted him as gregarious and outgoing. He was even a Syracuse U. football star in his day. There's also reason to believe that he had an affair or two while married to Clarice, so I don't think there was any love lost between them. And Clarice, by the way…she passed away only four years ago, at the ripe old age of ninety-eight."

"Did she have any children?" Charlie asked.

"You continue to impress me," Paul told him. "Turns out there is a record of her giving birth to one child, a son, two years after Frank died."

"Then who the hell is the father?" Charlie asked incredulously.

"Don't know," Paul answered.

"And you got all this from Jasmine's research?" I asked.

"Donald Riggins helped, too," Paul said. "Not every bit of information is on the internet waiting to be hacked."

"I could use a drink," Charlie said wearily, while hanging his head so low I thought it was going to fall into his lap.

"Now, let's move to facts and circumstances in real time," Paul added, while tapping on his pad with his pen. "We have Mia—the teenage girl with her own demons to deal with and multiple personality disorder to show for it. She said that she was put in a wooden crate or box, but— and this is important—unlike the missing boys, she lived to tell about it. She also said that she was taken to a cabin in the woods. Meanwhile, the remains of three other boys are found in wooden crates: two unearthed at a construction site, a third near the bank of the Seneca River, while another boy, Billy, went missing simultaneously with our arrival here. And upon investigating Billy's disappearance, we found a tire tread at the scene with a lump on it from mud, manure, or a maybe just a bubble. We can't be sure. We also discovered that the boy found by the bank of the Seneca River was buried with his clothes on, along with a book entitled, *Christmas Moon,* published in 2005. To make matters worse, there is evidence to suggest that he was buried alive. So there goes the 'poor family interment' explanation, not that anyone with half-a-brain believed it, anyway. Then, upon hitting the pavement ourselves up here, we find that this town has, at best, an inept police department, no real detectives to speak of, and one particular deputy who's an asshole floating the proposition that Billy—the boy who just went missing—might have run away from a bullying stepfather, despite neighbors' accounts that the stepfather was anything but. Besides, no little boy would run away in the middle of nowhere and leave his bicycle by the side of the road."

Paul took a deep breath. "In conclusion, we know that crimes were committed. We even have a suspect, but where is the proof that our suspect committed those crimes? Where is the proof that Richard Holcomb kidnapped and murdered young boys—whether it be in 1955 or at any time? Furthermore, since he's now too old or dead, who continues to be responsible for committing those same crimes today? And where is young Billy?"

# CHAPTER 60

Madeline sat up straight and took a deep breath, as the topic of discussion was about to change from alters to a darker inquiry—a recounting of the madness she was witness and victim to.

Lauren began with: "What can you tell us about—"

"Marnie was the strongest of all of us," Madeline interrupted.

"By 'all,' you mean the personalities?"

"We're not personalities. I know you mean well, but we're not personalities. We are people, separate and apart from each other, with many of the same physical characteristics, but different—inside a mind that has been severely victimized."

"You are very articulate," Lauren said in a flattering tone.

"I read a lot, which is why I'm the smartest. This is probably why many of us are still alive." Madeline continued to speak with a maturity well beyond her years. "Mia's biological mom was an actress who lived alone with Mia until Uncle Greg moved in. He wasn't anybody's uncle. He was just a boyfriend of her mom's, an actor also—and a creep who had a drug problem and eventually gave her mom one as well."

"That's really sad," Lauren said.

"It gets even sadder," Madeline continued. "He was also a dealer, and when Mia's mom had to go on tour, she would leave Mia alone with him.

Over time, Uncle Greg's drug problem got worse, but Mia's mom loved the guy and couldn't see past it. One night, while her mom was out of town, he hurt Mia in the worst kind of way. Mia was seven at the time, and Uncle Greg was high on coke, pills, and probably booze, too. He promised he would never do it again if Mia just kept quiet about it. But there was more. He was not only dealing drugs in the city, but outside the city as well. That's where he made his 'real dough,' as he called it. He also owed some bad people a lot of money. I'm not sure exactly why. All I know is that his trips out of the city became more frequent. I'm sure of this because I was the one who almost always went with him. Melanie started going too, but then the trips became too much for her. There were mountain walls along the highway, and she was afraid that a large rock would roll down and crush her. She has an unnatural fear of things falling on her from the sky. As for me, I'm more afraid of heights, but while on the ground, I just love the outdoors, so I took over for her."

"Was it after Uncle Greg hurt Mia that you and the others first appeared?" Lauren asked.

"As far as I know, Melanie and I were the only ones to appear right after. Uncle Greg thought Mia was just being moody, but it was us he was referring to. I wasn't entirely crazy about those long trips Upstate, either. I remember being on the highway for hours, and once we got where we were going, I would stay in the car, while he would leave with a paper bag in his hands, meet up with someone, and return with a different bag. What was really scary though, was when he made his first stop at the local police station. He was carrying a larger bag than usual and parked behind the building instead of in front of it. I remember sitting alone in the car after he went inside and being deathly afraid that we would both get arrested. After he calmly returned with a package and later pulled over to open it, I saw that it was stuffed with cash. He did these transactions with the police over a dozen times as best I can remember. Then...when I thought his crimes were bad enough...they got even worse."

"How so?" Lauren asked.

"Seems that there were these men who wanted to do terrible things to little boys. And for the right amount of money, Uncle Greg was up for just about anything. This is where it gets a bit fuzzy for me. I remember a pretty town, bright green trees, and Disney movies—but it's almost all in slow motion, like a series of photographs. Judy would relieve me at times, and then Marnie. I remember feeling Marnie—her strength and her courage during the worst of it. I also remember Mia—and not just in the playground with the alters, but near a real playground in the real world."

While Madeline was reciting events of a childhood that would have made any other teenager weep, she remained perfectly poised and composed as if the story was not hers or Mia's, but someone else's—sounding more like a seasoned detective recounting a cold case than a young victim violated by her experiences.

Then, as if an alarm went off in her head, or a buzzer sounded that she was wanted elsewhere, she stood up, said—"Sorry, I have to go now"— and left the room and the building before Lauren could even get a word in.

# CHAPTER 61

As we sat in Paul's hotel room, eating pizza and washing it down with beer and ginger ale (my choice), I wasn't sure if we were each hoping to hear something that would keep us in Cartersville, or send us home packing. A half-an-hour later, and we were still awaiting Lauren's call. Paul eventually went on his computer, while Charlie nodded off in his chair, and I kept checking my cellphone's ring volume. When after two notes of *Moon River*, I heard Lauren's voice, I hit the speaker button and we all immediately came to attention.

"A Madeline showed up," Lauren began.

"We were afraid that would happen," Paul responded.

While Charlie and I listened in silence and Paul jotted down notes, Lauren filled us in on the meeting. She had been afraid to ask too many follow-up questions for fear that another alter might suddenly show up and end the conversation, which is what she figured happened when Madeline hurried off. Maybe it was Judy who came to replace her again. But as far as Madeline's recollections went—'in slow motion, like a series of photographs'—none of us knew what to make of it.

"That may be how you remember things when you're drugged," Charlie said.

"Did she recall a school, like maybe the old Mount Seneca Seminary?" Paul asked.

"Madeline did recall seeing Mia play in a real playground, but she didn't say anything about a school, and I didn't ask." Lauren's voice had a hollow tone to it over my cell's speaker.

"But where's the connection to Cartersville and Upstate New York?" Paul asked, while becoming increasingly frustrated. "A pretty town with trees could be anywhere."

Then the bombshell came that we were waiting for.

"After Madeline left, I had many unanswered questions," Lauren said. "Like why did she show up and not Marnie? What would Marnie have told us if she actually had shown up? Now I don't know if this means anything, but I made a list of the alters' names that we know of so far: Madeline, Melanie, Judy, Marnie, and even Lisa."

"I was wondering about them, too," Charlie said. "I mean, where did they come from? Were they random picks? Were they the names of real people Mia knew?"

"But Mia was a child when the alters came," Lauren interrupted. "So, after Madeline left, I ran some searches on my laptop. Naturally, the first category I checked was Disney, and I thought I had hit pay dirt because Madeline said she had a vague recollection of seeing Disney movies. But that was a no-go. After exhausting a few other ideas and getting nowhere, I just plugged the names into IMDB, the online movie and television database. I did this because one name, in particular, stood out to me, and though I figured it was a long shot, it paid off, or at least I think it did." Lauren paused for a moment. "For what it's worth, and for whatever it means…the name that kept ringing in my ears was Marnie, which wound up pointing me in the right direction. Put simply, all the alters' names, without exception, are female characters in Alfred Hitchcock movies, namely *Psycho, The Birds, Vertigo, Rear Window,* and of course, *Marnie.*"

All three of us sat looking at each other, said nothing more, then gave our thanks to Lauren and ended the call.

Charlie could barely contain himself. "Holy crap!" he shouted. "Those Hitchcock posters in the back of the sewing shop! These alters—these kids—have been trying to tell us something."

I turned to Paul. "I saw the same posters and more stacked on the floor."

"Damn," Paul said. "We're going back in, only this time we're not just going down into that basement. We're going down into that tunnel too."

"And this time I'm bringing my pistol," Charlie said.

"You're lucky you're coming," Paul answered back. "And you are not bringing any pistol, especially an illegal one."

Surprisingly, Charlie sat silently reprimanded for a moment. "Okay," he said. "But only because it's illegal. Otherwise..."

Paul dropped his head in exasperation.

"So, when are we going in?" I asked nervously.

"Just after midnight. I'll lead the way, since you'll be carrying your buddy, Charlie, here."

Charlie looked at me, waiting for a rebuff, which I aptly delivered to him. "If my back goes out, you'd better hope that I'm not the one carrying heat."

"Oh, but you will be," Paul said. He then reached into his suitcase and handed me a Glock.

# PART 4

# THE TUNNEL

*It's up to me now.*
*No way the others can handle this.*
*It's just too painful.*
*And Mia is too good.*
*That's the problem.*
*She's too good.*
*And she is suffering for it.*

*Marnie*

# CHAPTER 62

Paul suggested we change into darker, more comfortable clothing. Charlie huffed and refused to take off his marine fatigues. "If we're going into battle," he said, "this is what I'm wearing."

"Other than sewer rats, I doubt you're going to see much action," Paul responded.

"Then I'll be ready for the sewer rats," Charlie said vehemently.

Charlie and I retired to our separate rooms, but not before we agreed to meet Paul by my rented Altima in one hour. Figuring I had at least thirty minutes to rest, I lay down in bed and attempted to do just that. Then, the expected/unexpected happened. More *Moon River*. It was Donald Riggins calling.

"Having fun in Cartersville?" he asked in his usual carefree fashion.

"Not really, but we're getting there," I answered wearily.

"Just be careful," he said. "There's a devil behind every door the closer you get to the truth. Don't forget that."

"And I thought my nightmares were behind me."

"Speaking of doors, I searched your house after you gave me the alarm code. Picking the lock on your back door was child's play. You should change it."

"Duly noted. So, what have you got for me? I'm trying to get some rest before we go out again."

"Well, after you hear what I've got to say, I don't think that rest is going to come easy."

"Lay it on me, Don."

"Your house was bugged. I found four devices. One in your kitchen, another in your den, your dining room, and your bedroom—long-term listening devices—the sophisticated kind—small and high-tech."

"But...why?"

"I'm not sure yet."

"Do you think Maureen planted them?"

"You mean, Olga?"

"Whatever the hell her name is."

"Could be—or maybe it was the guy I caught on your cameras going in on the night of the fake assault. My money is on him."

"Again, but why?"

"To hear what you have to say when she's not there with you."

"No kidding."

"Listen, I'm not really sure. Have you checked your bank accounts?"

"I just sent money to an attorney. It's all there."

"And your investments?"

"I have everything with one company, and even if you knew my password—in order to withdraw—you have to put in a code that I get on my cellphone. I haven't received any such code, and while we've been talking, I checked the app. All my money is still there, too."

"Do you have any passwords written down in the house?"

"What do you mean?" I thought again. "No. They're all in my head, mine and my daughter, Charlotte's."

Riggins huffed. "They were planning something. You can be sure of that. Their goal: to take your money and a good chunk of it."

"I got it, Don."

"Sorry, Nick. I realize this is upsetting."

"It was, but for some reason, less so now."

"I don't believe you. In the meantime, watch out for yourself. From the nature of those listening devices, we're dealing with high-level con artists, which in my view makes them all the more dangerous."

"But why should I be concerned? If they kill me, they don't get any of my money."

"I wouldn't be too sure about that," Riggins answered, and then, once again, hung up on me.

# CHAPTER 63

The center of town was damn near deserted; at least that's the way it appeared when Charlie and I had driven through it earlier that day. At 2:00 a.m. in the morning, with only half the streetlights on—a fiscal directive to be sure—it looked like the aftermath of a dystopian apocalypse. Other than a slight wind filtering through the telephone lines and the sound of the Altima's tires on the pavement, there was bone silence.

I parked the car a block away and out of the line-of-sight of the sewing shop—the inside of which was shrouded in darkness, like every other store in town. Paul and I were in dark blue sweats, while Charlie wore his camouflage jacket and pants. Since the back door of the sewing shop was bolted, and we hoped to enter and leave undetected, Paul slid open the lock on the front door with a slim jim, and we were inside. Using small flashlights that Paul provided to light our way, we moved past the narrow counter opening that Charlie's wheelchair couldn't fit through and used the office chair on wheels (which I had forgotten to return) to push him around.

After we passed the office and storage room, we got to the door of the rear apartment and found it unlocked with the key in the tumbler. Apparently, along with forgetting to return the office chair, I had also forgotten to lock the apartment door.

Since Paul and I were wearing sneakers, the only sound we heard as I navigated Charlie through the long dark hallway, past the kitchen and into the parlor, came from the wheels of the office chair.

Paul went right to the framed movie posters stacked upright in the corner of the room. Just as I recalled, *The Lady Vanishes* was up front. Six others were behind it. Paul recited the movie titles as he flipped through each of them: *The Man Who Knew Too Much, Notorious, Dial M for Murder, Family Plot, Spellbound,* and *Frenzy.* He then pointed his flashlight at the walls where posters of Hitchcock's oldest films were hanging: *The 39 Steps, The Pleasure Garden, Sabotage, Blackmail,* and *The Lodger.*

"I hope we're not pissing in the wind here," Paul said. "None of these are movies that Lauren mentioned. None of these have female characters with the same names as the alters."

"So what?!" Charlie exclaimed. "There's enough posters here to fill a Hitchcock convention."

Paul turned to the door with the three deadbolts on it that led to the basement. "The keys?" he asked begrudgingly.

I went over to the loveseat and reached under the cushion.

No keys.

"I put them back. I know I did," I said anxiously, as I stuck my hand in deeper and frantically felt around until my index finger scratched against something metal. Apparently, I had left the keys farther under the cushion than I thought.

Either that, or someone else did.

"Are you sure about this woman, Johanna?" Paul asked.

"She said she bought the place like this," I said. "And I believe her."

"She also left us here with her dumbass nephew to explore as we wish," Charlie added. "So I believe her, too. She's clueless. I'm convinced of that."

After I handed Paul the keys, he opened the locks. Without a moment's reflection, he moved quietly and quickly down the long steep flight of stairs, while I slowly followed with Charlie on my back. The second time around seemed easier than the first, probably because I was no longer worried that each step would be my last. I also felt more comfortable with Paul leading the way.

By the time Charlie and I got to the bottom, Paul was alternating the beam of his flashlight from the rock-laden walls to the dirt floor. "I thought you said the hatch was hidden," he said. "I can see the metal quite clearly."

"I didn't see any metal when we left," I replied, as I knelt down and Charlie lowered himself off my back.

"Me, neither," Charlie added. "Our hands were filthy from covering that plate back up."

"Maybe when we went to leave, we disturbed it somehow," I added.

Paul looked around. "What is this place anyway? Cave walls, cave ceiling, dirt floor with a hatch in it—and why build a basement so deep?" He shined his flashlight up the staircase, then back at the walls and floor. "My guess? This basement predates the shop, and the building owner wasn't the one who put it here. This was a municipal dig that was done a long time ago—and by hand—probably by miners. You can see the chisel cuts."

"So, what does this mean?" I asked.

"Aside from the timing of the dig, hell if I know, but look." Paul pointed his flashlight at the stairs again. "If this area was dug up fifty-plus years ago, those stairs were put in long after. Check out the wood." Paul ran the beam of light up and down the steps. "It looks no more than twenty-to-twenty-five years old. It barely creaked as we came down."

"I can vouch for that," I said.

"This metal hatch, though, is quite old," Paul said. "Look at the hinges, and the turn latch that locks it. It's ancient. By the way—did you turn it to the locked position when you left?"

"No," I answered. "I didn't even know it could turn. I just lowered the hatch down."

"Well, it's turned and locked now," Paul said.

"Holy shit," Charlie mumbled, then turned to me. "Maybe you locked it when you closed it."

"I couldn't have locked something I didn't see or know about. No way. And I'm also sure that we covered this hatch with a lot more dirt than this before we left."

"Yeah, we did," Charlie said definitively.

"So, you're telling me that there was either an earthquake that moved the dirt and locked the hatch, or someone else did." Paul spoke with an unsettling seriousness. He then reached down and turned the latch back to the open position. He needed two hands to do it. "I think you would have remembered turning this thing," he said to me.

"I do remember...and I didn't turn it," I repeated.

Paul nodded in acknowledgment while Charlie sat nearby on the dirt floor. I reached for the Glock Paul had given me that was snapped into place in a holster at my side. It was a reflexive move that both comforted and frightened me.

"You both go back to the hotel," he said. "I think it's best if I take it from here."

"Bullshit," Charlie howled. "No way, and unless you want a wheelchair ass-kicking, you'd better forget it."

"I'm not leaving you either, Paul," I said. "I didn't leave you in the basement of that kill house eight years ago and I'm not leaving you here. If this is just a municipal sewer access, we'll find out soon enough. If not, we'll deal with it."

"You have one less kidney thanks to that Long Island caper, plus a limp to show for it," Paul said.

"I don't have a limp. I just carried this crazy bastard down a hell of a long flight of stairs. I don't have a limp," I repeated—not sure why I was suddenly denying it.

"Sorry, buddy," Charlie said. "You do have a slight limp." I glanced at him. "But it's hardly noticeable," he gently added.

"All right," I said. "Now are we going down into this sewer or not?"

"Let's go," Paul said, as he pulled open the hatch cover and light from the tunnel poured into the basement.

We immediately shut our flashlights, looked down, and sized up the iron stepladder bolted to the sewer wall below.

"How are we going to get Charlie down there?" I asked Paul.

"I can get down myself," Charlie answered defiantly.

"And how is that?" Paul asked.

"Just watch me," he said.

"Wait, I'll go first," Paul said. "This way I can spot you."

"Fine," Charlie said. "But I won't need any spotter."

Paul turned and stepped down the ladder. I then stood next to Charlie and watched as he slid backward on his belly. Then, using his arms, slowly and carefully lowered himself onto each rung until he reached the tunnel floor. As he swatted the dirt from his clothes, I turned and stepped down the ladder.

When I reached bottom, I noticed Paul eyeballing the hatch. "Something I can't figure," he said. "Why is the lock to the hatch only on the basement side? Why is there no way to lock or unlock it from the tunnel side?" Paul went back up the ladder and examined the hatch more closely. "Ha. Look at that. There was a lock latch on the tunnel side, but it was broken off. So, if the hatch is locked from the basement side, there is no way someone in the tunnel can get out this way."

"I suppose once this tunnel was abandoned that made some sense," I said. "If I was the owner of the sewing shop, I wouldn't rest knowing that someone down here could creep up into my building."

"You would think the three deadbolts on that parlor door upstairs would be enough," Charlie said.

"Not enough for me," I said.

"Or there's another explanation we haven't thought of," Paul added.

"I'm not liking where this is going," Charlie said.

"You're not supposed to. That's why we're here." Paul turned and examined the wall of rocks about a dozen feet away that closed off the side of the tunnel leading into town.

"What do you think?" I asked, as I stamped my feet to rid my sneakers of the dirt from the basement floor.

"Definitely man-made," Paul said.

We each looked up and down at the wall of dark stones the size of footballs, then turned and stared down the opposite side of the tunnel, which was lit by a series of ceiling lights in small metal cages. I looked down. The floor below us was curved like a basin to allow for the easy flow of sewer water. Dry as a bone, it was covered with a thin layer of caked-on dirt, while the oval walls consisted of dingy yellowed tiles that were probably a bright white when installed. We could only see about a hundred feet or so before the tunnel turned to the right. Otherwise, it looked like any other underground sewer that provided passage for water or waste. And the longer we stayed there and took in our surroundings, the greater the queasy feeling in my gut became.

We were below the surface of the earth in a place we'd never been before, having no idea who or what we might encounter around the bend of the tunnel. Was it just more of the same that led deeper into the woods, or to a culvert, or simply somewhere underground and far removed from the civilized world—some desolate place no one knew or cared about?

I imagined how Charlie must have felt—boots in the jungle mud, insects in his hair, his heart beating to the danger beyond every patch of brush, every tree, every clearing—every step forward a potential precursor to suffering and death.

I was certain that no one was more nervous than I was as we stepped deeper into the tunnel. With Paul leading the way, Charlie was on my back, his chin on my shoulder and breathing as calmly as if we were bicycling through Central Park on a sunny afternoon.

And it was at that moment that the memory of Eleanor and me, doing just that, returned.

"Sad, isn't it," I said to Charlie. "That we don't appreciate all the beautiful moments in life until we experience the horrible ones."

"And hard for decent people to truly understand the depths of depravity in the underbelly of our existence," Charlie said softly. "It's why the world needs men like us to fight on."

Taken aback by Charlie's philosophical musings, all I could think of to say was: "You continue to surprise me, Charlie. Now, that was deep."

"I read a lot, too," he replied. "I was saving that one for the right moment."

"Or the wrong one," I answered.

# CHAPTER 64

From a distance it looked like the turn in the tunnel was sharper than it actually was, but in fact, it was barely a turn at all. I do believe I had suffered from a bit of self-inflicted vertigo (excuse the Hitchcock pun), as the tarnished yellow tiles seemed to morph into a dizzying blaze of tiny squares and the blurry visual began to strain my equilibrium. I also broke into a sweat that I was certain would have occurred with or without Charlie on my back. It was that warm and unsettling in the tunnel.

After two hundred feet or so, we could no longer see the ladder we had dropped from, or the wall of rocks behind it. Apparently, as we moved forward, we were turning—but ever so slightly. To make matters worse, the number of working lights along the ceiling was dwindling.

I had no gauge on how far we walked until my back and legs began aching to such a degree that I had to stop. "Paul, you've got to take him," I said, as I knelt down and lowered Charlie to the floor.

"I can walk on my thighs," Charlie announced, and proceeded to do just that in the semi-darkness. "It just hurts like hell if I do it for too long."

"No, I'll carry you," Paul said, and Charlie got on his back. "You okay, Nick?" Paul asked.

"I am now," I said.

As expected, we came to a point in the tunnel where we were engulfed in total darkness but for the use of our flashlights. At first, we figured that the nonworking cage lights were either broken or just didn't have electricity running to them, but a closer look revealed a more obvious explanation—the lights had no bulbs in them.

We continued walking and pointing our flashlights straight ahead—looking for something, anything—but all we saw were more curved tile walls and the same repetitive shades of blackness. Several hundred feet later, nothing had changed. There was no point of reference—nothing around us that was different or unusual to mark our way. But the more we moved forward, the warmer it became.

"Charlie, is it me, or is it stifling in here?" I asked.

"It's got to be at least eighty degrees," he said.

We walked about another hundred feet, maybe two, until we could go no further. Another wall of large rocks and stones blocked our way. But even more unsettling was the steel utility door framed into the tunnel wall next to it.

After Paul jostled Charlie on his back to get more comfortable, he approached the door and felt it with his hand. "It's warm," he said, shutting off his flashlight. "I don't see any sign of light around the frame."

"Me neither," I said, as I turned my flashlight off as well.

Paul put his ear to the door. "I can't hear much of anything—maybe a humming. I'm not sure."

"There could be generators in there," I said. "That would explain the heat. Maybe it's some kind of underground utility station."

"Yeah, but where's the high-voltage sign and the DO NOT ENTER warning?" Charlie asked.

"I smell something, too," I said. "Like fireplace ashes."

There was a knob on the door, and without saying a word, Paul turned it, and pulled the door open.

This was no municipal utility room.

# CHAPTER 65

Flashlights back on, we pointed them at the open doorway. With Charlie on his back, Paul motioned for me to step away while he reached around the doorframe for a light switch. Then he found one but didn't turn it on. Since we had no idea who—if anyone—was inside, Paul was allowing for the worst-case scenario. Standing in the doorway, we would be sitting ducks. And what we saw using our flashlights gave us little comfort.

It was a room of sorts, sunken three steps down to a concrete floor about a hundred square feet in size and under a ceiling about fifteen feet high. Once completely inside, Paul dropped Charlie onto a long beige couch in front of a coffee table the shape of a wagon wheel. With flashlight in hand, he walked straight ahead and up another three steps to a second steel utility door, which he opened easily. Paul shined his light in. "There's a passageway here that looks like a cave," he said quietly.

"I smell ashes, like something's burning," Charlie said.

"Me too," I added.

"It's a funny smell, too," Paul said, then closed the door and pointed his flashlight at the switch beside the entrance door. I was about to flip it on, when he said: "Wait." He gestured at a wall to my right, stepped down onto the concrete floor, and navigated in the semi-darkness around numerous scattered chairs until he walked up another three steps to a third

228

door. He grabbed its handle and opened it. "There's another room here," he said. "It looks like a bedroom, but…"

"Paul, what is it?" I spoke louder than I meant to.

"You'll see when you get over here," he said. "You can hit that switch now."

A large bundle of florescent lights hanging on chains from the ceiling brightened the room we were in. I turned off my flashlight, looked around, and felt as if I was in a cross between a ski lodge and a western hacienda. Three of the four walls, which I was certain had previously been painted an unknown shade of white, had dulled and yellowed over what I estimated to be decades. The wall to the right—the one with the third door in it—was a putrid green. It had a stucco finish and chips had begun to form on its surface.

Charlie remained sitting on the couch beside the entrance door to the tunnel. Across from him—on the other side of the wagon wheel coffee table—was a small desk. On it was an open laptop computer. Its screen was dark.

The rest of the room was cluttered with upright cushioned chairs of different styles, but what was most unusual were the large decorative carpets that hung from the ceiling to the floor about a foot away from each of the walls. On them, threaded into the fabric and design, were faded poster images of classic Disney movies—*Snow White and The Seven Dwarfs, Pinocchio, Dumbo, Bambi, Cinderella, Alice In Wonderland, Peter Pan,* and *Lady and the Tramp*. Were they hanging in effigy or in tribute? I couldn't be sure. Their images were so terribly faded over time that Snow White was no longer white, and you could barely tell Lady from the Tramp. I had no doubt, however, that once upon a time they were adored works of fabric art, pleasing to the eye of any child or adult.

You would think that these strange hanging carpets would have been enough to send us packing as we looked and listened for anyone or anything that would give us a clue as to the peculiar purpose for this underground bunker. Nor did we take comfort in the knowledge that we were in a desolate place under the woods and outside the town limits, which meant that if someone left us there to die, we would never be seen again nor heard from again—another unmarked grave.

As I sized up our bizarre surroundings, I kept glancing at Charlie, who

229

was fiddling with a coffee table drawer that was misaligned from its compartment. He kept tugging on it until it burst open and a bunch of pamphlets fell to the floor. As he picked one up, the vile purpose of the wall hangings and their false sense of childish merriment became apparent.

The pamphlets were published and printed by an organization called AMBLA—The American Man-Boy Love Association.

Charlie was dumbstruck. "You won't believe what it says here."

On page one, the organization claimed to be 'misunderstood.' Its members were merely 'standing up for the rights of male youths to be mentored, guided, and loved by older men,' as if it was perfectly reasonable to espouse such a mantra. There was no mention of sex, just generalized notions of 'love.' A quote from Oscar Wilde and the sonnets of Shakespeare and Michelangelo (out-of-context references to be sure) were noted as testimonials to the validity and justice of their cause célèbre.

Paul left his perch by the third door and walked over. He picked up one of the pamphlets and stuck it in his pocket, while the one in Charlie's hands fell to the floor as if it had suddenly become contaminated.

"I can't believe what I just read," Charlie said. "This is sick and can't be legal."

"It's legal as long as they don't talk or write about having sex with underage boys," I said.

"I bet years ago it was a lot easier for them to recruit," Paul said. "Society was much less accepting of gay kids than it is today. With nowhere else to turn, I'll bet the open arms of AMBLA seemed like the right choice…and maybe the only choice for some of them."

"It's like walking into the open arms of the devil, if you ask me," Charlie said. "And who are these grown men who participate in this shit?"

"They are from all walks of life," Paul answered. "Men with money who can't get their rocks off any other way except by having sex with young boys. But make no mistake about it: Getting these boys here has got to be one costly venture."

"I just wanted to find out who killed my sister," Charlie said. "But this sick stuff…I could have done without."

"You never know where an investigation is going to take you," Paul said, while walking back to the third doorway. "It's rarely a pretty picture."

With pamphlets scattered on the floor below him, Charlie stared blankly across the room. "I nearly got killed in Vietnam,' he said. "And if I have to risk my life up here, so be it if it means finding out what happened to my sister and Mia."

"Well, whatever they did to that little girl…I'll bet it was in here," Paul said, as he stood beside the third doorway that led to the adjoining room. Once he stepped inside and turned on the room's overhead lights, I hurried over and followed him in. The first thing that caught my eye was the set of twin beds against the wall. There was also a stairway in the far corner that led to another hatch in the ceiling. But what I had missed, until the moment that I walked over and looked up those stairs, was a most peculiar but familiar sight.

Hanging on all four walls were Hitchcock movie posters.

Paul reached for his phone. "After we spoke to Lauren, I made a list of the characters and their Hitchcock movies that coincided with the names of the alters." He spoke loud enough so that Charlie, who had remained on the couch in the next room, could hear. Then, like a teacher in a classroom, he pointed to each poster and recited its female lead. "Let's start with *Psycho*," he said. "Remember Janet Leigh in the famous shower scene? She played the character, Marion—an alter. In *The Birds*, Tippi Hedren played Melanie—also an alter. The movie, *Vertigo*, starred one female actress who played two parts. I'm talking about the beautiful Kim Novak, who played the roles of Madeline as well as Judy. Ring a bell? It's no coincidence that the alter Madeline said that she is closest to the alter Judy." Paul kept looking down at his phone and then up at the walls. "Then over here we have my mother's favorite—*Rear Window,* where the name of the female lead is Lisa, another alter. And last but not least, sitting on a wall all by itself, where the leading female character shares her name with the title of the movie, is *Marnie*—the alter who was supposed to show up at the meeting with Lauren, but didn't." When Paul was done, he put away his phone, lifted his head, and again spoke loud enough for Charlie to hear in the next room. "Gentleman, and I'm referring to you too, Charlie." Charlie didn't respond. "As we examine these underground rooms, which are becoming more sordid by the minute in sight and smell, one thing is undeniable: We are in one horrible and very dangerous place."

I watched as Paul's eyes simultaneously widened with the declaration and his pupils appeared to dilate under the bright florescent bulbs overhead.

Then, before any of us could utter another word, the steel door between the rooms slammed shut, the lights went out, and we were thrown into complete darkness.

# CHAPTER 66

Not a glint of light appeared, anywhere, as we stood frozen in blackness. If I hadn't felt a rush of air when the door between the rooms closed hard and fast, I would have sworn a shot rang out.

Paul immediately turned on his flashlight. Shaken by the startling jolt to my eyes and ears, I had dropped mine when the door violently closed. I knelt down and anxiously felt around the darkened floor, searching for it.

"Forget it," Paul whispered. "Just take out your gun." Paul already had his in his hand.

I quickly unlocked the strap of the pistol holster at my side and with my thumb and index finger began searching for the Glock's safety release. "How do I take the safety off?" I whispered with a nervous energy in my voice, unsure of what frightened me more—the source of the blackout and the closed door, or that I couldn't find the safety.

Paul spoke quietly into my ear and killed the mystery. "It's a Glock. There is no safety. You just cock it and pull the trigger." He then moved toward the door, turned the knob, and slowly pushed it open.

As the smell of ashes and spoiled meat filled the air, Paul beamed his flashlight into the main room where we had left Charlie. He was looking for something—anything—that could have caused the lights to go out and the door to slam shut. But there was nothing. And worse still, no Charlie.

Paul stepped through the doorway pointing his flashlight at the chairs, the couch, the wagon wheel coffee table, the desk, the laptop, and the concrete floor. Everything seemed undisturbed, yet there was still no sign of Charlie. Paul then beamed the light on to each and every Disney carpet that hung alongside the walls, except for…the one behind him.

As I followed him in, unable to find my flashlight, I reached for the only light source I had—the one on my cellphone.

"Charlie?" I whispered.

I listened for a response, but all I heard was the sound of something cutting through the air and Paul groan just before he hit the floor. A split second later, a sharp pain coursed through my neck and head. I had lost control of my arms and legs. My collapse on to solid concrete was gratefully broken by the cushion of a nearby chair.

Semiconscious, eyes glazed, the Glock no longer in my hand—and the only light around me coming from the screen on my cellphone that lay face up on the floor—I looked up at the dark figure of a man standing over me. My vision blurry and having little ability to gauge time in the condition I was in, I had no idea how long he stood there before he walked over to the second door that led to the cave passageway and opened it. Feeling faint, I tried hard to remain conscious. Call it the brain's 'protective mechanism,' but when the stranger returned, my head and vision had cleared just enough to watch him drag Paul over to the doorway, up the steps, and into the cave. I tried to move but couldn't. I managed to reach for my phone. Seconds later, I heard a grunt and something heavy drop into what sounded like muddy water. My head aching and my vision growing hazy again, I looked up.

Inside the doorway to the cave—a bleak light shining behind him—stood the dark figure.

As he stepped down and moved toward me, the light on my cellphone timed out, and the world around me went dark again.

# CHAPTER 67

The overhead lights flickered and then came on—painfully bright. Though my vision was spotty at first, after a second or two, I recognized my assailant. He was the same smiling man I had seen walking past when Charlie and I left the sewing shop. With eyes that appeared enlarged because they were magnified behind thick bifocals, he was dressed in beige corduroy pants and a matching blazer with patches on the elbows.

As he stood over me, his arm extended, a pistol in his hand, my vision began to clear again. Despite the pain in my head, I sized him up to be about my height and weight—five-foot-nine (or ten) and about a hundred and sixty pounds. He had short blond hair and a light, almost pale complexion.

Since there was no way he or anyone else could possibly know that Charlie and I would be crossing Main Street when we did, the odds of passing him were damn lousy ones—odds we didn't deserve to die over. Then again, I'd already beaten the probabilities of my demise on more than one occasion. But to lose my life at the hands of a monster who kidnaps and kills little boys? That was hard to accept, whatever the circumstances and whatever the timing.

I was always keenly aware of the imperfect and unjust life we are all born into. I often wondered whether we were really put on this earth to be happy, or if life is just one long search for meaning amid an ever-constant struggle. Convinced at that moment that I was going to die, my journey in life—from Brooklyn to the Bronx, then to Long Island, and finally to Tennessee—flashed like a photo reel in my head, as fright turned into sadness and the awful realization that I would never see nor hear from my kids again swelled inside me. I would wind up like the young boys we were trying to save—under a mound of dirt in the woods, or in a crate by the river, or as a mere pile of ashes inside a putrid furnace. There would be no body to bury. I would just disappear.

I thought about Charlie. Hadn't he suffered enough?

Though the pain in my head escalated each time I moved it, I looked around. The wall carpet with the poster image of *Lady and the Tramp* sewn onto it was on the floor. There were bloodstains on Lady's face and on the pants of the man standing over me—no doubt from Paul's head. I tried in vain to shake off the fear as the man relaxed his arm and bent it to the side—the pistol still in his hand—the barrel still pointed in my direction.

"Where's Charlie?" I asked.

"Never mind about Charlie," he said. "He's where he belongs." He spoke like an apathetic store clerk—monotonous and unremarkable.

Having no real sense of my own body, I realized that I was gripping the back of my head with my right hand while lying on the floor. "Who are you?" I asked.

"Never mind who I am. Now get up." He sounded more like a bratty computer nerd than a schoolyard bully. Why I took comfort in this, I'll never know. I was in no position to defy him. He had gotten the jump on Paul, which meant he was as quick and strong as he was devious.

I slowly turned to my side. One knee at a time, and one leg at a time, I rose to my feet. Though I tried, I couldn't seem to stand up straight. The room was spinning. I reached for the arm of a nearby chair, grabbed, and held on.

"Sit down," he commanded. "And face me."

I turned and fell backward onto the couch. The AMBLA pamphlets that had fallen to the floor were now under my feet. With my body barely taking messages from my brain, and my head springing back, then forward—for a moment I was seeing double. Two evil monsters were standing over me, each pointing a gun at my head. Then the two morphed into one—one diabolical demon.

An anger that I had no control over began stirring inside me. If I was going to be killed, I damn well wanted to know who my killer was, so I asked again. "Who the fuck are you?"

"Your worst nightmare," he said contemptuously.

"Seems you're not only *my* worst nightmare, but the worst nightmare of innocent young boys as well."

"You don't know what you're talking about. You never did."

"*I* never did?" I asked. "Have we met before?" I took my right hand off the back of my head and rested it on the arm of the couch. I forced my eyes to open wider, which only worsened the throbbing in my head.

"Let me put it this way," he said cavalierly. "I've been following your so-called illustrious career for quite some time."

"Interesting…except I couldn't give a shit. You're not the only one following my *illustrious* career, but maybe—if you tell me who you are—you'll also start making sense."

"You know me—but you don't know me," he said blandly.

I winced as a bolt of pain shot down my left leg—the side minus a kidney—the side the Jones Beach killer left his mark on—a zigzag scar from the hatchet job he did on me.

My grimace did not go unnoticed. "That war wound you caught a few years back acting up on you?" he asked snidely.

But despite the pain swirling around in my head and down my leg, I still pressed him, firmly believing that I was soon about to die. "I'll ask you once again: Who the fuck are you, and what is this place?"

He smiled slyly down at me while tilting the pistol back and forth in his hand. He was relishing the control he had over me. "I think you've got this place figured out quite well already," he said.

"This room…What is it, some kind of a waiting area or meeting place?"

"Very good."

"But for whom?" If I was going to die, I wanted to know the truth. And if it all possible, I wanted the world to know it, too. Meanwhile, the monster was enjoying himself. Standing over me, pistol in his hand, he was practically gloating. My biggest fear though, was that he was also looking to enjoy himself *after* he pulled the trigger, which meant that my death would not come quickly. If quick was his intention, he would have killed me already.

"For whom?" he asked back, with sardonic glee in his voice. "You really have no idea who comes here, do you?"

"Maybe I do and maybe I don't." I winced again. The pain in my leg had waned, but the pain in my head had not.

"For a pretty smart guy, you do know that you're only still alive because you got lucky."

Not sure what he meant, I continued to goad him. "You think too much of me. Lucky? I never thought I was lucky. You're the lucky one. Right now, I'm looking pretty unlucky, don't you think?" Thoughts of my son John and my daughter Charlotte filled my head along with an irrepressible sadness.

He stepped back and sat down in a red wing chair that was near the desk by the cave door. For the first time since getting hit, the pain in my head began to lessen as my stress level went from DEFCON I to DEFCON II. "Fuck you," he shouted. "There's no such thing as lucky. There's only ambition and the mind you're born with. You either use it to create your own destiny, or you don't."

"In your case, a criminal mind."

"Ha! *You* should know." He leaned forward in his chair. The barrel of the pistol that had been pointed at my head was now pointed at my chest. "Your uncle...now *there* was a degenerate murderer. And are you so different? That criminal mind...that may be something we both have in common."

"Oh, sure. We're so alike, you and me. Wanna order a pizza now?"

"Keep talking. You've got some sense of humor for a man who's about to die."

"We all have to go sometime."

"And your sometime is very soon."

"So then...considering all we have in common, tell me...who is this place or waiting room for, anyway? I don't think I'm going to be surprised by your answer." I was baiting him and silently praying to God he wouldn't catch on.

"Oh, really," he said brashly. Too full of himself at the moment, he took the bait. "You think you're something, palling around with the rich and politically connected with that center of yours for those loser veterans. I, however, have got real connections." He poked himself in the chest several times with his thumb. "Your money gained you those contacts. My power got me mine."

"What power? What are you talking about?" I had a good idea, but I wanted to hear it from him.

He then rose, extended his arm, and again pointed the pistol straight at my head. As he did, the tentacles of an intensifying throb that had begun at the back of my neck reached my eyes and stayed there—a mass of pulsating pain.

I pressed my palms against my temples in the hope that by doing so I might make the pounding subside as it had before.

He sat back down and accidentally knocked the chair against the desk, which jostled the computer and caused the monitor to light up. Boldly displayed on the computer screen was the search page for TOR—the access browser to the dark web—the perfect anonymous router for running a criminal enterprise like child sex trafficking.

I glanced over at the screen. "So, this is the way you contact and gather all the miscreants?"

"You really are pressing your luck," he said, with a calm, but no less scary seriousness.

"C'mon, you don't want to kill me...at least not yet," I said. "You're having too good a time."

"Ha." He chuckled, then looked toward the open door behind him that led to the cave tunnel he had dragged Paul into. In the silent break in our banter, I could hear the sound of wood crackling, along with another sound I couldn't get a fix on—like the slow stirring of a pot of stew. "I have stage four pancreatic cancer," he said, matter-of-factly. "So, you see, I don't have much longer, either—another thing we have in common."

"Happy to hear it. That explains the missing boy on the bicycle. Got sloppy there. He was not an orphan or foster child, or a boy from a broken home. This was a child of a living, breathing mother and stepfather—teachers. And if I check the tires on your car, wherever the hell it may be, will one of them have a bulge in it?"

"By the way—no need to keep looking for that boy."

"What the hell does that mean?"

"I don't know. You tell me. You've got everything figured out."

"Can I ask you a favor?" I bit my lip so hard in an effort to contain my rage, it started to bleed.

He didn't answer, but just looked at me amusedly.

I wasn't done. "Hey, you think you might drop dead before you pull that trigger?" The funny thing was, I believed that the more I joked and insulted him, the more he seemed to like it—the more an odd, pathetic loneliness appeared to rise to the surface. I glanced at the computer, having no doubt that it contained enough information to bring crashing down the lives of countless men in the highest levels of business and politics.

He chuckled again. "Would you believe that I had the Secretary of the Treasury down here, along with the CEOs and CFOs of several Fortune 500 corporations?"

"Sadly, I do believe it."

"You read and hear about sex scandals," he continued. "These people aren't rich and powerful because they are good, honest people. They are rich and powerful because they are unscrupulous and relentless."

"But how are you involved?" I thought to myself: *Was there a part of me that in some small way was becoming sympathetic to this wretch of a man?*

"I'm my father's son. It's in my DNA. I never had a choice. I was genetically predisposed, no—possessed—is more like it." He looked down at the pamphlets on the floor. "As for AMBLA, there are thousands of us who believe that our desire would not be as great as it is—if it wasn't real and natural and right for adult men and young boys to be together—just like it is real and natural and right for adults to be together."

"You are truly making me sick."

"Which is why we go underground."

"Is it real and natural to kill the boys, too?" I scowled in disgust as I spoke. "I swear...if there's a God in heaven—"

"Fuck you," he said, matter-of-factly.

"No, fuck you. Are you so warped as to actually attempt to find some common ground with me by talking about DNA, and comparing having sex with children to sex between two consenting adults? Let's be clear: And if these are my last words, so be it. We have no common ground. You're a degenerate. I'm not, and if you think you're powerful, think again. You and your ilk are the weakest among us. Real men suppress their darkest urges, especially when it causes harm to others—especially children."

Somehow my determination to make my case caused the pain in my head and eyes to subside. But make no mistake about it: I was keenly aware that I was soon going to die, which explained why I momentarily lost my voice. I took a breath, swallowed, and continued. "Like you said so calmly before, you are 'your father's son.' So, I suppose he was a piece of shit, too. But answer me this—if you can—because I'm having a hard time with it." I was breathing heavily, and my voice was cracking with every word spoken. "Who the fuck is your father, anyway? And who the fuck are you?"

"You're just buying time, because you *have* to know the answers to both those questions by now."

"Maybe I do and maybe I don't—but what I truly can't figure out, is who your mother is."

"That's the bigger mystery, isn't it?" he asked, as he sat there looking at me with a Cheshire grin. "After all, if you're not certain who my father was, and who I am, it might not be as much fun killing you."

"If you're your father's son, your father has to be Richard Holcomb. Just tell me who your mother is, and then you can blow my head off."

"But do you deserve to know who my mother is?" He seemed to be enjoying the cat-and-mouse conversation, which didn't surprise me in the least.

"If anyone deserves to know, it's me. Besides, you've got the gun. You win. I lose. Take your victory lap, but at least let me know who gave birth to the man about to kill me."

"None of this patronizing shit is going to work with me, but since you're going to die anyway, I'll reward you with the simple truth. My mother is my great aunt—my father's aunt. She used to own the shop upstairs."

"The old sewing shop lady?"

"She wasn't that old when I was born."

"Wow. No wonder. You poor bastard. After your Great Uncle Frank conveniently dies from food poisoning, your father shacks up with his aunt—your great aunt—and wonder upon wonders, a chip off the old block is born to continue the legacy of Richard Holcomb—kidnapper and murderer of little boys. And aren't you lucky—getting that double-dose of DNA evil? I almost feel sorry for you." As I spoke, his head dropped slightly and so did the barrel of the gun. Had I gotten to the son of a bitch?

Not a chance. "And your father is the same Richard Holcomb who was attacked at Mount Seneca Seminary, and who later murdered his college girlfriend."

"A charge that was never proven." He picked his head back up and looked straight at me.

"It never could be. He jumped bail, a sizable one at that—but not to the family who posted it."

"Since you appear to know everything…" He straightened his arm again, seeming quite intent on pulling the trigger.

"But I don't know everything," I said boldly. "I still don't understand how your father—who, by my count, was preying on young boys most of his adult life—could have also had a girlfriend in college, who he incidentally killed. Is he attracted to young boys? Is he attracted to women? Which is it?" Not that I could have cared less about the distinction. I was biding time, hoping there would be an earthquake, or a plane engine falling from the sky, or just about anything that could provide the earthly miracle that would save me. And whether this beast was amusing himself or simply enjoying the discussion, I couldn't be sure. But as long as he was continuing to engage me, I was going to keep him talking—and stay alive, even if only for only a few minutes longer.

"My father was abused by a priest. That phony profligate of the Catholic Church hurt him almost as badly as those students did. Where was the justice for him then? He tried to live a conventional life, dating women in college, but he couldn't."

"So, are you saying that what happened to your father provides some justification for him becoming a pedophile and mass murderer—and for you to follow in his footsteps?"

His face turned dead serious. "This conversation is over," he uttered with an indolent and frightening indifference as he straightened his arm, leaned forward, and pointed the barrel of the gun at an imaginary bullseye on my forehead.

I held my hand up. "One more thing—don't leave me hanging without a happy ending. Tell me: What ever happened to your father, Richard Holcomb?"

He dropped his arm again like a bratty child would who was asked a question he'd rather do anything else but answer. "He took his own life in

1996. He was sick of living and hiding, and he was about to die anyway of the same fucking cancer I got."

"And after he came back to Cartersville a wanted man, what about his next-door neighbor?" This one was for Charlie. I owed him that much.

"What are you talking about?" He appeared genuinely confused.

"I'm talking about Peggy Malone."

"Who the fuck is Peggy Malone?"

"In 1965, while on her way to her high school prom in a pretty pink dress, she was abducted and killed. She was only sixteen years old."

I watched as he thought for a moment, until a light appeared in his otherwise cold, demonic eyes. "Too bad for you. I'm tired of talking."

He stood up and again pointed the barrel straight at my head. "It's time now," he said. "No one will find your remains. No one will ever know the secrets of this place. It will all die with you, and then with me soon enough." He straightened his arm, the pistol firmly in his hand, my forehead a dead-on target.

"Wrong again," I said, as I pulled my cellphone from my pocket and held it high in the air, while his eyes widened in a furious rage and his face contorted into a wretched mass of confusion. "When I was on the floor, and you were dragging Paul away, I dialed a close friend of mine at CNN. She's been listening this whole time—and recording everything."

All I remember after that was watching his hand tighten around the pistol and his index finger press against the trigger the instant I shut my eyes to the gun blast.

# CHAPTER 68

B lood was streaming down the side of my face. *I'll be dead soon,* I thought to myself, if I wasn't dead already. When several shots in succession rang out, I could hear bullets ricocheting off the concrete walls and floor. The fate that I thought was sealed for eternity—in a bloody mess in an underground hellhole—was becoming more uncertain. All I knew for sure was that the pain in my head had reached a level so severe that I believed I was going into shock as I struggled to retain consciousness.

Then I heard my name—and I wasn't sure if it was God, or Saint Peter, or an alternate personality of my own speaking inside my head. I was that disoriented. But the more I listened, the more familiar the voice became.

It was Charlie's voice and getting louder. He was crawling toward me, and as he got closer, leveled a slap across my face so hard it awakened me to a world that I was certain I had left behind.

"No passing out!" Charlie shouted. "You stay awake!" He slapped me again.

"Enough," I said, straining to speak as I slowly opened my eyes to a room filled with the residual smoke of gunfire.

"You took a bad hit to the head," he said.

"Am I shot?"

"I don't think so. You're bleeding because he clobbered you with his pistol."

"I could swear I saw him pull the trigger," I said, as I struggled to talk and catch my breath at the same time.

"When you think you're about to die, your mind plays tricks on you. He wasn't letting you off that easy."

I grabbed Charlie by the jacket and pulled him close. "I thought you were dead."

"Nah. I rushed behind one of the hanging carpets when I heard him coming through the passageway door. Last he saw me; I was crossing the street in a wheelchair. He never expected to find me here."

"But how come he didn't see you?"

"I stood on my thighs. My camouflage cutoffs must have blended right into the wall and carpet."

I patted him on the cheek. "You survived. And I survived, thanks to you. But tell me…Paul?" My voice cracked. "Is he dead?"

"I don't know. Maybe," he said sadly.

"We've got to find him." I gestured toward the cave door.

"You're not going anywhere right now. Can you even walk?"

Charlie gripped me under my arms and propped me up against the couch.

"I just need a minute or two." I grabbed Charlie's jacket again, more for balance than anything else. I was sitting up, and the room was spinning in lockstep to my pounding head. I needed to get my wits about me—get my body oriented and my equilibrium back. I needed to see clearly. Charlie's face was coming into focus. "So, you really did have a gun?" I asked.

"Yes, pal. This time I had a gun."

"I didn't feel it when I was carrying you."

"It was behind my back, which is why it took me so long to get it out. I was in a tight space between the wall and the carpet, so I had to inch my arm around, careful not to make a sound or shake the carpet. I thought for sure I would be spotted, but you did help by keeping him busy with that question-and-answer session."

"I just hope Lauren got it all. I pressed her contact number on my phone when he was dragging Paul out. I lowered the volume so she'd be able to hear us while we couldn't hear her."

"That's great, but we're going to have to wait to find out." He handed me my phone off the floor. "Your battery needs charging. The red warning light is on." Charlie slipped the phone into my pants pocket.

Though the slightest movement of my head put me in excruciating pain, it didn't stop me from looking down at the monster sprawled out on the floor in front of us and bleeding profusely from several bullet wounds. His eyes were open and staring blankly—eyes without a trace of humanity. The dead eyes of a psychopath.

"Get me up," I said. "We've got to get to Paul." With Charlie acting as a crutch, I slowly rose to my feet, only to take a step, lose my balance, and fall forward. But for the arms of a nearby chair that I used to brace myself, I would have hit the floor, and hard. Fortunately for me, the room was filled with chairs.

"Let me call someone," Charlie said. "I still have two bars on my phone."

"No," I insisted. "Who are you going to call? The cops here are as corrupt as they come. We know that for sure now. You call them and they'll finish us off for good. We've got to find Paul. Then we'll contact Lauren and get the press here." I looked down at Charlie. "And what about you? Are *you* alright?" I put my hand on the back of his neck. "You're not hurt, are you?"

"Nah. That creep didn't know what hit him. My only problem was that I'm left-handed, but I was on the right side of the wall carpet, which meant I had to shoot around the carpet with my right." Charlie looked over at the body on the floor. "Not bad, considering. I think I hit him two or three times."

"Why didn't you just shoot through the carpet with your left?"

"I didn't want to risk hitting you."

"But I was a dead man anyway. You would have saved yourself."

"Save myself? There's no saving myself and leaving you and Paul behind. I'm a marine—or did you forget that?"

Gathering what little strength I had, I took one hand off the arm of the chair holding me up, placed it on Charlie's shoulder, and squeezed. "Can't ever be sorry I brought you along, now can I?" Despite the unrelenting bass drum pounding in my head, I smiled a weak but sincere 'thank you' at my loyal friend, then thought again. "But why do I think he got off a round?"

"Because he did. And I may have been wrong before. He might've caught you in the left ear. You're bleeding pretty bad there."

Charlie then ripped the sleeve off his shirt and handed it to me. "Wrap this around your head before you pass out."

I sat down in the chair that had been holding me up and did just that. Grunting in pain when I pulled the fabric tight, I noticed for the first time that my ears were ringing from the gun blasts.

Charlie grabbed my arm. "I hear something," He whispered. "Do you hear it?"

"I don't hear a thing," I said.

Charlie pointed toward the cave passageway Paul was dragged into.

# CHAPTER 69

By using the chairs in the room for balance, I made it past the monster on the floor to the foot of the open door. I then stepped up and into a passageway carved out of cave walls that were just like the basement of the sewing shop. It was barely large enough to walk through, and it came to an end about forty feet away.

Soot coated the tips of my fingers as I reached out to the walls for balance, while Charlie followed behind me—walking on his thighs and using his hands and arms for support. "I think my head is clearing a bit more," I said as I stopped to catch my breath under a cage light that dimly lit up the walls of black rock.

"You must have lost your sense of smell," Charlie said. "This putrid odor is friggin' nauseating."

"If I had, it's coming back." I winced and turned to check on him. "How are you doing?"

"I'm fine," he said sharply. "You're the bloody mess, not me. Any sign of Paul?"

As I looked down the short tunnel, Paul was nowhere to be seen. Refusing to believe that he was badly injured or dead, I called out his name.

I got no response.

"There appears to be a sinkhole at the end of this path," I said with an odd strain of hope in my voice—like the sound of false optimism that precedes a grim discovery.

"Just be careful," Charlie insisted. "I'm right behind you, and I reloaded."

The farther we moved into the passageway, the stronger the stench became and the warmer it got. When we could go no farther—a cave wall in front of us—I saw why.

Built into a side wall of black stone and rock was an old cast iron furnace, and although I didn't see a single lit ember inside it, it was still burning hot. Across from the furnace door and bordering the other side of the passageway was a short wall of black stone about two feet high and five feet long. Searching for Paul and the source of the awful smell—while praying the two were not related—I looked over the wall.

In the bleak light, I saw glimmers of surface water. As I strained to get a better look—sweat and blood dripping from my head—a smell so foul that it was nearly asphyxiating, floated up and into the air.

Charlie handed me his flashlight so I could get a better look.

On the surface of a well about twenty feet down, face up and motionless, was Paul.

# CHAPTER 70

A rope ladder bolted into the floor was crumpled at my feet. I quickly tossed it over the wall, then handed Charlie back his flashlight. "Shine it down," I said.

Charlie hesitated. "Are you sure you're up for this?"

Seeing Paul was like a shot of adrenaline and one monster shock to my senses. Alive or dead, I wasn't leaving him. "I'm fine," I said.

The rope rungs were thick, and the ladder was secure—but with each step down, my initial steadiness wavered, and the ladder shook in response. As I descended closer to the surface, I noticed that the lower rungs were submerged, but for better or worse, Paul wasn't. And despite the ladder shaking feverishly, I saw why.

He was floating.

I stepped down two more rungs after my feet touched water. Immersed up to my knees, I pulled Paul toward me. He was unconscious but breathing and moved rather easily across the surface. I called out his name and smacked his face like Charlie had smacked mine. "He's alive," I yelled. "We've got to get him out of here."

"Is he responding to you at all?" Charlie asked.

"No!" I shouted back.

"How then do you figure we do that?" The beam from Charlie's flashlight flickered off the surface water as his hand shook with every word spoken.

"I'm going to hook him on to the rungs, and we'll just have to pull him up somehow."

"I can do that," Charlie said proudly, and I immediately recalled his rock-solid arms.

"We'll do it together," I said.

With one hand on the rope ladder, I pulled Paul closer with the other. It was then that I realized that he wasn't floating at all. There was something holding him up. Concentrating hard on saving him, I secured one foot on a submerged rung and rested the other on what felt like a bag of sand. Since Paul was too heavy to lift, I had to drop further down into the water and whatever the source of the awful smell was, I would be chest high in it.

"Fuck it," I said, convinced that if I left Paul in this disgusting well a second longer, he would drown.

Whether it was my tugging at Paul in the water, or my body stirring the contents of the well every time I moved, whatever was holding him up was beginning to reveal itself—and to make matters worse, Charlie's flashlight was starting to dim.

Wasting no time and without too much difficulty, I managed to hook Paul's arms over the lowest ladder rung above the water line, and like a scarecrow on a clothesline, he hung on. As far as I could tell, he was unconscious and unaware of my efforts to save him, but he was breathing, nonetheless.

I yelled up to Charlie. "I can hardly see. Can you turn on your cellphone's light also?"

Charlie complied and before he could say, "Nick, don't look down," I did—unaware that the memory of what I would see would haunt me for the rest of my life.

Floating in the well water—were the bloated and decomposed bodies of dead little boys.

# CHAPTER 71

Charlie had seen the bodies before I did, but he kept it to himself. "Not to freak you out," he later told me.

It freaked me out anyway and I quickly climbed over Paul, up the ladder, and out of the well faster than I ever thought possible. Soaking wet and smelling like death, I fell to my knees and puked my guts out. I then crawled over to Charlie and tried single-handedly to pull Paul up, but quickly gave up. Adrenaline rush or not, I was just too tired and weak.

"I can do it," Charlie offered. "But you've got to anchor me."

"How the hell am I supposed to do that?"

"Just sit down behind me and brace your legs against the retaining wall. Then wrap your arms around me and hold on tight."

I didn't think Charlie's plan would work, but it was all we had. I just wasn't sure that I would be able to hold him. And I didn't believe he was strong enough to pull Paul out of that well by himself.

I was wrong on both counts.

One-by-one, he grabbed each rung of rope and pulled. Three rungs later, he turned to me, my head over his shoulder, my arms locked around him. "Just tell me how the hell we're going to get him out of here without calling someone?" he asked.

I was in no mood for questions and told him so. "My head is throbbing, and after what I saw today, the world will never look the same to me again. So just keep pulling up on that fucking ladder."

"Alright, already. Cool your jets. I got this." Another ten rungs and Paul's head rose to the top of the well. "Just don't let go of me," Charlie howled. "I'll grab him. You just hold on."

"Just hurry," I pleaded breathlessly. "My legs are about to give way."

In a matter of seconds, Paul's body was lying on the ground in front of us. Miraculously, he appeared to be regaining consciousness. His left eye was nearly swollen shut and the back of his head had two masses on it the size of golf balls.

I whispered in Charlie's ear. "We've got to get our guns and get the hell out of here."

"No shit! And exactly how do you suppose we do that all by ourselves?" he asked. "We're never going to get Paul down that tunnel and up that ladder...not to mention that basement's long flight of stairs."

"Just wait here. There's got to be another way out." I got up and returned to the so-called waiting room.

The monster was lying in the middle of three large puddles of blood. I picked Paul's gun up off the floor, held it firmly in my hand, and went into the adjoining room with the two twin beds and the Hitchcock posters on the walls. Before the lights went out and I got clobbered—not once, but twice, on the head—I remembered seeing a set of stairs.

In the far corner of the room and behind a large artificial plant, stood a walnut-stained staircase with a baluster rail that led to a hatch in the ceiling. I immediately went up the steps and pushed open the hatch to a brightly lit living room inside of what appeared to be a log cabin decorated like something out of a page from *Country Living* Magazine. An assortment of deer and moose heads was mounted on the walls. Stuffed chairs and a couch filled with pillows encircled a bearskin rug and a fireplace. Off to the side were a kitchen, a small dining room, and a bar stocked from floor to ceiling. I climbed out of the hatch. With Paul's gun in my hand, I walked over to the nearest window and peeked through the curtains. It was pitch black outside, while assorted stained-glass lamps lit up the rooms inside. And though it was apparent to me that no one was in residence, there was no sign of a hurried departure, either.

I checked the rear of the cabin and found a large nondescript bathroom, and a bedroom that was decorated in an 'early American' style. There was even a large steamer trunk at the foot of the bed, circa 1940s. Concerned about Paul, and getting us the hell out of there, I had seen enough. I stepped quickly down the hatch and across the underground room with the twin beds and posters on the walls. Once back in the so-called waiting room, I knelt down, and picked up my own gun. It was lying on the floor within a few feet of the killer's body. I snapped it back into the holster at my side. Fearing that in my condition I would not be able to crouch back down and up a second time, I turned, avoided the puddles of blood on the floor, and crawled over to the killer's dead body. After rummaging hastily through his clothes, I found cash, credit cards, a driver's license, and a car key—all of which I stuffed into my back pockets.

When I returned to the cave passageway, Paul was lying on the ground next to Charlie. Sounding more lucid than before, he asked for his gun, and no sooner did I take it out of my pocket than he grabbed it from my hand and snapped it back into its holster. He was still quite dazed and weak. From the looks of it, he had broken his ankle and maybe even his leg in the fall. I told him we had to get the hell out of there. When Charlie rolled his eyes at the prospect of moving Paul in the condition he was in, I told them both that there was a shorter way—an exit we could probably manage.

Paul was in a lot of pain and ignored me. "I was unconscious," he said. "Why didn't I drown in that well?"

He demanded Charlie's cellphone. Though he grimaced in pain, he wasn't satisfied until I turned him toward the well, where he was able to lean over the wall and shine the phone's light down at the water. After a few seconds, he called out to me and I turned him back around. Gripping him by his armpits, I lowered him slowly to the floor, his back resting against the cave wall.

Then he said something I would never forget.

"Such a cold-blooded monster, he didn't even realize that he had filled the well to capacity with their bodies. And these kids, whom we couldn't save…wound up saving me."

# CHAPTER 72

I asked Charlie, who had the only working cellphone (my battery was dead, and Paul's was waterlogged), to take pictures of absolutely everything—especially the surface of the well, even though I doubted there was enough light to do so.

As a testament to Paul's strength and perseverance—and to my utter amazement—when we got him to his feet, he put his arm over my shoulders and managed to hop alongside me as I walked. Charlie followed as before by walking on his thighs or swinging himself forward using his hands and arms, pausing only to take out his phone and click away.

After we made our way down into the waiting room where the killer lay dead, Charlie called out to me. "Forget something?" He reached under the couch and picked up another pistol. It was the killer's gun. It had gone flying when Charlie shot him. Considering it was prima facie evidence, I asked Paul if we should leave it.

"No fucking way," he answered. "No telling who will find it and make it disappear. Once we're out of here, I'm calling the FBI."

Charlie stuck the gun in his pocket, looked around the room, and took more photos with his phone. "Holy shit!" he shouted, while gesturing at the laptop sitting on the desk. "I guess I have to think of everything."

"Grab it," I said. "Even if it means you can't take any more photos."

"Who said I can't take any more photos?" Proving more useful by the minute, Charlie stuffed the laptop down his shirt, tucked the shirt in his pants, and kept moving.

"By the way, did you get that killer's ID?" Paul asked, while grimacing in pain as I helped him along.

"Yes, I did," I said, as I struggled to catch my breath.

"Well, who the fuck is he? What's his name?"

"I didn't look at the ID yet, but what I do know is that he's Richard Holcomb's son, following in his father's footsteps. That much I can tell you."

"You didn't look?" Paul asked incredulously.

"Sorry pal, but getting you the hell out of here alive was a higher priority. And don't worry. His ID is in my back pocket, along with his credit cards."

"Credit cards?" Paul grunted as he spoke. "I say we have a steak dinner on the prick." He didn't sound like he was kidding, either.

I was acting as a crutch for Paul and doing my best to keep us moving. We had already managed the three steps down just outside the cave passageway door, but there were still another three up, and then down again into the adjoining room. Finally, there were the ten steps that led up the staircase to the cabin, which would be especially difficult for Paul to climb. As we plodded along, I wondered if Paul's head was throbbing as much as mine. Though he seemed to be focused on the pain in his ankle, I was convinced that he was toughing it out since his entire leg was beginning to look like a tree trunk. Meanwhile, Charlie apologized for not being able to help and was moving along quite well but perspiring to such a degree I thought he was going to short-out the laptop under his shirt.

In a matter of minutes (which seemed like hours), and despite more than our fair share of internal bleeding, Paul and I made it up the steps and into the cabin.

After we plopped ourselves down on the couch by the fireplace, Charlie took a seat on the floor next to us. "Mia was right about a cabin," he said, while wiping sweat from his forehead with the sleeve of his shirt.

"She was right about a lot of things," I added.

"Except she was a little girl, and all the kids that were abused and killed up here were boys," Paul said, while continuing to breath hard.

"I may have that little inconsistency worked out," I answered.

"How's that?" Charlie asked.

"Can we get out of here first?" Since I didn't believe that the son of Richard Holcomb had acted alone, the longer we stayed in the cabin, the more worried I became.

Charlie left us on the couch, and while walking on his thighs, managed to pull himself onto a nearby window seat. With all the moving around and traveling up and down stairs that he had done, I had little doubt that he had his share of pain to deal with as well. But he never complained or gave me reason to be more concerned about him than I already was.

"I see an SUV parked outside," he cried out.

"It's probably the dead man's," Paul said, his voice growing hoarser with each utterance.

"If it is, I have the car key," I said. "It was with his ID and credit cards. Now let's get the hell out of here while we still can."

# CHAPTER 73

I managed to get Paul and Charlie into the SUV—Paul in the back and Charlie up front.

"Now I see why this place didn't show up on my drone," Paul muttered, while looking back at the cabin, his swollen leg stretched out across the rear seat.

"It's completely covered by trees," Charlie added, looking up.

"Right," Paul answered. "I wonder what would have shown up in winter?"

"I told you already," Charlie said. "Come November, it's cold as ass up here. What's now covered in trees would have been covered in snow, and lots of it."

"Cold as ass?" Seriously sleep deprived, I laughed as I spoke. Paul chuckled, but then howled in pain.

"Maybe you two clowns can shut up so we can get the fuck out of here," Charlie barked.

Paul and I weren't the only ones in the car who were dead tired.

"Relax, Charlie," I replied. "We're alive. An hour ago, I never thought I would ever be laughing again. Shit. I never thought I would ever be breathing again." I started the car then suddenly reached for the door handle and stepped out.

"Where are you going?" Charlie asked irritably.

"He's checking the tires," Paul answered.

Sure enough, the rear tire had a bubble in it, which coincided with the tread mark on the shoulder of the roadway where Billy's bicycle was found.

"Son of a bitch," I said to Paul as I got back behind the wheel. "Just as you thought."

After I turned the car around and started speeding down a dirt road covered by overhanging tree limbs, Paul didn't waste a second. He called Donald Riggins on Charlie's phone. Mustering up whatever energy he had left, he filled him in on the horrors of the evening, while emphasizing that the local police could not be trusted—especially Deputy Carter, whom Paul suggested Riggins run a full historical on. "I'm fine…I'm fine," Paul kept repeating. Concerned about Paul's injuries, Riggins made him promise to get to a hospital, and fast. He also told Paul that once they hung up, he would be calling the FBI Field Office in Syracuse. Considering the FBI is federal, Paul said: "Tell them it's an interstate child trafficking ring. And they'd better get forensics here, too—and bring facemasks. There's a well full of the decomposing bodies of dead children under the cabin, and we believe they're all boys. We've also got the ringleader's laptop with us." Then Paul sounded less certain. "It should provide us with a whole lot more information."

Paul then moaned in pain and added: "By the way—and for the record—we're driving the ringleader's car. It's our only way out of here." Then the cover of overhanging trees ended, and we found ourselves approaching the dead-end street behind the sewing shop. "Tell the FBI to cross over the railroad tracks when they get into town," Paul's voice became raspier and more restricted the more he spoke to Riggins. "When you get to the sewing shop on the corner, make a left. It's a dead end, but there's a road back there. You can't see it from the air and barely from the ground. Tell the FBI to follow it to a cabin. Once they get in, they'll see an open hatch in the living room floor."

It was some time after 5:30 a.m. The sunlight was beginning to rise over the treetops as I drove faster than I should have off the dirt road, past the shop, and into town.

I parked the killer's SUV behind my rental and threw its keys under the front seat. I was completely exhausted, but with the remaining adrenaline in my system keeping me awake, I managed to get Paul and Charlie back into the Altima—all the while afraid that a confederate of the killer or a corrupt deputy would pull up with a shotgun in his hands. Though considering the time of day and one lazy police force, I figured no one could possibly have known what transpired down in that tunnel just yet. But despite how anxious I was to get out of there, as soon as I started the car, Charlie had other plans for me.

He tapped me on the shoulder. "Nick...my chair?"

"Shit," I blurted. The last thing I wanted to do was go anywhere near the shop again. Just the thought of going back inside made my skin crawl. But I had no choice in the matter. Charlie needed his chair. So I got out, crossed the street, and walked over to the shop's front door. Using one of the monster's credit cards, I slid the lock aside in the door jam, and I was in.

Garth must have closed up because the wheelchair was bedside the rear counter, exactly where we had left it. Completely exhausted, I grabbed it more quickly than I meant to and accidentally tipped over a mannequin nearby. Fearing I was being attacked from behind, I nearly jumped out of my skin as it knocked into me before it fell to the floor. Spooked as a result, I didn't even bother to pick it up, but just rushed out the door, and left it there.

Returning to the Altima, I threw the chair in the trunk, jumped behind the wheel, and gunned the accelerator.

# CHAPTER 74

While heading back to The Red Mill Inn, I used Charlie's cellphone to call Lauren. Since she didn't know Charlie's number, I had to call three times before she picked up. When I heard her voice, I didn't waste a second. "Did you get it? Did you get it all?"

"Get what?" she asked.

"The details, the killer's confession while he had a gun on me."

"Nick, you called me at two-thirty in the morning. It was a terrible connection. I stayed on the line, figuring it must have been important, but you were fading in and out. I repeated *"I can't hear you,"* but you didn't answer."

"I had turned the volume down on the phone so he wouldn't know you were on the line."

"I'm sorry, Nick. But are you okay? What happened? Who had a gun on you?"

"The killer. I'm okay, I guess...banged up, but okay. I didn't think I was going to make it." I then told Lauren everything and gave her the same directions to the cabin that Paul gave Riggins.

"Just take care of yourself. And have Charlie send all the photos to this number," she answered. "I'll get a crew together and catch the next plane out."

"Better hurry. Once the wrong people get wind of what happened, no telling what they're willing to do to cover it up."

When we got back to The Red Mill Inn, I didn't go anywhere near the main entrance; I looped around back and parked behind a dumpster. I was about to cue Paul in on my plans to make a quick and surreptitious entry and exit, but he was visibly in a lot pain and barely conscious. Since I not only had to pack his bag, but empty the safe in his room, he did manage to give me the combination. "It my wife's birthday," he said sadly. This was the very first time I heard Paul even remotely sentimental, which only worried me more.

After we snuck into a service elevator and got to our floor, I told Charlie he had five minutes to pack. I then went to Paul's room and opened the safe in his bedroom closet. A box of ammo and another pistol were inside it; but it wasn't until I reached all the way in, that I made the best discovery of all—two cellphone chargers, one for the wall and one for the car.

I threw the gun and ammo into Paul's suitcase then stuffed the chargers into my pocket. Keenly aware that Charlie's phone was the only working one we had, I expected—like the three of us—it would soon lose all power and ability to function.

After I checked the room one more time, I grabbed Paul's suitcase, packed haphazardly, and hurried to my hotel room where I found Charlie waiting outside. He had changed his clothes and was sitting calmly in his chair. A duffel bag was across his lap. I slid my key into the door, and he followed me inside. Though he appeared to have freshened up a bit, his eyes were still red and watery from lack of sleep. Once inside, the first thing I did was pull my own phone charger out of the wall and give it to him. "Charge your cell while you're waiting. I'll use Paul's to charge mine," I said anxiously, but then thought again. "Where's the killer's gun and where's your gun—the one you had in the tunnel?"

"Mine is in my pocket. The killer's is in my duffel bag."

"Give them to me."

"But mine is illegal."

"Doesn't matter. It saved our lives. I'll put it in my bag as evidence, along with the killer's."

After Charlie handed the guns to me, I tossed them into my suitcase, then hurried into the bathroom, undressed, and stepped into the shower. My big mistake—I didn't cover my head, and it started to bleed again. When Charlie saw me enter the bedroom with a dry washcloth pressed against my ear, he immediately pulled a First Aid kit and camouflage hat out of his duffel bag. He handed both to me and said: "Bandage yourself, put the cap on your head, and let's get the hell out of here while we still can."

After I threw on some fresh clothes, I grabbed a stack of cash I had placed in the safe, took half, and stuffed the rest inside the sleeve of my suitcase.

After I finished packing my bag, I casually said to Charlie: "You know, for a veteran with PTSD, you've handled yourself quite well today."

He looked up at me and smirked. "That's because I don't have PTSD."

"What the hell are you talking about? It's on your medical chart, along with your anger issues. It's no secret that you've been known to be quite difficult at times."

"You try going through life with no legs. See if you don't act out once in a while."

"C'mon Charlie, you've been evaluated by experts. You may not think that you have PTSD, but you do."

"You think if I had post-traumatic stress disorder, I would have made it through the last twenty-four hours? Nick, there's a simple explanation. Sure, I've got anger issues, so when the shrink suggested I have PTSD, I just went along. To bolster her case, I even added that I zone out sometimes when I hear loud noises."

"Well, we know that's not true."

"Of course, it's not true."

"Then why *did* you go along with it—why did you let them diagnose you that way? Why not just object?"

"I not only didn't object, I pretty much confirmed it."

"Now you're confusing the hell out of me. We're in a hurry, and I'm stressed out enough already."

"Have you met the shrink that I get to spend forty-five-minute sessions with—two times a week, every week?" he asked.

"No," I said, impatiently.

"She's given me all the reason I need to get up in the morning. I think I'm in love with her."

"Dear God, Charlie. You have got to be kidding!"

"You brought up the PTSD, not me." He looked worried. "You're not going to drop a dime on me with the shrink, are you?"

"Not exactly tops on my list of things to do right now."

# CHAPTER 75

Once I started driving, I realized that it was impossible for me to get us to Syracuse safely. I was tired to the bone, stressed to the max, and could not stay awake behind the wheel for more than a few minutes at a time.

I pulled over onto a quiet street in a residential neighborhood somewhere south of Cartersville and called the closest limo service I could find on Google. I told them I would pay double and in cash to get a driver to take us to the best hospital in Syracuse.

I described the Altima we were in, and when the driver arrived—a small, heavyset man in his seventies—he knocked on the car window to wake us. Kind and considerate, he tried his best to move Paul and Charlie into the limo with what little help I was able to provide in my weakened state. He asked no questions—even when he saw Paul wearing a holster and pistol—which until that moment I had forgotten to remove and pack. That's what "double and in cash" buys you. No surprise there.

It was a stretch limo, so Charlie's wheelchair fit easily into the rear seating area. Evidently, the driver had his instructions: He drove us to the emergency room at Saint Joseph's Hospital.

A crew from the Syracuse affiliate of CNN got to the cabin first, but they were under strict orders from their programing head not to go in. It was a crime scene. But that didn't stop them from airing a **BREAKING NEWS** story, along with Charlie's photos preceded by a warning that the pictures would be disturbing.

Ten minutes later, the FBI arrived at the same time as the Cartersville Police. Interim Sheriff Rifts was there, along with Deputy Carter, who complained the loudest about the FBI involvement in what he termed "a local matter." Off-duty at the time, he became so belligerent that the chief FBI field officer threatened him with arrest if he didn't "stand down."

Rifts was visibly embarrassed by Carter's behavior. He had, on prior occasions, noticed Carter's mood swings and questioned whether he suffered from bipolar disorder. But each time he confronted him about it, Carter just apologized, disclosed that he was on antidepressants, and insisted that he was getting better. Rifts apparently didn't buy any of it and had documented his concerns.

While on the scene, the FBI was more interested in speaking to the three of us than the local police, who appeared clueless to the goings-on in and under the cabin—all of which became a cordoned-off crime scene where experts in all aspect of forensics—serology, toxicology, blood splatter, and firearms—as well as on-site photographers, documented and gathered whatever evidence they could find. That the late Richard Holcomb and his son were guilty of heinous crimes was without question. That they weren't acting alone was also clear from the waiting room full of chairs. That they had the protection of certain members of the local police was no longer in doubt. That Richard Holcomb chose to lay roots in the small town of Cartersville back in the mid-1950s could only be explained by family ties to the area—and the police protection he was able to buy. Before and after his son was born, Cartersville provided him with a convenient, accessible, and clandestine small-town location to act out his perverse desires, and encourage others like himself to join in. In a terrifying way, Cartersville—as a home base for his criminal mind—made perfect sense.

I suppose father and son figured that someday, before or after their deaths, their criminal enterprise and club for miscreants would be discovered. Regrettably, the precautions they took proved largely effective in averting any and all investigations. One such precaution was located in a hutch next to the front door of the cabin, where stacks of surgical gloves lined the drawers which every guest was required to wear to ensure fingerprints were not left anywhere in the cabin or the rooms underground. As a result, the only prints the FBI found were those of Paul, Charlie, the killer, and me. As far as witnesses to the crimes, the only one they found and identified was the killer himself; and since he was no longer breathing, he was no longer talking. Then there were the victims. From the body count in the well and the bone fragments later found in the furnace, the killer made certain that no child lived to talk about their ordeal. As far as adult participants were concerned, I was convinced that he kept a list somewhere. Such a list, however, was never found. As for the TOR app and the dark web from which all communications and searches emanated, it was impenetrable—one big dead end.

But there was yet one more source of information that was almost entirely untapped and locked away in its own secure and guarded vault.

And that was Mia's subconscious memory.

# CHAPTER 76

While CNN waited outside and broadcast footage of FBI agents going in and out of the cabin, Paul and I were in the emergency room of Saint Joseph's Hospital in Syracuse, where I was getting stitches to my head and Paul was being examined by a team of doctors for his head, leg, and ankle injuries.

When the doctors heard that we were headed to New York City, they suggested that we get Paul to the Hospital for Special Surgery, since his bone breaks from the knee down were excessive and severe. After they gave him a heavy dose of morphine, they wanted him to have an MRI and EEG of his head to determine if there was any blood buildup in his brain that required immediate attention. Since I wanted to get him to back to Manhattan, and fast, I asked the chief surgeon if the tests were just precautionary or if he really thought the lumps on Paul's head would require emergency surgery. In response, the doctor said that he was more concerned about Paul's leg and my lumps, which was all I needed to hear to make a final decision for both of us.

Paul and I immediately checked ourselves out of the hospital.

Since I had paid the limo driver an additional five hundred dollars to wait outside until he heard from me, I had him take us right to the airport, where I had arranged to have a chartered plane fly us to LaGuardia.

Though Charlie nearly jumped out of his wheelchair when he heard the cost, Paul needed specialized emergency medical care and the boarding protocol, or lack thereof—no baggage check and no inspection for guns and ammo by airport security, which would have seriously delayed our departure—made a flight in a private plane mandatory. Besides, despite the morphine, Paul was still in severe pain. Not the best patient myself, I still wasn't sure he grasped the seriousness of his injuries. I had to ask him several times before he finally agreed to let me call his wife.

The knowledge that all three of us had left the scene of a crime—though the crime was not ours—was not lost on me. Using the phone on the plane, I called Donald Riggins. After I brought him up to speed, he immediately put me on hold and called the FBI's field supervisor in Downtown Manhattan. When he got back on the line, he told me that two agents would be meeting us at the airport.

"And, Nick," Riggins added. "I've got more information on that former girlfriend of yours. I know you've been through a lot, but you need to hear this."

"Now? I need to hear this now?"

"Yes, now."

"You know, you're like a bad Santa with bad tidings. But why should this call be any different from your others? I suppose after what I just went through, I should be able to handle anything."

As was often the case, Riggins ignored my comments. "You said that she sometimes stayed over at your house. Am I right?"

"Yes."

"How many times?"

"At least a dozen."

"You ever go out to the store, for example, or to pick up a pizza, and leave her alone there?"

"Yes. I'm sure I have. She was a waitress. Sometimes, after her shift, I would pick her up and take her back to my house. She would be tired, so I would go out by myself to do a little shopping for us—to get some food—while she would remain at the house. Come to think of it, she would often ask me for something to eat or a snack that I didn't have. So, I would go out and get it for her."

"You had life insurance, didn't you?"

"For estate tax purpose, yes. Both Eleanor and I had policies."

"Those policies were not under lock and key, were they?"

"Come to think of it, no. They were in a desk drawer in the kitchen. I had taken them out of a combination fireproof safe we kept in the master bedroom closet. It took me months before I cashed in Eleanor's, and I would have completely forgotten about it if not for my daughter, Charlotte, reminding me to take care of it. That's why the policies were in the kitchen desk—so I would take care of it."

"Well, guess what? Either your former girlfriend—or her hooded partner—got hold of your policy, and I'm referring to the one for two million dollars—"

"How did you—?"

"It's still in your desk drawer. I was in your house, remember?"

"I may have gotten hit in the head more than once, but my brains are still intact. Yes, I remember, Don."

"Well, guess what? Someone went on the insurance company's website and changed the beneficiary from your two kids to the not so lovely Olga Sokolov, alias Maureen."

"And how the hell do you know this?"

"I checked naic.org—the site for the National Association of Insurance. I also checked with Tennessee's State Insurance Department. Their site has a free policy locator. I then made a phone call, pretending to be you, and confirmed it."

"What made her think she could get away with this?"

"If questioned, all she needs to prove is that you cared deeply for her—which you did—and that she was dependent on you for financial support, which, after her hit in the head was kind of true. By the way, she quit her waitressing job and told her landlord and her boss that she was moving out of her apartment to go live with you—her boyfriend—and that you would be taking care of her now. She used those very words. She was covering her tracks but good, alright. How she planned to collect is what concerns me."

"I suppose it should concern me, too."

"Listen…I know you've been through hell and back, but you still need to continue to be very careful. Meanwhile, I'll do more digging, because there's something else I need to figure out. Just give me twenty-four hours."

"Really, that long?" I asked sarcastically. "I'll try to contain my goose-bumps waiting for your call. And what is it that you need to find out?" He didn't answer. "Don, are you there?"

Once again, Riggins ignored me and without another word, hung up.

After we landed in New York City, our luggage and Charlie's chair were put in the trunk of an unmarked car, courtesy of the two FBI agents sent to pick us up—via Riggins' legacy of influence with the bureau. In turn, Paul was placed on a stretcher and taken away in a waiting ambulance. The unmarked car that Charlie and I were in followed, as the ambulance made its way through the busy streets of Queens and Manhattan, headed for the emergency room of the New York Presbyterian Medical Center—home for the Hospital for Special Surgery.

The two agents sat up front, while Charlie and I sat in the back. Even though there was no place else to put us, we couldn't help but feel a bit like suspects in a crime. Since Charlie was, after all, the shooter, and this was his first foray into civilian violence where the rules of engagement were quite different from those of jungle warfare, he had become quite nervous during the drive. Sitting sequestered in the back and fielding a barrage of questions from the agents didn't help. Overtired, and still rattled from the early morning melee, I assured our two stalwart FBI escorts that we would be more than happy to answer all of their questions after both a good night's sleep and when my head, in particular, got the proper medical attention. "I don't know if you're aware, gentlemen," I added, in a further effort to end the questioning and calm my loyal friend. "But if Charlie here hadn't shot the mass murderer and mastermind of the child trafficking ring we uncovered, Paul Tarantino and I would be dead—not to mention many more young boys." I left out the part about the killer's pancreatic cancer seeking its own form of final justice. Since it's been my experience that the evil miscreants of this world seem to find a way to claw onto life longer than most, Charlie deserved all the recognition and reward I could give him. And I wasn't done by a long shot.

"You're a hero, Charlie," I bellowed. "Once a marine…always a marine."

# PART 5

# THE EMERGENCY ROOM

*Money, money, money...*
*To someone who will never find true love,*
*It's everything.*
*And it's nothing.*
                              *Marion*

# CHAPTER 77

When we arrived at New York Presbyterian Medical Center, Paul was quickly taken to the Hospital for Special Surgery for an MRI, while Charlie and I remained in emergency room triage. Since my injuries weren't as severe as Paul's, my MRI was done on the premises. and once it was determined that I had no internal bleeding, an intern put a few additional stitches in my head. Charlie was examined also, and though found to be in generally good health, he was severely dehydrated, so the nurses hooked him up to an IV and pumped him with fluids while he slept.

With Charlie in dreamland, I remained lying in my emergency room bed, stitched up, exhausted—but for a mind and body tingling with nervous energy. I was overtired but couldn't fall asleep. There was also something I was forgetting, and I knew it—the cards I took out of the killer's pocket. I immediately checked the pants I was wearing until I remembered that I had changed them at the hotel. I leaned over slightly and spotted my suitcase on the floor next to my bed. Between the stitches, the painkillers I had been given, and my general state of debilitation, I feared that if I rolled over and reached down for it, there was a good chance I would wind up flat on my face. Since my head had already been split open once, maybe twice, I decided to call a nurse.

When I told her I merely wanted to get a pair of pants out of my bag, she huffed and hurried off—not exactly the call for emergency she was there for. A few seconds later, a sweet elderly man peeked through the opening in my curtain. His wife of fifty-five years was in the bed across from mine. He had heard my plea, called me 'young man,' and said he would be only too happy to help. I asked him to open my messy suitcase and retrieve the pair of black pants I had been wearing.

"I suppose packing is not your strong suit," he said cheerfully as he looked inside.

Fortunately, the pants were on top of the heap of clothes. If the kind old man had explored further, he would have come across three pistols, a few thousand dollars in cash and there's no telling what would have happened after that.

As he handed me the pants, I thanked him and wished his wife well. He smiled weakly, then graciously nodded. I had a strong suspicion that she was not going to make it back home this time. It was in his expression of resolute sadness.

After he left and the billowing curtains around my bed came to a close, I inspected the pants. They were still moist from my foray into the well to get Paul. Fortunately, they didn't smell as bad as I recalled—or at least not bad enough for the old man to comment upon. *God forgive me,* I said to myself for complaining about the odor, when the source of the smell conjured up the frightening and grotesque images of the remains of the little bodies we left behind.

While Charlie snored loudly nearby, I retrieved the cards out of the back pocket. A driver's license was on top and face up. On it was a photo of the killer that must have been taken twenty years earlier. The name on the license was Richard Norris—a combination of his father's first name and his mother's (his father's aunt's) last—giving the false impression that he was his great aunt and uncle's son. No one the wiser that his real father, Richard Holcomb, was alive, and well enough to sire a son with his father's sister.

Under the license was a police officer's courtesy card—the kind that gets you a pass when pulled over for a traffic violation. To an officer in New York City, it's called a PBA card, which stands for Police Benevolent Association. What I was looking at, however, was an honorary membership in the Sheriff's Association of Oswego County. *Serving our members for 65 years.* Penned on the flip side: *To Richard Norris from Deputy Phineas Carter.* Carter's cell number was added for verification.

Had I not felt emotionally and physically debilitated at the time, I probably would have let out a cheer. In my hand was a key element of proof connecting the monster, Richard Norris, to the arrogant, asshole Deputy Carter.

# CHAPTER 78

D espite aching in pain from head to toe, I refused morphine. Double doses of Tylenol were all I would take. I wanted to remain clear-headed. Between nearly losing my life at the hands of a degenerate killer, my concern for Paul, and wondering what more would come from the FBI's investigation of the cabin and its underground sanctum, it was a small wonder I could close my eyes to rest even for a minute. Though I had relegated the care and control over my body to a hospital staff with the best of intentions—which never seemed to include letting a patient sleep for any prolonged period of time—I tried anyway. And despite my protestations that I wanted to rest but remain alert, the nurses gave me a sedative anyway.

Lying in the noisy emergency room, machines beeping and buzzing, and Charlie snoring as loud as a train engine in the bed next to me, thoughts about the woman I had called Maureen saddened me deeply. Since the in-vestigation into missing young boys had come to a violent and tragic end, she kept drifting in and out of my mind—thin wisps of memory and feeling coating the empty hollow in my gut over losing someone I thought would continue to be very special to me—a last shot at romance—a last hope for true happiness. With Maureen, the barren sense of loneliness I had felt since Eleanor's passing had left me for a time. I wished Maureen was real.

I wished that at that very moment she was rushing to be by my side, to hold my hand, kiss me, and tell me that she loved me. And in my state of physical and emotional melancholy, all I wanted to do was close my eyes and imagine a Maureen that never was or ever would be—a Maureen I thought I knew but didn't—like a figment of a broken dream.

When I opened my eyes, the wicked realization of where I had been in the last twenty-four hours and what I had seen—what I had learned about pure evil, its depths, its partners, its obdurate path, and its victims—I felt deeply ashamed that all I could think about was a lost love and how sad I felt about it.

When my cellphone played *Moon River* once again—and once again it was Donald Riggins calling—I knew I would soon get what I deserved for my foolish and selfish imaginings. The black hole of awareness would see to that.

"My wife can be a pain in the ass," he began, without so much as a 'hello.'

"You sure you're not the one who's the pain in the ass, Don?" I snapped back.

"Oh, no question about it," he claimed rather modestly. "How are you doing by the way?"

"Hanging in there. Thanks for asking. Nice to know you really care."

"Hey, I wanna get paid when this is over," he said, while chuckling to himself. "And how's Paul?"

"He's got a road back, but he's tough as nails. I'm still worried about him, though. He's at the Hospital for Special Surgery. They're checking to see if he has internal bleeding. I'll let you know if I hear anything."

"Please do. Paul and I go way back. And your friend, Charlie, the vet?"

"Sleeping like a baby in the bed next to me."

"Good…that's good," he said tentatively, and I could hear in his voice that another shoe was about to drop squarely on my already swollen head. After I waited for a few seconds in silence, I could wait no more. "Don, what is it? I know you didn't call just to see how I'm doing."

"I started by telling you about my pain-in-the-ass wife, didn't I?"

"I can confirm that, bumps on my head and all."

"But I didn't tell you why she's a pain in the ass."

"Okay, Don. So, tell me. Why is your wife, whom I'm sure is a lovely woman that you don't deserve, a pain in the ass?"

"Because…" A woman's voice could be heard faintly in the background. "Though I love her dearly…"

"Are you home now, Don? Is that it?"

"Actually, I am. Back home in Bayside, Queens."

"Okay. I get it. Please go on."

"My wife is a lovely pain in the ass because she needs to know where I am every minute of every day."

"Well, Mr. Retired FBI, who isn't really retired, that's probably because she cares about you and is worried about you. I don't have to tell you what a lucky man you are."

"That's nice of you to say. She'll appreciate that. But back to my point. Do you know *how* she knows where I am without calling me constantly and asking me, which would drive me absolutely crazy and once did?"

"Other than having you followed, you got me."

"It's because of this particular setting app on our iPhones."

"Oh yeah, I did that with Maureen."

"Really, on which phone? The one Detective McCormick took, or a different one?"

"The new phone—a different one." It took a second or two for this information bomb to sink in. "Holy shit!"

"That's right. The only way for her to collect on your life insurance is—"

"For me to die. I get it. And to think how yesterday she almost had her wish."

"Get out your phone," Riggins blurted. "If she can tell where you are, you can probably tell where she is, or at least where her phone is."

"Did you really ask me to get out my phone?"

"Sorry, a senior moment. Now just go to the *Find My Friends* app."

I remembered when Maureen walked me through it. "I got it," I said.

"Good. Now, we both know where you are right now, and with that phone in your hand so does Maureen. So tell me, where is Maureen's phone—sorry, I mean Olga's? Like I said, if she can see where you are, you can see where she is."

"Okay. I get it, but I have to squint. I don't have my reading glasses."

"Well then, squint already."

"I'm trying." I held the phone closer for a clearer read. "Okay…

Maureen…or whoever…I'm calling her Maureen…is at 525 East 68th Street according to this app. Damn. What do you know? She's right here in New York City."

"Wait a second." I could hear Riggings fiddling with his phone. "For God's sake, Nick! That's the address for New York Presbyterian!"

# CHAPTER 79

After Riggins rushed to hang up, given the news about the location of Maureen's cellphone, I should have been wide-awake to the potential danger that awaited me. But I wasn't. Whether it was because I wasn't convinced of the accuracy of the *Find My Friends* app—perhaps I had incorrectly read the location of *my* cellphone and not hers—I can't be sure. But there was another reason why I didn't jump out of bed and hide the instant I became aware that Maureen, and maybe her partner in crime, might be soon paying me an unwelcome visit...

Having fought off the devil, with head injuries to show for it and little-to-no-rest thereafter, the sedative the nurse had given me was beginning to sink me into a stupor. My thoughts seemed to slow, while I simultaneously struggled to keep my eyes open. In short, I was physically incapable of getting out of bed—and more likely than not to wind up pancake-flat on the hard tile floor if I tried.

With my senses far from reliable and my vision a blur, when a doctor walked in, I wasn't sure at first if he was real or imagined. When without so much as a 'hello' or an introduction, he quickly stuck a needle into my upper arm, I physically reacted. Whether it was instinct or reflex—the product of my recent fight for survival—I can't be sure. But what I am certain of is that I shoved him away with such force that even in my weakened condition he was brushed back, and the needle that had been in my arm fell to the floor before it could be injected.

With eyes half-open, and more of my senses returning, I turned to the man.

In blue scrubs and about six feet tall with salt and pepper hair, looking more like a soap opera star playing a doctor than a real one, he regained his footing and smiled. "Whoa," he said blithely. "Sorry, Mr. Mannino. I didn't want to wake you." He picked the needle up off the floor.

I was in no mood to apologize to someone who needle-pricked me while I was dozing off into a desperately needed but perhaps poorly timed sleep. So I didn't. With a scowl on my face, I watched as he looked down and examined the needle, not for its cleanliness, but merely for its contents. I knew this because he didn't so much as wipe it clean; nor did he have anything in his other hand to do it with. I looked at my arm. There was a tiny bubble of blood where the needle had entered and exited. I also didn't recall feeling or smelling any alcohol-based wipe.

I looked around for a nurse, but the curtain around my bed was completely closed, and—along with it—my view of the corridor. I turned to my right. Charlie was still sleeping. I searched for the call button that had been by my side. It was gone. I felt my adrenaline pumping. More of my surroundings were coming into greater focus and clarity. Why wasn't a nurse or a physician's assistant accompanying the doctor? Why was I getting a shot to begin with? I already had two IV drips running into my veins—antibiotics and vitamins—plus a sedative. And why was a doctor himself giving it to me? And why was he holding the needle like he was ready to blow my brains out with it? As a multitude of questions ran through my mind, oddly enough, none had to do with Maureen or her current location.

"This will help you sleep," he said.

"But I got a sedative already, and don't need any help sleeping," I said firmly.

"It will also help you with the pain in your head." He raised his eyes and seemed to be examining my scalp. "We should change those bandages. I'll have a nurse do it when I leave." Again, he remained poised and controlled—like a doctor should, and like a patient would expect.

I looked down at the needle. My head was starting to ache again. The din in the emergency room was getting worse. My ears were ringing. They had never done that before. Charlie's snoring in the bed next to me was getting louder. Perception was overtaking reality. I could hear a man crying. It was the old man who handed me my pants. The chatter of hospital personnel and patient complaints was deafening. The doctor stepped closer. Everything was moving in slow motion. He leaned against the side of the bed, his scrubs brushing against my arm, a stethoscope dangling from his neck. I looked for his nametag. He wasn't wearing one. He smiled at me again. Then the smile disappeared, and his face took on the coarse pale look of a department store mannequin.

Lack of sleep, head injuries, plus a sedative, and I was feeling faint.

The needle penetrated my arm.

Like a ghost or an angel, the curtain parted on the opposite side of my bed and Maureen appeared. I reached out to her. *I missed you.* She had a pistol in her hand. It was pointed in my direction. She looked sad, angry too—yet resolute. I was happy and afraid to see her at the same time.

She raised her arm and fired.

My face was covered in blood. More shots rang out. The area around me was consumed with smoke. The needle was still in my arm. The doctor, who wasn't a doctor at all, was lying on the floor beside my bed, a bullet in his head. Maureen had shot him dead before he could pump me with a deadly overdose of the morphine that was still in the syringe.

I wiped the blood from my eyes. Maureen was gone. The same two FBI agents who had driven us to the hospital burst through the curtains, guns drawn, asking if I was alright. A nurse followed—the same one who huffed away earlier. She looked down at the man in scrubs on the floor and screamed. She then looked at me and carefully pulled the needle from my arm.

"What the fuck?" Charlie growled as he raised his head and turned toward me. "What the hell happened? Damn, Nick. Are you okay?"

"I wasn't hit," I answered, as the nurse wiped the blood from my face while muttering something about God and heaven. "Some phony doctor was about to give me a syringe cocktail. Maureen shot him and saved my life."

While the one nurse continued to clean me up, two other nurses and an emergency room doctor approached with hospital security. One of the FBI agents flashed his ID with one hand while making a call with the other. "We got this," he shouted to all who would listen, then glanced at his partner who was crouched down next to him.

Charlie gestured half-heartedly to the area in front of my bed and out of my line of sight.

I leaned over, despite the nurse cleaning me up, and demanding that I sit still.

Lying in a pool of blood, her beautiful blue eyes open and lifeless, was Olga Sokolov, alias my Maureen. The dead man in scrubs was a Russian national—and her husband.

# CHAPTER 80

As soon as I had hung up with Donald Riggins, he called the FBI field supervisor and insisted that the two agents who had dropped us off at the hospital be ordered to turn around, and fast. Once they arrived outside the emergency room doors, they bolted out of their car, and rushed in. Swatting curtain after curtain aside, they searched for me, until they turned down the corridor where my bed was located.

There, they spotted Maureen, gun in hand, pointed straight at me.

She never saw them coming.

After she put a bullet in her husband's head to save me, the FBI put three in her. From their vantage point, they thought I was the one they would find shot and killed. They were wrong about that—and wrong about Maureen. That controlling louse of a husband whom she had described to me when detailing her phony background—the one who cheated on her, treated her like an intangible possession, used and abused her—was real; only he was Russian, not American. The note that she left with the doorman to my building in Manhattan was also real. I would like to think that she had left it because in some small way—that I can't possibly measure or calculate the sincerity of—she cared about me, and wanted out of the life of crime she was leading under the iron fist of one obsessive and controlling husband.

In the end, she risked her life and lost it to save mine. As far as I was concerned, when she pulled that trigger, she attained her absolution. Whether it was also her salvation is up to a much higher power.

Did I ever really know her? Of course not. She made her choices long ago and, in the end, they worked out tragically for her—bad choices tend to do that. But when I look back and think about her, and what I thought we had, I always seem to find a proper way in which to remember it.

# CHAPTER 81

Both Charlotte and John rushed to see me shortly after I ducked yet another attempt on my life. Fortunately, by the time they showed up, I was an admitted patient and had been moved out of the emergency room crime scene.

Charlotte insisted on staying the night. Armed federal agents outside my room or not, I wouldn't hear of it. The following morning, she popped in on her way to work and John called right after she left to check on me as well.

Then—who would have guessed it—but lo and behold, later that morning, Donald Riggins showed up.

Since Charlie had been discharged—and I was already missing the quirky old bastard—I was looking forward to the company of yet another.

As it turned out, all Charlie needed was a good night's rest, some food in his belly, and he was fine. The hospital arranged for his transportation back to the Veterans' Center.

When Riggins walked in, a broad smile was draped across his face. In his mid-seventies, he had a short white beard and a twinkle in his eye that reminded me of a Macy's department store Santa—a good Santa, not a bad one. We shook hands warmly.

"Guess I screwed up by calling the FBI in here yesterday," he began.

"Don't be ridiculous. Nice to know you cared enough to call back up. I was beginning to think you were only in this for only the sheer adventure."

"Let's not get carried away," he said with a slight smile. "After all, you are my employer, and I do like getting paid. It's kind of hard to collect from a dead man, you know."

I chuckled. "Nothing you say should ever surprise me, Don, but for the life of me, it continues to." I then noticed the red and white bag in his hand filled with Denny's hamburgers.

"Want one?" he asked. "I got you a burger and fries."

"Hell, yeah. Give it here," I said eagerly. Hospital food was never my favorite.

As we ate our lunch, he briefed me on the follow-up investigation in Cartersville. "From the deer and moose heads mounted on the cabin walls, it seems that Richard Norris was a hunter of sorts. By the way, it's illegal to hunt moose in New York, but that didn't stop him."

"You mean a law-abiding serial killer he was not?"

Riggins smiled weakly and continued. "It wasn't until the FBI got hold of a series of photo albums, kept in a large steamer trunk at the foot of Norris' bed, that additional proof surfaced pointing to the overtly friendly and corrupt relationship he had with the local sheriff's department. Seems the arrogant Deputy Carter was an avid hunter also, as was evident by the dozens of photos they found of him and Norris taken during their hunting trips together. And that's not the only pastime the two shared. When a local drug dealer—who's in jail and awaiting trial—saw the commotion at the cabin on the news, he called the local district attorney's office. For a nifty plea deal, he was more than willing to turn state's evidence against the dirty deputy. A warrant was quickly issued to search Carter's house, and when a few loose floorboards in the guest bedroom were removed, keys were found to a rented garage full of cocaine, heroin, and bags of cash. The lessee of that garage? None other than Richard Norris. Needless to say, Deputy Carter was immediately placed under arrest and held without bail. I'm sure I don't have to tell you what the seizure of such a large quantity of cocaine means for the deputy."

"It means he's facing serious jail time," I answered. "No wonder he went nuts trying to stop the FBI from going in that cabin. He wanted to get to Norris before the FBI did. Little did Carter know, but Norris was already dead."

"In the end," Riggins added. "It was all about drugs and money—dating back to when that teenager who started us on this adventure was just a little girl entrusted to the care of her mother's drug dealer boyfriend, who happened to have his own arrangement with the local police."

I listened and shook my head in sorrowful resignation.

But Riggins had one more bomb to drop on me. "Seems that steamer trunk in the cabin at the foot of Norris's bed was an heirloom—a 1940s edition with drawers and compartments. In other words, it had been in the family for at least fifteen-to-twenty years before that degenerate, Richard Norris, was even born."

"I remember seeing that trunk, but I paid it no mind. I was crazy out-of-my-mind at the time and couldn't get out of there fast enough."

"Seems that trunk also had a false bottom."

"Why am I not surprised? More photos?"

"Not exactly. Try the pink summer dress of a teenage girl."

"And this was the father's trunk—Richard Holcomb?"

"From the age of the trunk, no doubt."

"And the dress…did you tell Charlie about it?"

"I even sent him a photo…and I do believe I heard him crying over the phone. He told me that his mother bought his sister, Peggy, that very dress. It was the one she wore the night she snuck out of the house to meet her prom date. He said that he could never forget that dress as long as he lived."

"So, Richard Holcomb killed Peggy—but why?"

"You mean why does a kidnapper and killer of little boys—kill the teenage girl next door?"

"We know he's a maniac, but it's got to be more than that."

"Well, without becoming too much of a psychotherapist, there is more to the story."

"Isn't there always?"

"I know you've heard the expression 'follow the money.' Well, money is not the only type of evidence that can provide answers. The same goes for weapons, which can be traced all the way back to the manufacturer—illegally obtained or not. And if not illegally obtained, to its rightful owner."

"Weapons? What weapons? I thought Peggy was strangled, her body sawed to pieces. They only found her skull for God's sake."

"That's not where I'm going. I'm talking about the gun Charlie used to kill Richard Norris."

"What? Charlie said it was an illegal gun that he got from an old Upstate friend—someone he served with in Vietnam."

"And you know who that friend is?" Riggins was smiling, and though I didn't think he was one for dramatic pauses, I suppose this was an exception. "Does a Howie Hendricks ring a bell?"

I thought for a moment. "No, not at all."

"How about Howard Hendricks?"

"Do you mean, Howard, Peggy's high school boyfriend?"

"Bingo."

"I never did know his last name. I don't think Charlie ever mentioned it. So, Howard is the old friend Charlie was referring to?"

"Yep. They served in Vietnam at about the same time; only Howard got drafted while Charlie enlisted. They ran into each other overseas and remained good buddies ever since. Howard married a few years after he returned home, had three kids—all girls. It was his wife who started calling him Howie. I supposed she thought it was cute or something, and it stuck from there."

"So, Charlie probably never thought he would use the gun, and figured he would just get it back to Howard before he left, with no one the wiser."

"I suppose. After the shootout in the emergency room yesterday, the agents searched the area for weapons. That included your open bag."

"I had asked someone to get the pants I was wearing out of my suitcase. The killer's ID was in it."

"We know."

"Come to think of it. Where is my suitcase anyway?"

"The FBI has it."

"And they traced the gun Charlie shot the killer with that fast?"

"It's 2018. That's not hard to do—especially if you've got a legit weapon with serial numbers on it."

"So, the pistol was not legal and got traced back to Howard. Is that what you're telling me?"

"Once they gave me the owner, I wasted no time reaching out to him.

Nice guy, he picked up the phone when I called. He's still married to the same woman. He still lives in Phoenix, outside Cartersville. He has three daughters. All have moved away, and from what I gathered, life as a whole, has been good to him."

"I'm glad to hear that. But let me think about this for a minute...so, when Charlie told me the gun was illegal—he was lying just trying to protect Howard and keep him out of this?"

"Likewise, I assured Howard that there would be no charges brought for giving Charlie the gun, especially since it saved three lives and stopped a serial killer dead in his tracks. And you know what he said when I told him that? He said if he had to go to jail for the rest of his life because he gave Charlie that gun, it would have been worth it."

"I'm not surprised, but you still didn't answer my question. Why in God's name did Richard Holcomb kill Peggy?"

"The answer, I'm afraid, was also in the steamer trunk. Seems Holcomb not only kept the pink dress, but Peggy's purse as well. I haven't told Charlie about this part yet, but I will. When he started crying over the photo of the dress, I stopped there. I plan on going to see him when I leave here, unless you think I shouldn't."

"He's a pretty tough guy—but we are talking about his sister," I huffed. "Besides, Donald, I can't answer you until I know what the hell you're talking about."

"Peggy's purse was in the trunk also. It was also pink. In it was a tube of lipstick, makeup, tissues, a five-dollar bill, and here is where we hit pay dirt—a camera. A 1965 Kodak Instamatic with undeveloped film inside it."

"That figures. She was on her way to her first prom, after all."

"Of course, that figures, but it's the photos she took that told us what we needed to know."

"You mean—you were able to develop them?"

"Not me—the FBI. They have a lab that can develop just about anything."

"But she never made it to the prom, so what could...don't tell me?"

"There were only two pictures taken. Both were outdoors and apparently snapped on her way to Howard's, along a road somewhere between her house and his. It's hard to place the location exactly."

"And now you're about to tell me is that she saw something she shouldn't have, and to make matters worse, took pictures of it."

"Unfortunately for her, yes. First, she took a photo of a woman walking ahead of her on the other side of the road. The shot was taken from about thirty feet away. You couldn't see the woman's face because she had her back to Peggy. The woman was in low heels, had shoulder-length blonde hair, and was wearing a dress. A pocketbook was hanging off her arm. Nothing unusual about that—until the lab developed the second photo. In that one, the woman had stopped walking and is looking over at Peggy taking the picture. She appears to be engaged in conversation with a boy, eight or nine years old, hanging off a two-wheeler. Apparently, Peggy had walked past them and for some reason decided to turn and snap this second photo. We didn't find out why until we enlarged it. And I've got to tell you, for a 1965 Kodak Instamatic, it took one hell of a picture."

"You're doing it to me again, Don. Please just tell me what you found."

"It's what the FBI found. I just confirmed it. Seems this woman… wasn't a woman at all. It was Richard Holcomb dressed up as one. And I can only figure that once he saw Peggy snap that photo of him with that little boy, she was done for."

"She must have had her suspicions. Her bedroom window overlooked his aunt's house. I wouldn't be surprised if she had seen him in the same get-up before. Maybe she had her suspicions already."

"And when she saw that same man stop that little boy when no one else was around, or should I say when *he thought* no one else was around, Peggy must have known something wasn't right."

"But why the first photo?"

"When the FBI blew that one up, you could see the bicycle's front tire in the frame. Holcomb had probably flagged the boy down first. Once Peggy saw that, she got wise, took out her camera, and snapped the photo."

"Any theory on why he dressed up as a woman, other than he may have liked to?"

"Keep in mind, when Peggy saw him on her way to Howard's, he was hiding out and wanted in Manhattan for murder. Maybe that's how he got around in Cartersville—in disguise."

"Maybe that disguise served another purpose as well," I added. "It was probably a lot easier to lure little boys as a woman, than as a man. But what I can't figure is: Why keep Peggy's purse and dress to begin with?"

"It's quite common for serial killers to keep mementos. Also, there were short blonde hairs found under the shoulder straps of the dress. Peggy's hair was dark brown. For all we know, while playing dress-up he probably wore the dress a few times himself."

"Don't tell Charlie that."

"I won't."

I sighed, looked down at my half-eaten hamburger, and lost my appetite. "The dark hole just keeps getting darker and wider," I said dolefully. "I should start going to church again. Can we talk about something else now? How are the Mets doing?"

"Don't ask."

"Wonderful," I said sarcastically.

Riggins eyes appeared to light up slightly, though it was hard to tell. They were quite puffy and sunken under thick wispy eyebrows. "I have more news for you," he said with a barely discernible tone of merriment.

"Donald, before I drop dead, I swear you're going to tell me something positive that has nothing to do with murder, evidence of it, or someone out to kill me. Otherwise, I beg you—let me try and finish this hamburger."

Riggins didn't flinch. "In that big steamer trunk—before the feds got to search its compartments and secret drawers, guess what they found—or should I say, *who* they found?"

"Can't wait until after I finish eating, can you?"

As usual, he ignored me. "They found a little boy, hog-tied, hands and feet bound, his mouth taped. It was Billy—the last boy to go missing. And he was very much alive, but better yet—he was unharmed."

"Thank God! Finally, news worth waiting for."

"He had been drugged, which probably explained why he slept through most of the ordeal and remembers little of it. By the way, do you know why he wasn't harmed?"

"Knowing there is no depth to the evil that is Richard Norris, son of Richard Holcomb, I have an inkling. But tell me, and maybe I can finally put the haunting mental images of child abduction and abuse behind me."

"Sorry, Nick, but that is going to take some time, and I speak from experience."

"Go ahead anyway and confirm my worst imaginings."

"After little Billy was found and questioned, he told the agents how Richard Norris cut him off with his SUV while he was riding his bike along the side of the road. As the boy remembers it, Norris grabbed him, then put a cloth in his mouth with a funny smell to it."

"Chloroform."

"You got it. Sweet smelling, he said. He was surprisingly quite calm and lucid with the agents, but I figure that was because he was drugged and unaware of what was happening to him. Tie me up, stick me in a box, and I'll be ready for the loony bin. By the way, I also called the FBI in Syracuse this morning to see how he was doing. Call it a miracle, but he's doing fine."

"Let's just be thankful he wasn't hurt."

"But if you ask me, the real reason he wasn't touched is because some miscreant ponied up a lot of money to be his first."

"Dear God in heaven, I'm just grateful we got there in time." I needed a moment to gather myself as my head was beginning to ache again. "And thank God, too, that Richard Norris is dead—may the bastard burn in hell. Now on a much happier note: Tell me…the boy's mother and stepfather? They must have been thrilled to get him back alive and well. Now that's what I want to hear about the next time you call me."

"It's a reunion you made possible."

"Nice of you to say, Don. I only hope God sees it that way, and maybe—just maybe, when my time comes—there might be a place in heaven for me yet. After all, I have two wonderful women—my mother, and my Eleanor, waiting for me—and I don't want to disappoint them by not showing up."

# PART 6

# THE LURE

*But why am I here?*
*This seems pleasant enough.*
*A real playground with boys in it.*
*A flowing river behind it.*
*Fenced in and safe.*
*I want to play, too.*
*But I can only smile and wave.*
*And why am I afraid?*
*Now I know why I'm here.*

                                        *Lisa*

# CHAPTER 82

I n our efforts to obtain Mia's psychiatric records, our goal was simple. Dr. Field's session notes would open a window into what Mia and the alters saw and heard while trapped in the cabin and the underground rooms. It was our last hope at cracking the dark web of secrecy concealing the rich and powerful participants and co-conspirators whom Richard Norris bragged about.

Instead of cooperating and turning over her records, however, Dr. Field hired a top Manhattan law firm to oppose all demands and applications. She even moved to quash an FBI subpoena for the very same material.

In an affidavit that accompanied her attorney's opposition papers, Dr. Field claimed that Mia was still suffering from multiple personality disorder, thereby rendering her incompetent and legally incapable of giving her consent, even at the age of eighteen. Fortunately, the judge hearing the case didn't buy the argument and ordered the notes and records to be turned over immediately—a decision we celebrated, but not for long. The reason: There were no notes and records to speak of. Doctor Field had destroyed them, and lied about it.

In way of explanation to the court, her lawyer wrote: "We regret to inform Your Honor that the material in question caught fire in the process of being transported to a storage facility." When the judge demanded further clarification, more spurious details were provided. Seems that Dr. Field had temporarily stacked the papers on a patio table while cooking steaks on a nearby barbeque. When the grill was left unattended, a spark ignited, and the notes and records were burned to a crisp. Curiously, the fire department was never called.

One bright spot: The no-nonsense judge ordered Dr. Field to submit to an FBI Q&A on the content of the destroyed notes and records. Since lying to the FBI is a felony, the question-and-answer session—more like an interrogation—wouldn't prove to be without its worthwhile moments.

But it wasn't until June of 2019— after a year of litigation and further delay tactics by her attorneys—that Dr. Field finally complied. Though the FBI had no problem with her request to have the Q&A in her office, retired agent Riggins persuaded them otherwise. Paul, who only a month earlier had finally recovered completely from his injuries, wanted the cagey doctor to feel the intimidating atmosphere of the FBI's sterile interrogation room after she walked into the confines of 26 Federal Plaza. But what all of us really wanted was to watch and listen behind the feds' one-way mirror installed for exactly that purpose.

With a weak scowl on her face, Dr. Field took a seat in one of two plastic cafeteria type chairs on each side of a small metallic table. Since she hated lawyers—starting with her ex-husband—she didn't want or need one to accompany her. Besides, the FBI made it clear that she was not a person of interest in any alleged criminal activity, and that the subject of the inquiry was the content of the lost notes and records—nothing more.

Conducting the Q&A were two midcareer agents in their forties: — tall, milky-white, clean-cut men with dark hair—like two stereotypical FBI handbook cutouts of old. They were polished and good-looking, which— in addition to their pleasant manner—seemed to have a relaxing effect on Dr. Field. One did all the talking, while the other just stood nearby and looked on. Although Dr. Field's initial scowl was replaced with a less off-putting smirk, I remained skeptical about our chances of getting anything of value out of her. After all, she had already—and literally—cooked the books to hide what was ever in those notes and records. And as she was quite the professional at posing questions herself, I could only assume that she was just as crafty at answering them.

When the agents began by asking how Mia came to be adopted by Beatrice Langley—a softball question, to be sure—Dr. Field appeared circumspect, and said that Beatrice had a social worker friend who 'started the ball rolling' some time before Mia's birth mother passed away. "The mother was a drug addict," she added brashly. "And her live-in boyfriend, whom Mia called 'Uncle Greg' was an addict, as well as a dealer. Mia's mother was found dead from a fatal overdose around the same time that Uncle Greg disappeared."

As we huddled behind the one-way mirror, Riggins whispered: "Untrustworthy drug addicts become quite disposable in a criminal enterprise."

"Maybe someday justice will truly be served, and Uncle Greg will turn up in a wooden box of his own," I whispered back.

Though I was certain that Riggins heard me, he didn't react. He seemed to be studying Dr. Field. "You know, for a gal who hired a high-priced law firm to go to battle in court, she seems rather complacent...even chatty," he said.

"Maybe she just feels comfortable with the agents," I answered.

"No," Paul joined in. "It's something else." He looked down at his phone. "Jasmine just texted me. One hour ago, Beatrice Langley was found dead in her apartment—an empty bottle of Ambien by her bed."

"Holy shit! What about Mia?" I asked. "Is she alright?"

"She doesn't know yet," Paul said. "She's at Great Adventure with her senior class."

I then came to understand the reason behind Dr. Field's air of cooperation. With Beatrice Langley dead, there was no one left to protect—and no reason to risk felony prosecution by lying to the FBI.

The agent then moved on to 'forbidden ground' and asked Dr. Field about her conversations with the alters.

"All my conversations were with Mia," she answered abruptly. "The alters are creations of Mia's subconscious mind. They're multiple personalities, but they are all Mia's personalities. If you want me to distinguish one from the other, I won't be able to, especially since I don't have my notes to turn to."

"Just tell us what they told you about Mia and Cartersville." The agent spoke firmly.

Dr. Field huffed. "Richard Norris was a dangerous, cold blooded killer—."

"Tell us something we don't know," he interrupted.

Suddenly uncomfortable in her chair, she adjusted her seating position. "Mia is as beautiful on the inside as she is on the outside, which makes this so difficult for me." Dr. Field apparently had her own rehearsed answers.

"I'm sure," he remarked sarcastically. "I'm sure you thought she was extraordinary, just like the amount of money you were getting paid for your sessions with her. What was it, seven-hundred-and-fifty a clip? A little high, wouldn't you say?"

"I'm sorry, sir, but it wasn't just about the money."

"Of course not. It was also about horrible crimes against children and reporting what you learned about them—only to your friend, Beatrice, and no one else."

"I resent that."

"You can resent it all you want, and you can resent this, too: I want to hear it all, Doctor. You didn't walk in here as a person of interest, but I can't say how you're going to walk out."

"You're being rude."

"That's the least of it. You're here under a court order—and may I remind you that lying to an FBI agent is a felony punishable by incarceration in a federal prison. Martha Stewart did a year for lying about a stock trade. How much time do you think you'll do for lying about the murder of little boys? Now, are you going to tell us what you know—or do I place you under arrest for withholding evidence?" The agent was bluffing about the arrest, but doing such a good job of it, he had me convinced.

Dr. Field put her hand on her chest, and whether it was a by-product of grief over Beatrice's death, I couldn't be sure, but she leaned forward and began to cry. Though the agent was unaffected by her tears, he did hand her a tissue and give her a moment to gather herself. "Beatrice wanted to help Mia, but she also wanted to keep secret her husband's activity in Cartersville," she said woefully.

"What activity?"

"The worst kind. I'm not sure exactly what Beatrice knew, but be assured of this: She loved Mia very much—but she also cared deeply about protecting her family name."

"You also kept a few secrets, too, Doctor."

"Those were past acts—what Mia said happened before I started treating her. I'm not the FBI, and I'll swear to anyone who asks that I had no reason to believe that crimes were continuing. Therefore, I had no obligation to report anything to anyone, even the authorities."

"No reason—except maybe the exercise of decency and the use of your common sense."

"You're not making this easy."

"It wasn't easy for those boys found in that well, either," the agent snapped back.

While Paul and I glanced at each other in recollection of the horror we shared, Dr. Field thought for a moment. "I was never told anything about a well, but I *was* told about a playground."

"I'm sorry, did you say…playground?"

"According to Mia, it's where the boys were chosen."

"Doctor, I'm paying close attention—and I'm still not following."

"Mount Seneca Seminary in Cartersville. It started as a school for young men who wanted to become priests, but years later, it became an orphanage, and then a group home."

"I know, but where does a playground fit into all this?"

"The little ones…this is so hard to hear, no less tell…the little ones— boys five, six, seven, and eight years old—would play in a playground along the Oswego River—on the seminary grounds. Understand that…back then…the record keeping on these children was poor. Corrupt is more like it. I have no doubt that many files on birth and placement were intentionally destroyed—so that when certain boys went missing, they went missing without a trace."

"What do Mia and the alters have to do with this?"

"Mia was the lure."

"The lure?"

"She's now a beautiful young woman. She was a beautiful little girl back then too." The doctor choked on her words, then took a breath to compose herself. "Little Mia, petite and adorable, would be brought over to a fence that encircled the playground, whether it was by Richard Norris or somebody else. Don't ask me who, because even Mia didn't know. Once at the fence, she was told...no...ordered...to wave to the little boys. When one would run over to the fence to talk to her...sadly...that boy would be sized up and taken."

"Did Mia know what she was doing?"

"Not at first. This began when she was only six or seven. Once she realized...even at that age...that something terrible was going on, not only did she refuse to wave—she wouldn't even face the playground. That's when she would get stuck with a pin—or I should I say...one of the alters got stuck with a pin."

"Did you say...pin?" The agent was taken aback.

"Yes, or a lit cigarette or cigar. If she still refused, she got stuck twice more, or burned. And then, if she still failed to cooperate, she would get put in the box."

"The box?"

"It's where they put the boys before and after doing whatever they would do to them. Mia may have been hurt...I mean abused...also. She wouldn't say. Even her alters wouldn't say. After all, they were created to protect her. But alters or not...surviving that horror is a testament to what an extraordinary young woman she is."

"How often did Mia act as the lure?"

"Every other month for about four years, until she was adopted by Beatrice."

"And what ever happened to Uncle Greg?"

"He just disappeared."

"Mia's adoption also occurred right after Beatrice's husband, Reginald, died as well. Could this be a coincidence? Beatrice had to know about Mia's abuse. So, c'mon. She adopted Mia to keep her quiet, and then got Mia therapy sessions to find out what she knew about her dead husband's Upstate visits."

"Mia was a child. Beatrice was her mother. She had a right to know—to help Mia. As for Beatrice's true intentions? Only she can answer that." Dr. Field dabbed her eyes again with a tissue.

"And I assume you told Mia not to discuss these awful childhood experiences with anyone but you?"

"For her own protection, any psychiatrist would. You must believe me when I tell you that Beatrice came to love Mia. She always took great care of her. She saved Mia...and Mia saved her." Dr. Field's voice cracked. "With Mia turning eighteen, and the court battles over the subpoenas, Beatrice knew the truth would come out about her husband. And that's something she could never live with. But there was a mountain of goodness in that woman, and if anyone has any doubt, all they have to do is read her will. She left a fifty-million-dollar estate, and to show you the kind of woman she was or...wanted to be...one-half is going to the National Center for Missing and Abused Children, and the other half is going to Mia. As for her apartment, she left it to me under the condition that Mia be allowed to live there as long as she wants to."

As the agent pressed on—asking Dr. Field what the alters saw and heard concerning Richard Norris, Reginald Langley, and anyone else—he got the same answer: "It was so long ago that Mia and the alters talked about Cartersville, I just can't remember."

I suppose Dr. Field didn't need a lawyer, after all. She knew how to answer without answering, and without revealing a single thing that would incriminate her or anyone else. With her office located in Downtown Manhattan, I had no doubt that Beatrice Langley wasn't the only high-priced client the doctor was looking to protect. And although the Cartersville kidnapping and murder enterprise had come to an end—with many wealthy and powerful men scared out of their wits for fear of being discovered—it was hard not to feel like we had only done half our job. But evil minds don't stay idle for too long, and when they do eventually burrow out of their tunnel, cave, or bunker—and they will—Paul, Riggins, and now the FBI, will be there to meet them. As for me, I'll gladly sacrifice every penny I have, and more, if given the opportunity to shut them down somewhere else again.

As I left the Federal Building, I couldn't stop thinking about Beatrice Langley—the sad life she led and her ill-conceived attempts at love in a world she was irreversibly anchored to since birth—a world far too powerful and cruel to allow her the happiness she longed for without paying the ultimate price. I thought about her attempts at absolution before and after her death. But absolution without penance is no absolution at all. And considering the number of little boys who continued to be abused, tortured, and killed while she and Dr. Field remained silent—good tidings in a will or not, Beatrice Langley might just be spending eternity in a furnace, or well—or buried box of her own.

# PART 7

# THE NEW WORLD

*Maybe there's hope for me yet.*

*Mia*

# CHAPTER 83

though it took Paul about a year to heal from the fall and the multiple concussions he suffered, he claimed to be just fine long before that. As for me, I was fully recovered after a few months—physically that is. I spent the next year attempting to put my personal life back in order; not that it had completely fallen apart, but I did lose a girlfriend and some of the respect of my two kids for falling for the Maureen/Olga con. They denied it, but I knew better.

Since there was nothing left for me in Tennessee, I decided to sell the house in Franklin and return to New York. It's where my children were, and like my daughter, Charlotte, once said to me: "Home is where there is someone who loves you."

As for Charlie Malone, he was more than happy to return to the life of a crusty old man with nothing more to look forward to than therapy sessions with an attractive psychologist for a PTSD condition that he never had to begin with.

But I, however, had other plans for him.

In December of 2018, I closed on a house in my hometown of Merrick, Long Island, and set up a trust fund with enough money in it to pay the real estate taxes and utility bills on the home for the next twenty years. The beneficiary of the trust: Charlie Malone.

It was a two-bedroom ranch with a rear patio, an outdoor gas bar-beque, and a large backyard. The inside did need some minor alterations (I called them 'design changes') to suit the unique characteristics of its newly entrusted inhabitant—like ramps and widened interior doorways for easy wheelchair access and navigation.

In short, after all was said and done, it was perfect for him. But with-out even asking, I knew what Charlie wanted more than anything in the world.

He wanted to stand up and walk again.

Which brought me to 'Phase II' of the Charlie Malone project: Getting him fitted for a pair of prosthetic legs. As expected, he resisted at first. But the more he said he didn't want them, the more I knew that he did. Either way, this man had saved my life, and I wasn't taking no for an answer.

I bought him two pair, which, with therapy and training, he easily adapted to.

Cleaned up—hair trimmed, face shaved, dressed up and out on the town—you would never know that he was standing on artificial limbs.

Then came the biggest surprise of all—the wedding.

On July 27, 2019, Charlie Malone married a sixty-two-year-old wait-ress he had met in a Peruvian restaurant in Mineola, Long Island. And after having had dinner with them on numerous occasions, I was able to witness firsthand how genuine her love and affection for him really was. As a result, I was only too happy to give Charlie my wholehearted blessing, and it touched me to my core how much it mattered to him. That tough, cantankerous curmudgeon—who growled at everyone from his wheelchair—turned out to be one big (at six-foot two-inches) teddy bear in the presence of his lovely bride. The man who gave his legs for his country, risked his life for Paul and me, and would not quit until we put an end to the horror in Cartersville, New York, had finally found happiness in a world that had sold him terribly short. And no one deserved it more. Charlie was, and still is, an American hero—my hero—and a great man.

# CHAPTER 84

August 24, 2019.
New York Harbor.

The view from the penthouse deck of the cruise ship is nothing short of breathtaking—a vacation gift from John and Charlotte "for no special reason,"—or so they claimed. They wanted me to get away. But I knew better. They wanted *us* to get away as a family.

Though I have grown closer to my son and daughter with my return to New York—and have a new granddaughter to fuss over—when I'm alone at night, that unrelenting sinking feeling returns. Maybe that's why I went down into that tunnel, knowing in my mind and heart that nothing good was waiting for me there.

But even when I was certain I was going to die—whether it was a death that would come quickly or slowly at the hands of a monster—deep down I wanted to live, even if it was in a world without my Eleanor. A world without the deep, abiding love of the life partner I adored. And though the happiness my children and their families bring sustains me, they have their own lives, and I must have mine. I just need to stop feeling sorry for myself (I hate that I sometimes still feel sorry for myself). I also need to stop feeling sad. But with each successive day that passes with Cartersville behind me I am imbued with a greater sense of hope. And it's that hope, however fleeting it may be sometimes, that makes me believe that there is still something worth living for—like a light in the offing beckoning me onward.

If I garnered anything from Mia and her alters, maybe it was that.

It is on this same special day that Mia begins her freshman orientation at New York University in Downtown Manhattan. Her dorm room is on Fifth Avenue and 10th Street in the same building that was once Mark Twain's personal residence. Though she has not yet selected a major, I'm expecting it will be journalism, given her close personal relationship with Lauren, whom she now resides with—something I couldn't be happier about.

Though Charlie and I have been anxious to see more of Mia—and I'm told she feels the same way—since we are vivid reminders of Cartersville, her new psychiatrist has recommended we keep it to a minimum for the time being. And although alternate personalities creep in and out of Mia's psyche on occasion, it is becoming less frequent. Consequently, we are hopeful that we will be able to see more of her as time passes. Until then, Lauren will continue to keep us updated on her health and well-being—and I rest easy knowing that Mia has a champion caretaker, mentor, and best friend. The two have become nothing short of inseparable since Beatrice Langley's death. And considering the tragedy that befell Lauren's sister, I couldn't have hoped for a better ending for Lauren, and an even better beginning for her and Mia.

As for Mia…she is brilliant. She is kind. She is a beautiful young woman in every way, who now not only has Lauren, but also Charlie and me as a support system. Together or apart, none of us will ever let anything bad happen to her again.

As our ship leaves New York Harbor—my eight-month-old granddaughter in my arms—Charlotte and John alongside me on the penthouse deck—I get a text from Charlie.

*Our little girl is little no more. I bought her an NYU sweatshirt. Can't wait to see her.*

I give my granddaughter a kiss, pass her to her father, and text back. *We'll get to soon enough. So proud. Two proud uncles we are.*

Charlotte, John, and my sweet Eleanor (her grandmother's namesake), soon return to their staterooms. Left alone with my thoughts, I lean on the deck rail and marvel at the expanse of the Hudson River and its connecting shores, while a tugboat nearby shoots a cone of river at the sun—a salute to our passing ship and New York City's glittering undaunted skyline.

We pass the Freedom Tower shining like a pristine rocket poised to launch unscathed into a cloudless sky. And I am awed by it, until it is gone from sight along with the tip of Lower Manhattan and its harbor of countless untold stories that swell inside me like a melancholy dream.

And I can't help but wonder what ran through the minds of those Dutch sailors who first lay claim to a trading post there—their sense of unwavering adventure, their daring, their bravery at confronting F. Scott's 'fresh, green breast of the New World.'

The ship continues past Ellis Island, Brooklyn, Staten Island, and New Jersey until it gently coasts under the Verrazano Bridge, but it is the vision of the singular majesty of the Statute of Liberty, beckoning those who dare challenge its shores that stays with me long after the city and all its monuments and symbols of struggle and achievement are left behind, and long after our ship meets the endless bounty of the ocean—content in the knowledge that when we return—freedom and hope will, as ever, be there long after...

**Thank you** for reading *The Criminal Mind*. I certainly hope you enjoyed it. I welcome your reviews, so please post on Amazon as you wish.

Please also feel free to connect with me on:
My Amazon author page http://amzn.to/3qTCsy5
Facebook www.facebook/thegoodlawyer
Twitter @thomasbenigno
Instagram @ThomasBenignoauthor

You can also connect with me on Goodreads, Tumblr, and Pinterest, or just shoot me an email at tombenigno@aol.com. I try to respond to all readers, even if it is to just say thank you.

Also check out my author website at BenignoBooks.com.
God bless you all. T.B.

# ACKNOWLEDGEMENTS

Thanks to my first draft readers: Maria Tullo, Bruce Ferber, and Kathy Gurrieri. Many thanks to my editor and story consultant, Anne Brewer, whose brilliance on this one I could have not done without, Diana Benigno, my supporting editor and initial copy editor, and Jonathan Baker, my final copy editor. Thanks to my friends and family for their continued support, A tremendous note of thanks to my readers. I try my best to write books I can be proud of but make no mistake about it—I write them for you and only you. Once again, to my children for their love and tolerance. And most of all, to my wife, Angie, "God only knows what I'd be without you." –Brian Wilson/Tony Asher.

# ABOUT THE AUTHOR

Thomas Benigno is a former trial attorney with the Criminal Defense Division of the NYC Legal Aid Society. Over the years he has dabbled as a Broadway producer and actor while continuing in the private practice of law on Long Island. Recipient of the Readers Favorite Award in Psychological Thriller Fiction, he is currently working on his fourth novel along with the television pilot to The Good Lawyer.

He is also author of the international bestsellers:
The Good Lawyer at: http://amzn.to/2drvzPl and
The Criminal Lawyer at: https://amzn.to/3a2Odfl.

Audiobooks of his novels, including this one, are available on Audible.com.